HARDCASTLE'S COLLECTOR

HARDCASTLE'S COLLECTOR

Graham Ison

This first world edition published 2015
in Great Britain and 2016 in the USA by
SEVERN HOUSE PUBLISHERS LTD of
19 Cedar Road, Sutton, Surrey, England, SM2 5DA.
Trade paperback edition first published
in Great Britain and the USA 2016 by
SEVERN HOUSE PUBLISHERS LTD

Copyright © 2015 by Graham Ison.

British Library Cataloguing in Publication Data

Ison, Graham author.
  Hardcastle's collector.
  1. Hardcastle, Ernest (Fictitious character)–Fiction.
  2. Police–England–London–Fiction. 3. Great Britain–
  History–George V, 1910-1936–Fiction. 4. Murder–
  Investigation–England–Hampshire–Fiction. 5. Detective
  and mystery stories.
  I. Title
  823.9'14-dc23

ISBN-13: 978-0-7278-8557-9 (cased)
ISBN-13: 978-1-84751-666-4 (trade paper)
ISBN-13: 978-1-78010-720-2 (e-book)

All Severn House titles are printed on acid-free paper.

Severn House Publishers support the Forest Stewardship Council™ [FSC™],
the leading international forest certification organisation.
All our titles that are printed on FSC certified paper carry the FSC logo.

MIX
Paper from
responsible sources
FSC® C013056

Typeset by Palimpsest Book Production Ltd.,
Falkirk, Stirlingshire, Scotland.
Printed and bound in Great Britain by
TJ International, Padstow, Cornwall.

GLOSSARY

ACT UP: temporarily to assume the role of a higher rank while the substantive holder is on detached duty, on leave or sick.

ALBERT: a watch chain of the type worn by Albert, Prince Consort (1819–61).

ANTECEDENTS: police slang for details of an accused person's general background, address, education and previous employment, etc.

BEAK: a magistrate.

BRADSHAW: a timetable giving routes and times of British railway services.

BUCK HOUSE: Buckingham Palace.

BUSY, a: a detective.

CID: Criminal Investigation Department.

COMMISSIONER'S OFFICE: official title of New Scotland Yard, headquarters of the Metropolitan Police.

DABS: fingerprints.

DARBIES: handcuffs.

DARTMOOR: a remote prison on Dartmoor in Devon.

DDI: Divisional Detective Inspector.

DERBY ACT or DERBY LAW: Military Service Act 1916, formulated by Lord Derby, that introduced conscription.

DIGS or DIGGINGS: rented lodgings, usually short term.

DIP: a pickpocket *or* to steal from the pocket.

DPP: Director of Public Prosecutions.

FLORIN: two shillings (10p).

FOURPENNY CANNON, a: a steak-and-kidney pie.

GANDER, to cop a: to take a look.

HAP'ORTH: half a penny's-worth; taken to mean worthless.

JIG-A-JIG: sexual intercourse.

KC: King's Counsel: a senior barrister.

LAY-DOWN, a: a remand in custody.

MANOR: a police area.

OCCURRENCE BOOK: handwritten record of *every* incident occurring on a police sub-division.
OLD BAILEY: Central Criminal Court, in Old Bailey, London.
ON THE SLATE: to be given credit.

PISSED AS A FIDDLER'S BITCH: drunk.
POLICE GAZETTE: official nationwide publication listing wanted persons, etc.
PROVOST, the: military police.
PURLER: a headlong fall.

REDCAPS: The Corps of Military Police.
ROYAL A: informal name for the A or Whitehall Division of the Metropolitan Police.

SILK, a: a King's Counsel (a senior barrister) from the silk gowns they wear.
SMOKE, the: London.
SNOUT: a police informant.
SOMERSET HOUSE: formerly the records office of births, deaths and marriages for England & Wales.
SWADDY: a soldier. (*ex* Hindi.)

TITFER: a hat (rhyming slang: tit for tat).
TOMMY or TOMMY ATKINS: a British soldier. The name 'Tommy Atkins' was used as an example on early army forms.
TONGUE PADDING, to give a: to scold.
TOPPED: murdered or hanged.

TOPPING: a murder or hanging.

TOUCH OF THE VAPOURS, a: to be overcome with faintness.

TURNIP WATCH: an old-fashioned, thick, silver pocket watch.

UNDERGROUND, the: the London Underground railway system.

UP THE DUFF: pregnant.

WIPERS: army slang for Ypres in Belgium, scene of several fierce Great War battles.

ONE

The Hampshire village of Thresham Parva was situated roughly halfway between the market town of Alton, famous for its ales, and the military encampment of Aldershot. There were probably no more than four hundred residents in the village, but in a war that seemed interminable quite a few of them had been killed fighting on the Western Front. Several had fallen on the first of July last year when thousands of British soldiers had been slaughtered on the opening day of the disastrous Somme offensive.

The close proximity of Aldershot had made villages like Thresham Parva fertile hunting grounds for the recruiting sergeants, and now that conscription had been introduced even more were likely to find themselves in the mud of the Flanders trenches ere long.

Police Constable Edward Jessop, an Alton man born and bred, had been a member of the Hampshire County Constabulary for nigh on twenty-five years. Six-foot tall and well built, with a flowing, Kitchener-style moustache, he was the archetypal English policeman, one who carefully weighed up a situation before taking any action. Although appearing ponderous, it would be a mistake to regard him as slow-witted or unintelligent, for he was well-read and beneath his constabulary helmet there existed a keen brain. If anyone were to be asked to describe a typical country bobby Edward Jessop would be the one most likely to spring to mind.

He and his wife Annie lived in the police house on the outskirts of Thresham Parva, the village for which he had been responsible these past seven years. It was a great disappointment to the Jessops that they had no children, but Edward Jessop had remarked, on many occasions since the war began, that it was perhaps a blessing. Several of his contemporaries had lost sons in the conflict and some of the younger policemen who had volunteered in 1914 now lay in hastily dug graves in France, Flanders and the Middle East.

The rainfall that July of 1917 had been unseasonably heavy and August was showing little improvement. In consequence,

Jessop, a cautious fellow, had brought his glazed waterproof cape with him and had strapped it neatly over the handlebars of his bicycle. It was a recognized feature of the Hampshire County Constabulary that its officers were always properly turned out. In fact, the Chief Constable insisted upon it and disciplinary sanctions would be the lot of any officer who allowed those high standards to slip. To appear out of doors without a helmet was, in the absence of a reasonable excuse, tantamount to seeking instant dismissal.

It was about seven o'clock on Tuesday morning, the seventh of August, when Jessop reached South Farm. He was surprised to see the owner, Joshua Blunden, leaning over the gate that led directly into his five-acre field, which at this time of year always contained a number of haystacks. Although Blunden was out on his rounds at dawn every day, those early morning chores were usually completed before seven o'clock, and he could normally be found indoors having breakfast at that hour.

Whenever he was passing the farm, PC Jessop always called in on the Blundens on the pretext of checking that there had not been a sudden outbreak of foot-and-mouth disease among the farmer's herd of cattle, or the onset of epizootic lymphangitis among those of his horses that had not been commandeered by the military. But the reality was that Jessop enjoyed a cup of Martha Blunden's tea, a round of toast and a chinwag. In common with most policemen, he would always listen to local gossip; a surprising amount of petty crime was often unwittingly revealed and there had only ever been petty crime in Thresham Parva. Until today. This morning, Jessop was in for a surprise.

'Morning, Josh. We'll be having a bit more rain today, I shouldn't wonder.' Jessop dismounted from his bicycle. 'It don't do my rheumatics any good. It's times like this when I think I'm getting too old for this job.' The constable wondered why Blunden was not inviting him in for his usual cup of tea. 'You're out and about later than usual this morning, Josh,' he commented, hoping for an answer that would satisfy his curiosity.

'I've found a body, Mr Jessop.' Blunden removed the clay pipe from his mouth with one hand, took off his worn cloth cap with the other and briefly scratched his bald pate.

'One of your sheep been got at by a dog, was it?' Jessop looked

concerned. Dogs attacking sheep was a serious matter and regrettably not uncommon.

'No. It's young Daisy Salter, the coal merchant's girl.' Blunden
was a phlegmatic character, not known to get excited about
anything. From the way he made this awesome announcement to
the local policeman, anyone could be forgiven for thinking that the
finding of a body was an everyday occurrence at South Farm.

Jessop frowned. He did not like the sound of that. 'Dead, is she?'

'Aye!'

'Where is she, Josh?'

'In the corner of the field right behind this hedge, Mr Jessop.'
Blunden indicated the place by pointing with the stem of his pipe.

'What time was it that you found her, Josh?'

'About a half hour since. I guessed you'd be on your rounds
already, and as you always pass here about this time, I thought
I'd wait for you.'

'Better take a look, I suppose.' Slowly and carefully, Jessop
propped his bicycle against the hedge and waited for Blunden to
open the five-bar gate.

'Stay, girl!' Blunden glanced down at the Border collie sitting
patiently at his feet and led Jessop into the field.

On the other side of the hedge closest to the road lay the body
of Daisy Salter. Her clothing was disarranged sufficiently to reveal
the lower half of her abdomen, her thighs and the tops of her lisle
stockings. The bodice of her cotton dress was torn open to the
waist, but Jessop noticed that there was no sign of any bloomers.
Shreds of hay were in her hair, now unpinned and hanging loosely
across one shoulder. Her face showed elements of powder and
there were traces of kohl around her eyes that she had undoubtedly
used to make herself look older. Most significant of all, however,
were the livid red marks on her neck.

Jessop bent down and felt for a pulse he knew he would not
find, but as has already been said, he was a careful man. Standing
upright again, he added, 'She's been strangled, Josh, of that I'm
certain, but I'll need the doctor to confirm it officially.'

'What happens now, then, Mr Jessop?'

'If I can use your telephone, Josh, I'll get in touch with
the station at Alton and they'll likely send for a detective from the
headquarters at Winchester. In the meantime, I'd better cover

the body.' Returning to his bicycle, Jessop took his cape from the handlebars and spread it across the body of Daisy Salter.

'Aye, right you are. And while you're doing that, I'll get Martha to make some tea and I daresay you could do with a slice of toast.' Blunden looked at his dog again. 'Stand guard, Bess!' he said, pointing at the girl's body. The dog sat obediently. 'No one will get past Bess, Mr Jessop.'

'A cup of tea and some toast would be most welcome, Josh. And perhaps Martha wouldn't mind me making use of her kitchen table while I make a few notes. They're very particular about notes at headquarters.' Jessop took his pipe from his tunic pocket and began to fill it slowly with Three Nuns tobacco as he and the farmer walked towards the farmhouse. 'How's your missus keeping, by the way?' It was a formal question: Jessop had seen the farmer's wife only yesterday morning.

TWO

S ince 1890 the headquarters of the Metropolitan Police has been housed in the imposing edifice of New Scotland Yard. Standing between Whitehall and Victoria Embankment in central London, it had been designed by Norman Shaw and constructed of Dartmoor granite hewn, deservedly some said, by convicts from the nearby Devon prison that took its name from its bleak surroundings. A.P. Herbert, lawyer, playwright, politician, author and wit, was later to describe the Yard as 'a very constabulary kind of castle'.

Immediately opposite the Yard was Cannon Row police station, headquarters of the A or Whitehall Division of the Metropolitan Police. As the officers of the self-styled 'Royal A' would proudly tell you, they were responsible for the security of Buckingham Palace and the other royal palaces including Windsor Castle and Holyrood House in Edinburgh, as well as the Houses of Parliament, 10 Downing Street, the offices of government and Westminster Abbey.

On the first floor of this police station was the office of Ernest Hardcastle, the divisional detective inspector in charge of A Division's criminal investigation department.

Hardcastle was forty-five years of age and had joined the Metropolitan Police in 1891. After four years walking a beat in the Islington area of London, he had joined the CID and had reached his present rank – which he firmly believed was as far as he would rise – just before the outbreak of war in 1914. His stocky, well-built frame was invariably clad in a dark suit, complete with waistcoat – no matter what the temperature – and box cloth spats over his polished black boots. Twenty-four years ago Hardcastle had married Alice Roberts, the daughter of a sergeant in the Royal Garrison Artillery; she had been born in Peshawar in India, where her father was stationed at the time.

Ever since their marriage the Hardcastles had resided at 27 Kennington Road, Lambeth, not far from where the famous actor Charlie Chaplin had lived as a boy.

Living with the Hardcastles were their two daughters and their only son. Kitty was a strong-willed twenty-one-year-old presently working as a conductorette with the London General Omnibus Company. Her younger sister, Maud, although only nineteen, was mature beyond her years, doubtless as a result of her harrowing experience nursing at one of the big houses in Park Lane that had been given over to the care of wounded officers. The Hardcastles' son, a boisterous seventeen-year-old named Walter, was a post-office telegram messenger, but wanted to become a policeman like his father despite Ernest's entrenched opposition to the idea. Alice Hardcastle agreed with her husband, and was often heard to say that one policeman in the family was one too many.

Although he was a good detective, Hardcastle was a very demanding one and somewhat short-tempered when his subordin-ates did not produce the results he frequently, and on occasion unreasonably, expected of them. The better educated of his detect-ives described him as cantankerous, an assessment with which Hardcastle's wife would not disagree.

On Tuesday the seventh of August 1917, he was standing at the window of his office, smoking a pipe of his favourite St Bruno tobacco and staring moodily at Westminster Underground station below, hands deep in his trouser pockets. He was fretting that he had little to do and on such extremely rare occasions had a tendency to roam about the police station interfering with the work of his junior detectives, or behaving similarly at the other two police stations – Rochester Row and Hyde Park – for which he had responsibility. Or even visiting the police lodge at Buckingham Palace and making a nuisance of himself.

But this period of inactivity was about to come to an end.

Hardcastle took his half-hunter from his waistcoat pocket, stared at it and noted that it was still only nine o'clock. Winding the watch briefly before returning it to his pocket, he looked around his office, sighed and crossed the corridor to the large room occupied by Cannon Row's detectives.

Charles Marriott, who held the rank of detective sergeant (first-class), supervised the junior detectives and was the only officer in the room privileged enough to have his own desk. He was also the officer always chosen by the DDI to assist him in major enquiries. It was a role known in the CID as a bag carrier.

'Good morning, sir.' Marriott stood up, as did the other detectives seated around the long wooden table. They too knew the signs of the DDI's boredom, but this morning he would not have the opportunity to meddle. 'I was just coming to see you.'

'What about, Marriott? Some murder occurred somewhere, has it?' asked Hardcastle hopefully, and waved at the other detectives to resume their seats.

'Possibly, sir. I've just had a telephone call from Mr Wensley's clerk. Mr Wensley would like to see you as soon as possible.'

'I wonder what that's all about,' said Hardcastle, half to himself. He returned to his office to collect his bowler hat and umbrella, without which he was never to be seen outside, before crossing the roadway to the main entrance of what policemen call 'Commissioner's Office'. When the senior detective at Scotland Yard, who had charge of all CID operations in London, requested the presence of a divisional detective inspector as soon as possible, he meant immediately.

The fifty-two-year-old Detective Chief Inspector Frederick Wensley, in every sense a big man, was soberly dressed in a dark suit, a wing collar and grey tie with a pearl tiepin. His impressive record as a detective included the solving of numerous murders and robberies, and in 1911 he had been standing alongside Winston Churchill, the Home Secretary, at the Sidney Street Siege. It was typical of him that on that occasion he had declined to carry a firearm. Described by journalists as 'Ace' on account of his detective prowess, he was known to fellow officers in the Metropolitan Police by the less complimentary soubriquet of 'the Elephant' because of the size of his nose. Originally a teetotaller, he had begun to drink when he found that informants did not trust a 'busy' who refused to drink with them.

'You wanted to see me, sir?' said Hardcastle as he entered the chief inspector's large office. Wensley was seated behind his desk, his back to a window that gave a sweeping view of the Thames. On the other side of the river was the half-built County Hall, the construction of which had been halted last year because of the war.

'Come in and take a seat, Ernie.' Wensley waited until Hardcastle had lowered himself on to one of the DCI's hard-backed chairs before asking, 'How do you like Hampshire?'

'Apart from going to Aldershot a few times on enquiries of the military, sir, I don't know the county at all well,' Hardcastle replied guardedly, wondering where the question was leading.

'In the circumstances a trip to Aldershot might prove to have been useful.' Wensley smiled and pulled a docket across his desk. 'The Chief Constable of the Hampshire County Constabulary has asked the Commissioner for assistance with a murder enquiry he's faced with. My detectives based here at the Yard are fully occupied so I suggested to Mr Thomson that I should send you, and he agreed immediately, not that he's got much time for us at the moment.' Basil Thomson, the Assistant Commissioner for Crime, was now almost completely occupied with Special Branch matters. It was a situation that pleased neither Superintendent Patrick Quinn, the head of that branch, who disliked interference, nor the rest of the CID, who felt neglected.

'When do I start, sir?'

'As soon as you can get down there, Ernie. That should give you a head start; the body was discovered early this morning.' Wensley glanced at the docket again. 'Around seven o'clock, apparently. Who d'you propose taking with you?'

'Marriott, sir. He's my first-class. A good man.'

Wensley turned over a page in the docket. 'As you don't know Hampshire, Ernie, I doubt you'll have heard of the village of Thresham Parva.'

'I can't say I have, sir.'

'You're not alone,' said Wensley with a chuckle. 'Neither had I until the Yard received this request. Apparently it's some six or seven miles from a place called Alton.' He raised his eyebrows questioningly.

'Haven't heard of that either, sir.'

'Nor me, but you're about to become very familiar with the area. I'll let you have the file in a moment, not that it'll be much help, but in short, the murder took place in Thresham Parva.' Wensley paused and tapped the docket with a pencil. He was a thorough and painstaking detective who never arrived at a conclusion unless there was evidence to support it. 'That is to say that Thresham Parva is the village where the body of the victim was *found*.'

'I wouldn't have thought a village murder would've exercised the Hampshire minds too much, sir.'

'Ah, but there are complications.'

'Oh!' said Hardcastle. 'What sort of complications, sir?'

'For a start, the murdered woman, a sixteen-year-old called Daisy Salter, is known to be free with her favours. And secondly, there are thousands of soldiers billeted at Aldershot, Ernie, and Aldershot is only seven miles from Thresham Parva. Put the two together and you could have the makings of a complicated topping.'

Hardcastle shook his head. 'I always seem to finish up working with the army, sir.'

'You must be good at it, Ernie.'

'I'll get on my way immediately, sir. Whereabouts is the headquarters of the Hampshire Police? I suppose I'd better start off by seeing the Chief Constable.'

'It's in Winchester, Ernie, but there's no need for you to go there.' Wensley opened the file. 'I've already spoken to Major Warde and he's happy for you to go straight to Alton and get on with the job.'

'That's refreshing, sir.' Generally, Hardcastle had no high regard for the average Chief Constable, particularly when the post was held by a superannuated naval or army officer who had no knowledge of policing. Many of them imagined the police to be an extension of the armed forces that should be commanded in the same way as a battleship or a regiment of cavalry.

'The Hampshire County Constabulary also has a number of detectives, Ernie. They should be all right: the Chief Constable sends them to us to be trained.'

'Wonders will never cease,' muttered Hardcastle as he rose to leave. 'Incidentally, sir, have you spoken to Mr Hudson?' Arthur Hudson, the superintendent in command of A Division, had no control over where Hardcastle was sent, but the DDI enjoyed a good relationship with him, and if Wensley had not told him then Hardcastle would.

'He's been advised as a matter of courtesy. I can see that there isn't too much outstanding crime on A Division at the moment so I'm happy for Detective Inspector Rhodes to act up while you're away. You and Marriott will be attached to Commissioner's Office for the duration of this case, Ernie. Let me have a report from time to time.' Wensley stood up and shook hands. 'But don't waste your time or mine sending in negative reports.'

* * *

'Come into my office, Marriott, *now*.' Hardcastle shouted his order through the open door of the detectives' office as he passed it.

'Sir?' Marriott was still buttoning his waistcoat as he entered the DDI's office.

'We've been given an out-of-town murder to deal with, Marriott.'

'Where, sir?' Marriott was never pleased with enquiries that took him out of London. He rarely knew how long he would be away, and his young wife Lorna had her hands full with the two children, a difficult enough task anyway, but made even more difficult when Marriott was not there.

'The village of Thresham Parva. Apparently it's just outside a place called Alton.'

'Which one, sir?'

'Which one?' Hardcastle raised his eyebrows. 'What d'you mean, which one?'

'There are four towns called Alton that I know of, sir. In Derbyshire, Hampshire, Staffordshire and Wiltshire.'

'You're much too clever for a sergeant, Marriott. In fact, you're a bloody know-all.'

'That's what I'm here for, sir,' said Marriott, risking a grin. And a reproof for insubordination.

'It's the Hampshire one,' said Hardcastle, 'and as you're so clever you can tell me how we get there.' He took out his pipe and began to fill it. Satisfied that he had not pressed the tobacco down too hard, he lit it and emitted a cloud of smoke towards the nicotine-stained ceiling of his office.

'I'll find out, sir.' A minute later, Marriott returned clutching a copy of Bradshaw's. 'Train from Waterloo, sir. According to the timetable it'll take about an hour.'

THREE

Hardcastle and Marriott returned to their respective homes to collect a razor and a toothbrush and such other items that they would require for a few days away, and after a tedious journey from Waterloo arrived at Alton railway station at four o'clock that afternoon.

A young man wearing a grey flannel suit, a shirt with a celluloid collar and a rather flamboyant tie was waiting on the platform as Hardcastle and Marriott alighted from the London train.

'Mr Hardcastle, sir?' The young man raised his straw boater.

'Yes.' Hardcastle studied the young man and wondered exactly who he was. Not yet thirty years old, he had chiselled good looks, eyes that were noticeably blue, and his hair, a little too long in Hardcastle's view, was blond. He certainly did not look like a policeman. 'What are you, a reporter?' he asked, assuming that word of the intervention of Yard officers in the murder had already reached the public domain.

'No, sir, I'm Detective Constable Yardley of the Hampshire County Constabulary, sir. I've been assigned to assist you.'

'Good gracious!' Hardcastle's two words could have been interpreted in a variety of ways.

'Mr Maddox sent me here to escort you to the police station, sir,' continued Yardley. 'I have a motor cab waiting.' He led the way out of the railway station and beckoned to a black car that was parked a few yards away.

'And who is Mr Maddox?' asked Hardcastle as he and Marriott settled themselves into the back seat of the taxi.

'He's the superintendent of the Alton Division, sir.' Yardley settled himself into the seat next to the driver.

'Is the police station far from here?'

'Less than a ten-minute drive if the High Street's not too crowded, sir. It's in Butts Road.'

'I'll take your word for it.' Hardcastle was not greatly interested in the location of the police station. 'By the way, this here is

Detective Sergeant Marriott. He's lost count of the number of murders he's solved.'

'Please to meet you, Sergeant.' Yardley stared at Marriott with undisguised admiration.

'What's your first name?' asked Marriott as he leaned forward to shake hands with the young detective. He was always concerned, when out of town, that local officers who were assisting the investigating officers should be made to feel part of the team.

'It's Richard, Sergeant, but everyone calls me Dick.'

'How did you know what time to meet me and Sergeant Marriott, Yardley?' queried Hardcastle, who had been wondering about that ever since the young policeman had greeted him at the railway station.

'I took the liberty of telephoning your office, sir. I spoke to a Mr Catto, one of your detectives, and he told me which train you were catching.'

'You were lucky to find him awake. In fact, you were lucky to find him at all,' muttered Hardcastle, who had no great opinion of DC Henry Catto, even though Catto was a good detective. Nevertheless, Hardcastle was impressed by the young Hampshire officer's initiative. Not that he had any intention of telling him so. 'Anyway, what can you tell me about this here murder, Yardley?'

'I'm stationed at headquarters at Winchester, sir,' said Yardley, 'and I've only just arrived in Alton myself. To be quite honest, I've not had the time to find out much about it yet, other than to say it occurred at Thresham Parva, a village a few miles from here, but I'm sure the superintendent will be able to tell you more about it. Ah, we're here,' he added as the taxi came to a halt outside a large white two-storey building.

'This is a big police station, lad,' said Hardcastle, who had not expected anything larger than the usual police house to be found in county constabulary areas. But he would be the first to admit, if only to himself, that he did not know very much about police forces outside London or how they operated.

'It's the divisional headquarters, sir, and the police court's here as well. A sergeant and some of the constables live here, and part of it is the superintendent's house.'

'D'you mean he lives next to the shop?' Hardcastle stared at the young detective in disbelief. At least when Hardcastle was required urgently, a message had to be sent to his local police station, and a constable had to be despatched from there to the Hardcastles' house in Kennington Road. But the thought that a PC would only have to go next door to get hold of him, day and night, was appalling. As things stood under the present arrangements, he knew that any of his detectives would think very carefully before making the decision to call him out.

'Yes, he does, sir,' said Yardley as he pulled open the main door. 'I'll show you to his office.'

The man who rose from behind the desk was tall and slim, and his uniform was immaculate. His neat moustache and carefully trimmed hair gave the overall impression of an army officer rather than a policeman, an impression that caused Hardcastle to wonder whether the Hampshire County Constabulary was in the habit of recruiting such men to the senior ranks. But it was not long before Hardcastle discovered that the Alton superintendent was what is known in the force as a policeman's policeman.

'Welcome to Hampshire, Mr Hardcastle. I'm Robert Maddox.' He skirted the desk and shook hands.

'Pleased to meet you, sir,' said Hardcastle. 'This is my bag carrier, Detective Sergeant Marriott.'

'Sergeant,' murmured Maddox as he shook hands with Marriott. He waved a hand to indicate that the two London detectives should take a seat. 'Ask someone to get us some tea, Yardley, there's a good chap.'

While the young detective was arranging for tea, Maddox took out his pipe and began to fill it. 'Do smoke if you wish, Mr Hardcastle.'

'What can you tell me about this murder, sir?' asked Hardcastle, once his pipe was alight.

'Only the bare facts,' said Maddox. 'The girl's body was discovered early this morning by a farmer on his land. He called the local constable and the body was removed to the mortuary here in Alton, where it awaits a post-mortem examination.'

'I'll want Spilsbury to do that, sir.' Hardcastle had great faith in Dr Bernard Spilsbury, whose reputation as a forensic pathologist had been established by his findings in the notorious Brides-in-the-Bath murders that culminated in the execution of George Joseph Smith. That case, in which Spilsbury had proved that the women had been murdered and had not drowned by accident, had placed him among the leaders of his profession, if not *the* leader.

'I'm sure that won't be a problem and, as you've been put in charge, I'll leave you to make the necessary arrangements,' said Maddox. 'The Chief Constable is very progressive in his outlook and he decided straight away that the Yard should be asked to investigate. This isn't one of those police forces that believes it can deal with everything. Quite frankly, Mr Hardcastle, we're not equipped to investigate complex murders – at least, not of the modern variety.'

'The modern variety?' queried Hardcastle, raising an eyebrow and fingering his moustache.

'A very famous case took place here fifty years ago this month, but it was an open-and-shut case,' said Maddox with a wry smile. 'It became known as the murder of Sweet Fanny Adams. Her killer, Frederick Baker, was arrested within hours by Superintendent Henry Rossiter who was in charge here at the time, and was hanged on Christmas Eve the same year.'

'I've certainly heard of Fanny Adams, sir, but I didn't realize it took place here.' Hardcastle accepted a cup of tea from Yardley, who had returned to the room with all the necessaries on a tray.

'Fanny Adams's decapitated body was found in Flood Meadow, not far from this police station,' continued Maddox, waving vaguely at his office window, 'but as I said just now it was a fairly straight-forward case. I fear the murder of Daisy Salter – she's the victim – will prove to be a little more difficult. But to get back to the details: as I said, her body was discovered this morning by a farmer, name of Blunden, at his farm in Thresham Parva. Thresham Parva is a village about six or seven miles from here and I would suggest that you speak first to PC Jessop, who is in charge of that area. He's a good man with twenty-five years' service, and frankly what he doesn't know about local goings-on in his village isn't worth knowing.'

'I'll need to get out there this evening, sir,' said Hardcastle, pulling out his watch and glancing at it. 'There's the question of transport, of course.'

'We haven't got any official transport in the force as yet, Mr Hardcastle, but the chief has assigned young Yardley here to assist you in every way possible, including arranging for taxis. The chief said that Mr Wensley spoke very highly of you, and he's hoping that Yardley might learn a thing or two about the investigation of murder while he's working with you.'

Hardcastle glanced at Yardley. 'Stick with me, lad, and you'll soon find out how we go about getting a killer dancing on the hangman's trapdoor.'

Yardley blinked at Hardcastle's uncompromising statement, but said nothing.

'I've taken the liberty of arranging accommodation for you and your sergeant at the Swan Hotel in the High Street, Mr Hardcastle. I trust that will be satisfactory.'

'I'm much obliged, sir,' said Hardcastle, 'and now we'll get about the business of murder. Come, Marriott.'

'I anticipated that you might want to go out to Thresham Parva straight away, sir,' said Yardley as the trio left the superintendent's office, 'so I kept the taxi waiting.'

'You'll be costing your Chief Constable a pretty penny if you've kept the meter running for that length of time, Yardley.' Not that Hardcastle cared how much it was costing the Hampshire force; a sharp contrast to his own attitude to expenses incurred on his own division. At least by his junior officers.

Yardley grinned. 'We've hired it for the duration of the investigation, sir, so it doesn't matter how long we keep him hanging about. Anyway, I'm sure that Jed Young – he's the owner and driver of the taxi – will be quite happy to be tied up with a murder enquiry. I doubt if he'll have to buy a drink for many a week after it's all over.'

'So long as he keeps his mouth shut until we've got a noose round our killer's neck, he won't upset me,' said Hardcastle, secretly impressed by the astute husbandry practised by the Hampshire County Constabulary in the hiring of taxis. Clearly the Chief Constable was a man after Hardcastle's own heart.

'I presume you'll want to register at the hotel on the way, sir.'

'No, Yardley, that can wait,' said Hardcastle. 'The first thing to remember about a murder is the sooner we get to grips with it, the sooner we get a result. What happened to our bags?'

'Still in the boot of the taxi, sir.'

The police house at Thresham Parva was situated on the edge of the village and was no different from its neighbours except for a blue lamp and a modest sign.

Clearly expecting the arrival of the Scotland Yard detectives, PC Edward Jessop had appeared in the open front door as the taxi drew up.

'Evening, Ted,' said Yardley. 'This is Divisional Detective Inspector Hardcastle and Detective Sergeant Marriott of the Metropolitan Police.'

'Welcome, gentlemen. Come along in.' Jessop led the way through a room containing a desk and into the parlour at the back of the house. 'This is my wife, Annie,' he said, indicating a plump, rosy-cheeked woman in her forties. Her grey hair was neatly dressed into a bun and she wore a white blouse and a plain black skirt.

'How d'you do, sir,' said Annie. 'Sit yourselves down. I daresay you could do with a cup of tea and a slice of cake while you're talking.'

'I can recommend Annie's homemade plum cake, sir,' said Jessop. 'But you'll want to know a bit more about this murder.'

'I want to know *all* about it, Mr Jessop,' said Hardcastle. 'Your superintendent has only given me very brief details.'

'Right you are, sir.' Jessop took out his pocketbook, opened it and rested it on his knee. 'Josh Blunden – he's the owner of South Farm – was out and about at five this morning as he usually is, and at about half past six came across the body of young Daisy Salter. She was lying behind a hedge not more than three feet from the road.'

'How old was this girl?' asked Marriott, making notes in his pocketbook.

'Sixteen, Sergeant,' said Jessop. 'She's the daughter of Alfred and Rose Salter. Alf Salter's the local coal merchant.'

'If Blunden was out on his farm at about five o'clock, how was it he didn't come across this body until half past six?' asked Hardcastle.

'Josh Blunden always works his way round the farm in a set pattern of a morning, sir,' said Jessop. 'He walks round the perimeter making sure the fences are intact and that there aren't any dead sheep. This time of year he always inspects the haystacks as well. So he wouldn't have gone anywhere near where the body was until the time he said. I was surprised to see him standing there because he's usually having breakfast at that time.' Jessop paused to glance down at his pocketbook. 'That'd be five minutes to seven, sir, when I arrived at the scene.'

'Where's the body now, Mr Jessop?'

'In the mortuary at the Cottage Hospital in Crown Close in Alton, sir.'

'Has a post-mortem been conducted?'

'No, sir,' said Yardley. 'The police doctor, Doctor John Mears, certified death this morning. He suggested that death was the result of manual strangulation, but I understand that you told Mr Maddox at Alton that you'll be getting Doctor Spilsbury down from London to do the post-mortem, sir.'

'Quite right, Yardley.'

'But Doctor Mears is a very good doctor, sir,' volunteered Yardley, somewhat unwisely.

'I daresay he is, lad,' said Hardcastle, 'but how many post-mortem examinations has he carried out on murder victims? And how many times has he given evidence in a murder trial?'

'Ah, yes, I see what you mean, sir,' said Yardley, determined that he would think carefully before he made any more observations.

'Well, Mr Jessop, now we know the details of the finding of the body, so to speak, what's known about this Daisy Salter? What's the local gossip?'

'She was nothing but trouble, Mr Hardcastle.' Annie Jessop spoke before her husband had a chance to answer.

Jessop frowned at his wife's intervention. 'I'm not sure the inspector wants to hear—'

'Oh, but the inspector most definitely does,' said Hardcastle, who had learned over the years that policemen's wives were mines of information. On the few occasions he had ventured out of London, he had found that the wife of a country copper often had her ears well attuned to local gossip. 'Do go on, Mrs Jessop.'

'It's not the sort of thing that Rose Salter would ever have talked to Ted about,' said Annie Jessop, nodding towards her husband, 'because once you tell the local bobby anything you sort of make it official. But when she tells me something she knows I'll tell Ted and so he'll know, but not official like, if you know what I mean.'

'I understand perfectly,' said Hardcastle. 'I take it that Rose Salter is the girl's mother?' That Rose was married to Alfred Salter did not necessarily make her the girl's mother, and the question was an indication of Hardcastle's thoroughness.

'Yes, she is, sir.' Mrs Jessop paused to offer second cups of tea and more cake. 'But Rose often poured her heart out to me about young Daisy. It wouldn't surprise me to know that she was the cause of Rose having her stroke. The long and the short of it was that Daisy was nothing but trouble to her parents. I'll speak frankly, Mr Hardcastle, but I understood from Rose that young Daisy had been with just about every boy in the village. And when I say "been with" I'm talking in the biblical sense.' She paused again. 'And from what I've heard it was usually in one of Farmer Blunden's haystacks.'

'And this girl's body was found on Mr Blunden's property.' Marriott, looking up from his note-taking, was also being thorough.

'That's correct, Sergeant,' said Jessop.

'In that case we'll have to have a word with the farmer, sooner rather than later,' said Hardcastle.

'I don't think he knew anything about this affair, sir.' To Jessop it sounded as though Hardcastle suspected Blunden of being implicated in the girl's death.

'I don't suppose he did, Mr Jessop, but he might have turfed the girl out of one his haystacks and said nothing about it to anyone else. In which case he'd likely know the boy she was with.'

'I think he'd have mentioned it to me if he had, sir.' Jessop was slightly aggrieved that he might not have known about something that had occurred on his manor, even something as trivial and commonplace as a boy and a girl canoodling in a haystack.

'Oh, come now, Mr Jessop. It's the sort of thing that's been going on since time immemorial. But when it comes to murder it's a different thing altogether.'

'D'you want me to have a word with him about it, sir?' asked Jessop.

'No, I'll put him on my list of things to do. Now then, is there a decent hostelry in the village?'

'The Thresham Arms is in the centre of the village, sir, opposite the village green.'

'Excellent.' Hardcastle glanced at his half-hunter, wound it briefly and dropped it back into his waistcoat pocket. 'Half past six. I imagine you're off duty about now, Mr Jessop.'

'I could be, sir. D'you have something in mind?'

'I've always found that the local pub in any community is the place where you'll pick up all manner of interesting information.'

'It's only a short stride from here, sir. I'll just get changed very quickly.'

When Jessop returned to the parlour, Hardcastle picked up his bowler hat and umbrella. 'Thank you for the tea, Mrs Jessop, and your excellent plum cake. I can see that Mr Jessop is well fed.'

'Oh, thank you, sir,' said Annie Jessop, only just preventing herself from curtsying.

As Jessop had said, the Thresham Arms was situated in the centre of the village opposite what appeared, at first sight, to be a ploughed field, in the middle of which was a pond.

'Strange place for a pond,' commented Hardcastle.

'It's because of the war, sir,' said Jessop. 'That's the village green, or used to be. It's been dug up for planting vegetables and the like. It's the food shortages, you see.'

'German submarines,' said Hardcastle.

'I suppose it would be, sir,' said Jessop, not quite understanding the Londoner's somewhat enigmatic remark.

There was an expectant pause in the conversation as the four policemen walked into the saloon bar of the inn. But whether it was the presence of PC Jessop or the arrival of the Scotland Yard officers in their midst was open to conjecture. One thing was certain: the locals would already have heard about the arrival of the London detectives and the reason for it.

A squat man with a bald head, save for tufts of grey hair at the sides, who looked as though he could have been a useful wrestler in his youth, wiped the top of the bar. 'Evening, Mr Jessop.' He looked enquiringly at Hardcastle and Marriott.

'This is Inspector Hardcastle and Sergeant Marriott, Tom, and Dick Yardley, one of our local detectives,' said Jessop. He turned to Hardcastle. 'This is Tom Hooker, the landlord, sir.'

'Pleased to make your acquaintance, I'm sure, sir,' said Hooker. 'You must be the gents from Scotland Yard come to deal with the murder of the coal merchant's lass.'

'That's right,' agreed Hardcastle, 'and I'll trouble you for four pints of your best bitter.' He assumed that was what everyone would be drinking and had not bothered to ask.

'Coming right up, sir.' Hooker busied himself drawing the beer and placing the pints on the counter. 'There we are, gents – best Alton ale, that is, and I defy you to find any better in the country.'

Hardcastle took the head off his beer and nodded. 'I believe you're right, Mr Hooker.' He laid a ten-shilling note on the bar.

'No need for that, sir.' Hooker pushed the note back.

'I insist,' said Hardcastle sharply. Out of his environment and working on the basis that everyone was a suspect until proved otherwise, he had no intention of being beholden to anyone.

'Very well, sir.' Hooker took the money and counted out the change.

Jessop moved closer to Hardcastle. 'I hope you won't think me impertinent, sir, but might I remind you of the "no-treating" order?' As the local constable, Jessop was obliged to enforce what he and other policemen saw as one of many footling regulations made under the Defence of the Realm Act and which was more often honoured in the breach.

'I'm well aware of the no-treating order, Mr Jessop,' said Hardcastle loudly, 'which is why you, Sergeant Marriott and DC Yardley here will all reimburse me later on.' He laughed and was pleased to see that the other customers joined in, but only Marriott knew that the DDI was being serious. Turning to the landlord, Hardcastle asked, 'Do you have accommodation here?'

'Indeed we do, sir,' said Hooker. 'Two or three very comfortable rooms and all empty at the moment.'

'And Amy Hooker's a very good cook, sir,' added Jessop. 'I can recommend her steak-and-kidney pudding.'

'In the circumstances, Mr Jessop,' said Hardcastle, turning to the local policeman, 'I was thinking that as my enquiries are likely to be in and around Thresham Parva, Sergeant Marriott and me don't really want to be travelling back and forth to Alton every day.'

'But you're booked into the Swan Hotel there, sir,' said Yardley, who until now had remained silent.

'Ah, well, that's a job for you, Yardley. You can cancel it the minute you get back. And now, Mr Hooker, perhaps you can accommodate Sergeant Marriott and me until we have our murderer with a rope round his neck.'

'No doubt you'll have your luggage at the Swan, sir. I can provide you with a razor and soap and flannel and that sort of thing until you can send for it.'

'My luggage is in the taxi up at the police house, Mr Hooker. Young Yardley here had the foresight to bring it with us. In the meantime, I think we'll have another round of your excellent ale.'

'Do you get many soldiers in the village, Mr Hooker?' asked Marriott. 'I understand that Aldershot is only a few miles away.'

'We used to get a few coming out here from time to time, sir,' said Hooker, 'to get away from the military atmosphere of Aldershot, so they said. It was mainly the older men who'd been used to a decent pub and a quiet pint afore they was conscripted. But then the younger elements learned about this place and they found out about the pretty girls in the village. Well, the upshot was we had a very nasty fight in here one weekend.'

'I finished up having to call out the mounted military police from Aldershot before order was restored, sir,' said Jessop. 'Anyway, a complaint was made and the whole village was put out of bounds by the general officer commanding Aldershot Garrison. Pity really because, like Tom said, there were a few of the older soldiers who came here to get away from it all.'

'And you've had no trouble since?' asked Hardcastle.

'No, sir,' confirmed Jessop. 'Some of the same mounted military policemen come out here from time to time just to make sure.'

'We offered to hide the quieter swaddies when the redcaps turn up,' said Hooker. 'It wouldn't have been a problem because you can hear the provost's horses clattering down the road a mile off, but the older men wouldn't risk it. So, no, we don't get any military here any more. Mind you, it's cost me quite a bit of money in takings,' he added gloomily.

'What was the fight about?' asked Hardcastle.

'More a case of *who* it was about, sir,' said Jessop. 'Daisy Salter.'

'Ah, I wondered if that might be the case.'

'As far as I could tell, young Daisy had promised to go out with both of the swaddies concerned, but on different days. Unfortunately they both turned up in here on the same night.

The next thing that happened were flying fists and about a dozen or more soldiers were knocking hell out of each other. There was quite a lot of damage done to chairs and tables and that sort of thing, but the general at Aldershot made sure it was all paid for.'

FOUR

When he was at home, Hardcastle always insisted that he could not go to work without having what he termed 'a proper breakfast'.

Alice Hardcastle usually managed to produce fried eggs, a rasher or two of bacon, two pieces of fried bread and a couple of sausages followed by two slices of toast and marmalade. This sumptuous banquet was washed down with three cups of tea, in each of which Hardcastle always put two spoonfuls of sugar.

He was never quite sure how his wife managed such a meal when, by the late summer of 1917, a voluntary code of food rationing had been introduced, led by the King. But it was a very confusing arrangement: some retailers enforced it, others did not. Among the other staples it was suggested that meat, including bacon, should be set at two-and-a-half pounds per person per week, and two large loaves of bread for each adult per week. Three-quarters of a pound of sugar a week was suggested, but this became an irrelevancy when it was more difficult to obtain.

Some time ago, Hardcastle had concluded that his wife was being afforded preferential treatment by the grocer around the corner in Lambeth Road, who was aware that Hardcastle was a senior police officer. It was not a matter, Hardcastle thought, into which it would be politic to enquire too deeply. If, as a result, the grocer imagined for one moment that Hardcastle would overlook any transgression of the law, which now included many minor regulations made under the Defence of the Realm Act, then he was sadly mistaken.

To his delight, Hardcastle found that Amy Hooker, the wife of the landlord of the Thresham Arms, was just as obliging as Alice Hardcastle when it came to the provision of breakfast.

'Just like home, Mrs Hooker,' said Hardcastle, rubbing his hands together as a plate of eggs, bacon, sausages and a slice of black pudding was placed in front of him. 'I really don't know how you do it.'

Amy Hooker made a parody of glancing around the deserted dining room as though fearful of a government eavesdropper before whispering in the DDI's ear. 'We have an arrangement with Josh Blunden up at South Farm, Mr Hardcastle. The fact of the matter is that Josh likes a bottle of Scotch and we're happy to supply it. And Tom and I, to say nothing of our guests, like eggs and bacon and Josh can provide them, if you see what I mean. But it's all very hush-hush, and I hope you won't tell the police,' she added, and laughed.

Hardcastle laughed too. 'Oh, I do understand, Mrs Hooker, I do,' he said warmly. 'You see, Marriott,' he added, turning to his sergeant, 'this wretched war has brought back the old system of barter.'

'That young Mr Yardley's just arrived,' said Amy Hooker, glancing out of the dining-room window as the taxi drew up.

'Perhaps we could have another pot of tea, Mrs Hooker, and then we must get to work.'

'Good morning, sir.' Yardley appeared in the dining room. 'I've just received a message from London to say that Doctor Spilsbury is arriving at Alton station at ten o'clock, sir.'

'Is he indeed?' Hardcastle took out his watch and stared at it. 'In that case we'd better get along there to meet him. Don't bother with the tea, Mrs Hooker,' he shouted as he and the other two dashed from the dining room.

'Good to see you again, my dear Hardcastle,' exclaimed Spilsbury effusively as he emerged from the railway station. 'Having a sojourn in the country, I gather.'

'You could call it that, sir, but I fear that it'll be more work than pleasure,' said Hardcastle, leading the way to the taxi.

'It was ever thus, my dear Hardcastle.' Spilsbury handed his Gladstone bag, top hat and cane to Yardley, presuming him to be the taxi driver.

'This is Detective Constable Yardley of the Hampshire County Constabulary, sir,' said Marriott hurriedly. He did not want there to be any bad blood between the Metropolitan Police and local officers, something that Hardcastle rarely thought about. In fact, Marriott wondered if the DDI sometimes forgot that he had local officers assisting him whenever he was away from London. 'He's helping us with his comprehensive knowledge of the conditions and people in these parts,' he added, anxious that Spilsbury should not infer that Yardley was a dogsbody who was there simply for the sake of appearances.

'Splendid!' exclaimed Spilsbury as he clambered into the back seat of the taxi. 'Stay close to Mr Hardcastle, young man, and you'll learn a great deal of the black art of investigating murder. Never lost a case yet, have you, Hardcastle?'

'No, sir,' said Hardcastle firmly. Nevertheless, he could not help thinking back to the murders just a year ago of Rose Drummond and Edith Sturgess, and the unsatisfactory conclusion to those two cases. The man he had strongly suspected of being responsible for the women's murders was killed by an artillery shell in the small Belgian town of Poperinge. Hardcastle had been there himself to make the arrest when the attack had occurred.

'Where have you put my cadaver, Yardley?' asked Spilsbury suddenly.

'Er, at the Cottage Hospital, sir. It's, um, in Crown Close, sir,' said Yardley, clearly taken aback at being asked a question by the great pathologist.

'Excellent! I suppose you know this area well, Hardcastle,' suggested Spilsbury, returning his attention to the DDI, 'otherwise they wouldn't have sent you down here.'

'On the contrary, Doctor. I'd only ever been to Aldershot, but Mr Wensley decided that I should come here to assist the local police.'

'I'd long ago concluded that the Metropolitan Police moves in mysterious ways, Hardcastle,' said Spilsbury.

'Will you require accommodation here, sir?' asked Yardley, now becoming a little bolder. 'The Swan in Alton town centre is a very good hotel.'

'I shan't be stopping, young man, but thank you for thinking of it. I shall make short work of carving up this young lady and then go back to London later today.'

'Oh!' Yardley was astounded at the pathologist's bluntness. Furthermore, he was rapidly coming to the conclusion that London people tended to move much faster than those in country districts.

Having been forewarned that the great London pathologist would be visiting, a reception committee was waiting at the door of Alton Cottage Hospital to greet him when he and the detectives arrived.

'Welcome to my humble hospital, Doctor Spilsbury, sir,' said a fussy little man with a toothbrush moustache and a foldover hairstyle. 'I am Doctor Clarence Willey, the surgical resident.' Beside the doctor stood the matron, a woman of austere countenance whose uniform was so heavily starched that Hardcastle thought she might have difficulty sitting down.

'Be so good as to show me to your mortuary, Willey. Don't have much time, you see, and neither does the inspector here.'

'Oh, er, certainly, yes, Doctor.' Like Yardley, Willey was taken aback by the haste of the London men, and somewhat disappointed. He had purchased a bottle of sherry and a selection of small cakes and had arranged them on a table in his office where, he had hoped, he would entertain the famous pathologist before he started work – and maybe pick up one or two pieces of advice.

Willey led Spilsbury along a corridor, through a set of double doors and into a white-tiled room. The body of Daisy Salter was laid out on a steel table, beside which a nurse was standing.

'This is Joan Attwood, my theatre sister, Doctor,' said Willey.

'How d'you do?' said Spilsbury, giving the sister a cursory nod.

'Very well, thank you, sir,' said Sister Attwood, bobbing a curtsy.

'You don't have to curtsy to me, Sister,' said Spilsbury. 'I'm just a simple doctor, not royalty.' He took off his jacket, tossed it on to a table and looked around for an apron. With all the solicitude of an unctuous head waiter, Doctor Willey rushed across the room holding up a rubber apron.

'This is the body of Daisy Salter, is it, Yardley?' asked Hardcastle, aware of the need for continuity of evidence.

'It is, sir. It was identified by PC Jessop as Daisy Salter and handed over to me. I took possession of it and gave it into Doctor Willey's custody here yesterday morning. There are signatures for each occasion the body was handed over.'

'Good,' said Hardcastle, and then added a rare word of praise. 'I see you know your business down here.' He turned to Spilsbury. 'We'll see you later on, sir.'

'Should be finished in time for lunch, Hardcastle. D'you happen to know a good place for a bite to eat?'

'The Swan Hotel, sir,' volunteered Yardley.

'I hope you're right, young man,' said Spilsbury. And with a perfectly straight face added, 'I'm beginning to wonder if you've got shares in that establishment.'

'Good heavens, no, sir,' spluttered Yardley. 'Police officers are not permitted to—'

But before the hapless Yardley was able to complete his protest, Spilsbury laughed uproariously and turned to Hardcastle. 'Perhaps you and your colleagues will join me for lunch if you have the time, my dear fellow.'

'Most kind, sir,' murmured Hardcastle, determined that nothing would keep him away from a free meal.

'Where to now, sir?' asked Yardley.

'We'll begin at the beginning, Yardley,' said Hardcastle, as though that course of action were obvious. 'We'll speak to the man who found the victim and get his version of events.'

'You must be the gentlemen from Scotland Yard.' The speaker was a man of no more than five-foot-six-inches tall, but what he lacked in height was more than made up for by his muscular build, and his weather-beaten face and arms testified to a life spent largely in the open air.

'Yes, we are. I'm Divisional Detective Inspector Hardcastle and this is Detective Sergeant Marriott.' Hardcastle had no intention of dropping the prefix 'divisional' just because he was temporarily attached to Scotland Yard; it was, after all, a rank above that of detective inspector. 'You probably know Detective Constable Yardley of the local force.' He indicated the Hampshire officer with a wave of the hand. 'And you, I take it, are Joshua Blunden, the owner of this farm.'

'I am, sir.' Blunden shook Hardcastle's hand with a firm grip. 'Come along in. I've been expecting you, and I daresay a cup of tea wouldn't go amiss. I'll get Martha to put the kettle on.' Hardcastle and Marriott were obliged to duck in order to get through the door, and Hardcastle surmised that the farmhouse was probably a hundred years old, at least. The farmer showed the two detectives into the stone-flagged kitchen and invited them to sit down at a scrubbed wooden table. The plaster-rendered walls were whitewashed and a row of copper saucepans hung from hooks on the wall adjacent to the range. A large copper-lined washtub stood in one corner alongside a mangle and a large porcelain sink. Hardcastle imagined that the room would be very snug in winter-time, and even now was a little too warm for comfort, despite all the windows being open. But he then realized that the warmth came from the kitchen range.

'What on earth are you doing, Joshua Blunden?' The farmer's wife turned indignantly from the range. She was a large woman with greying hair dressed into a single plait, but one or two strands had escaped and she flicked them away from her forehead with the back of her hand. 'Take our visitors into the parlour this minute,' she said, dabbing at the perspiration on her face with the corner of her apron.

'We're more than happy to sit here in the kitchen, Mrs Blunden,' said Hardcastle. 'It's much more homely.'

'Well, if you're sure you don't mind, sir, but it don't seem proper entertaining in the kitchen, particularly London folk,' said Martha Blunden, reluctantly admitting defeat. 'I'll make you gentlemen some tea, and then I'll leave you to talk business.'

'I'd rather you stayed, Mrs Blunden,' said Hardcastle, who always appreciated the value of a woman's contribution, particu-larly where there was a possibility that local gossip might reveal some telling information. 'Have you farmed here for long, Mr Blunden?' The DDI turned back to the farmer.

'All my life. I was born in this house, Mr Hardcastle, fifty years since, and I inherited the farm when my father died the Christmas afore the war started. Out cutting holly, he was, the old fool, and he stood up in his trap, overreached hisself and dropped dead.'

'Most unfortunate,' muttered Hardcastle gruffly. Never very accomplished at expressing condolences, he promptly switched to more familiar territory. 'I understand that it was you who found the body of Daisy Salter yesterday morning.'

'A terrible tragedy, Mr Hardcastle, and so young too.' Blunden moved his chair so that he was facing the policemen across the table.

'What time was this?'

'I explained all this to Mr Jessop. He's the local policeman.'

'I know, but I'd like you to tell me because I might have some questions, and so might my sergeant here. And then our Hampshire officer will take a written statement from you.' Turning to Yardley, he said, 'You'd better start taking notes, lad.' It was an order that caused Yardley some apprehension. Even though he had met Hardcastle only a short while ago, he had already concluded that the London DDI was not a man who tolerated mistakes or sloppy police work.

'I see,' continued Blunden. 'Well, it was half past six yesterday morning, give or take a few minutes, and I was just finishing my rounds—'

'What rounds are they?'

'Making sure everything is all right. That the fences and hedges were still in good order, and there hadn't been any dogs worrying my sheep. There's a lot to running a farm of this size, Mr Hardcastle, I can tell you, even though I've got three girls from this new Women's Land Army that the government started last February, and one or two prisoners-of-war what's brought over from Aldershot every now and then. Anyhow, I was making my way back across five-acre field for breakfast with Martha, like I always do at that time, when I happened across young Daisy Salter's body. I knew Mr Jessop would be along any minute, so I waited there for him.'

'You knew this girl Daisy Salter, did you, Mr Blunden?' asked Marriott.

'Yes, of course I did, Mr Marriott. Everyone knows everyone else in the village, apart from them up at the college.'

'College? What college is that?' Hardcastle looked up sharply. It was the first that he had heard of a college and he took a sudden interest.

'It's a private boarding school for the sons of the well-to-do, sir,' said Yardley.

'How old are these boys, Yardley?'

'From about eleven to eighteen or thereabouts, sir. Mind you, they've never been any trouble.'

'You mean they haven't been caught.' Hardcastle spoke bluntly, suddenly realizing that he may have a lot more suspects than he had first imagined. 'Anyhow, we'll talk about that later. Do go on, Mr Blunden.'

'I daresay you'd like a slice of upside-down cake,' interrupted Martha Blunden as she handed round cups of tea. 'Made with apples from our own orchard.'

'Thank you, Mrs Blunden, that would be most welcome.'
Hardcastle was beginning to realize that living in a country area
had certain advantages that outweighed those of living in London.
'I understand that you've had dealings with Daisy Salter in the
past, Mr Blunden.' The DDI turned back to the farmer. 'Found
her in one of your haystacks, I believe.'

'It hasn't taken you long to pick up the local gossip,' said
Blunden with a chuckle. 'Yes, only a week or two back, it was. I
thought I got a glimpse of movement in one of my stacks one
evening, 'bout seven o'clock it were, so I walked across and there
was Daisy with young Charlie Snapper, kissing and cuddling. I
bloody soon gave them the bum's rush, I can tell you.'

'Language, Josh!' cautioned Martha.

'Sorry, love. You see, Mr Hardcastle, if the boy was smoking
a cigarette there's always the possibility of a fire. I don't know if
you've ever seen a stack go up in flames, but it don't take long.
Mind you, it weren't the first time I've caught youngsters fooling
about in a stack.'

'There's no need to be so hoity-toity about it, Joshua Blunden,'
said Martha, her face suddenly breaking into a broad smile. 'I
seem to recall you and me doing something of the like in one of
them very same haystacks when your pa weren't about. Mind you,
that was more years ago than I care to remember now,' she added
with a laugh.

'I think what Martha's suggesting, Mr Hardcastle,' said Blunden,
'is that that sort of thing's been going on ever since the good Lord
invented haystacks for the benefit of Adam and Eve. I never paid
too much attention to two youngsters doing what comes naturally,
but now this terrible thing's happened, I s'pose I should have
mentioned it to Mr Jessop at the time.'

'You said it wasn't the first time, Mr Blunden,' said Marriott.
'D'you mean you caught Daisy Salter in one of your haystacks
on a previous occasion?'

'Aye, I did that. That were just afore Christmas. Her and that
young tearaway Harry Watts. Surprised they never caught the pneu-
monia, not having much on at the time. Freezing cold, it were.'

'Is Harry Watts a local lad?' asked Marriott.

'He was,' said Martha Blunden, 'but you could say he shaped
up all right in the end. Volunteered for the Hampshire Regiment

as soon as he was old enough. About six months ago, that'd be. Got killed almost straight off when the Messines Ridge was taken back in June.'

'You said that you'd come across Daisy Salter at about seven one evening, Mr Blunden,' said Marriott. 'Were you by any chance near that spot last evening?'

'Yes, I was, as a matter of fact.'

'Did you see anyone in the area? Anyone at all?'

'No, sir, I didn't. I usually have a last walk round afore it gets too dark, and to give the dog a run, but I never saw anyone last evening.'

'I think that'll do for the moment, Mr Blunden,' said Hardcastle, having decided that he had obtained as much information as he could from the farmer and his wife, at least for the time being. 'Mr Yardley here will take a written statement from you about what you've been telling us and then perhaps you'd show me exactly where you found the Salter girl's body. But while the statement is being taken, Mrs Blunden, another slice of your very tasty upside-down cake wouldn't go amiss.'

At last the laborious task of taking Blunden's statement was completed and Hardcastle stood up. 'Thank you for the tea and the cake, Mrs Blunden.'

'Always a pleasure for someone what appreciates a bit of home cooking, sir,' said Martha Blunden.

'I'll show you up to five-acre field, sir,' said Joshua Blunden as he put on his cap and selected a walking stick from a stand by the back door. 'We'll go along the road, sir, and that'll save you getting your boots too mucky. We've had a lot of rain this month – more than usual.' He clicked his fingers at the sleeping Border collie. 'Come on, Bess.'

It took over ten minutes to reach five-acre field. Joshua Blunden pushed open the gate and led the detectives in. 'It were just here, sir,' he said, using his walking stick to point at the place immediately behind the hedge where he had come across Daisy Salter's body.

'Is that haystack by any chance the one where you found Daisy Salter and Charlie Snapper, Mr Blunden?' asked Hardcastle, pointing to a stack that was only about thirty yards from the road.

'That's the one, sir. I'm thinking of building it much further back from the road next year. It's a mite too handy for youngsters who want to go canoodling and it's a long way from the farmhouse. Where it is now they can see me coming so they've time to escape before I reach 'em, so to speak. But like I said, it's the fire risk that worries me, and more and more youngsters seem to be smoking cigarettes these days.'

'Shocking habit,' said Hardcastle, shooting a glance at his cigarette-smoking sergeant. 'Was there a search of this area after the body was discovered, Yardley?' he asked suddenly, turning to the Hampshire DC.

'I was told that PC Jessop had a look round, sir.'

'Did he find anything?'

'Not as far as I know, sir.'

'I think we need a proper search of the area,' said Hardcastle, to no one in particular. 'How easily can you organize that, Yardley?'

'It would mean calling in officers from all over the county, sir,' said Yardley thoughtfully. 'On the other hand, there's the Alton troop of the Boy Scouts. They're all reliable lads and I daresay they'd be pleased to help.'

'Yes,' said Hardcastle. 'I think they'd probably be more diligent than policemen when it comes to doing an area search. Arrange for a good look at the ground between the haystack and here.' He pointed at the spot where the girl's body was found. 'And we might have to widen the search later, but that'll do for a start.' He turned to Joshua Blunden. 'I'm sure I'll have to see you again, Mr Blunden, but in the meantime I'd ask you to avoid going over this piece of land until it's been searched.'

'Of course, sir,' said the farmer, 'and if there's anything else I can help you with, you're welcome to call in any time.'

Hardcastle turned to the Hampshire officer. 'I take it you know where Mr and Mrs Salter live, Yardley.'

'Yes, sir. PC Jessop told me that they've a place at the other end of the village.' Yardley paused as he opened the door of the waiting taxi. 'I trust I did all right taking Mr Blunden's statement, sir. I know it's important and I hope I've not missed anything out.'

'Sergeant Marriott will cast his eye over it, Yardley,' said Hardcastle. 'He'll soon let you know if anything's wrong with it.'

It was a comment that did little to reassure the Hampshire detective.

FIVE

The Salters' modest house was adjacent to the coal yard from where Alfred Salter carried on his business. A four-wheeled dray, its shafts raised, stood next to a stable from which the head of a carthorse gazed inquisitively at the arrival of three strangers and occasionally pawed the cobbled floor with a hoof. A lean-to shelter attached to the stable was stacked high with logs and the whole of one side of the yard was taken up with a huge pile of coal. Two young men were busy filling sacks from this pile, but neither of them looked up at the arrival of the police. Their apparent indifference caused Hardcastle to be suspicious and he made a mental note to find out who they were. In his experience the arrival of police would usually attract the interest of bystanders, whereas those who avoided eye contact usually had something to hide. And there was no doubt that by now everyone in the village knew who they were.

A laurel mourning wreath hung on the front door of the house and although intended to dissuade visitors from imposing upon the Salters' grief, Hardcastle had no intention of being deterred by it. He rapped loudly on the lion's-head knocker.

The man who answered the door was probably in his mid-forties, although he looked older, and greeted the visitors with a melancholy face. Dressed in a dark suit, he wore a black tie and an armband of black silk on his right sleeve.

'Mr Salter?' asked Hardcastle.

'Yes, I'm Alfred Salter,' the man answered listlessly.

'We're police officers, sir,' said Hardcastle. 'I'm sorry to intrude at such a time, but we need to speak to you and I'm afraid our investigations cannot be delayed.'

'I quite understand,' said Salter. 'Please come into the parlour.'

It was a cluttered, gloomy room dominated by brown paintwork, brown curtains and sepia wallpaper with an uninspiring pattern of brown leaves. There seemed to be bric-a-brac on every available surface and where there were no ornaments there were numerous photographs, presumably of family, but at a quick glance there appeared to be none of Daisy Salter. A framed text hung on the wall over the fireplace. It read: *For whatsoever a man soweth, that shall he also reap.*

A woman turned from the net-curtained window out of which she had been watching the arrival of the three policemen. Her facial expression implied that she was bitter, argumentative and hard done by. It was the sort of belligerent face that Hardcastle's old mother would have described as likely to turn the milk sour. Her black hair was shoulder-length, straight and parted in the centre. The black bombazine dress she wore was of the style that had become customary mourning attire since it was adopted by Queen Victoria following the death of her beloved Prince Albert fifty-six years ago. Overall, the impression was of a woman who fully intended to observe the customary fifteen months of full mourning followed by three months of half-mourning, and may even have revelled in doing so.

'This is my wife, Rose,' said Salter.

'Good morning, madam,' said Hardcastle. 'I'm Divisional Detective Inspector Hardcastle of New Scotland Yard; this is Detective Sergeant Marriott also of the Yard and Detective Constable Yardley of the local force.'

Rose Salter said nothing but merely nodded in the detectives' direction. With the aid of a walking stick she limped across the room before sitting down in an armchair close to the fireplace. She stared into the empty hearth and at first appeared loath to talk to the police, let alone discuss her dead daughter with them.

'You have my sympathy,' murmured Hardcastle clumsily, affording Rose Salter a brief glance before returning his gaze to her husband. He was about to pose his first question when Rose Salter spoke.

'I hope you're going to catch whoever did this to my Daisy.' She burst into tears and immediately produced a lace handkerchief with which to dab at her eyes. It was almost as if she had been holding back her grief until she had uttered that one statement.

'You may rest assured of that, madam,' said Hardcastle. 'The net is closing already and her murderer will shortly be caught and hanged.'

Standing behind the DDI, Yardley was astounded at Hardcastle's confidence. From what he had learned so far, he had not the faintest idea who might have murdered Daisy Salter. What he did not know, of course, was that neither had Hardcastle.

'I'm sorry that we can't offer you a cup of tea or the like, gentlemen,' said Salter, 'but we told Maisie – our maid – to take a few days off. And we are teetotal: no alcohol has ever crossed the threshold of this house,' he added sanctimoniously. His voice sounded nasal, and he had an irritating habit of fidgeting with the square and compasses device on the watch chain that was strung between his waistcoat pockets.

'Why did you give her time off?' asked Hardcastle. 'Surely you need help around the house now more than ever.'

'I'm afraid Maisie was upset something dreadful about Daisy's death, Inspector.'

'Is there a particular reason for her distress, Mr Salter?' asked Hardcastle, as he and the other two officers accepted Salter's belated invitation to sit down. 'Were they close?'

'Yes, they were very close. Right from when they were at the village school together.'

'What's Maisie's full name and address, Mr Salter?' asked Marriott, looking up from his note-taking.

'It's Watts, Maisie Watts, and she lives at Lavender Cottage with her parents. Her elder brother Harry was killed in Flanders earlier this year and now her oldest friend's gone.' Alfred Salter, still sounding as though he were talking through his nose, shook his head slowly as though unable to comprehend the wickedness of the world in which he was living. 'It's this awful war, you know. It took our Leslie last year. He was drowned when HMS *Hampshire* was mined off Scapa Flow. That Lord Kitchener was drowned at the same time. Ordinary seaman, he was. Our Leslie, I mean, not Lord Kitchener,' he added hurriedly. Most men would have laughed at such a solecism, but not even the whisper of a smile crossed Salter's face.

'Apart from Maisie Watts, did your daughter have any other close friends?' Hardcastle realized that he would have to be circumspect about the questions he posed to the Salters. In view of what he had gleaned so far of their daughter's reputation, he did not want to alienate her parents by suggesting that she was a wanton hussy, even though that was rapidly becoming apparent and was very likely to have been a factor in her murder. 'Or was she walking out with a young man, perhaps?'

'She knew most of the girls in the village, Mr Hardcastle. It's a very small community and people tend to remain here all their lives. Nearly everybody in Thresham Parva made friends at school and continue to be friends – of the same generation, of course. I'm forty-five and I'm still friendly with people I was at school with.' Salter paused, a look of even greater sadness on his face than hitherto. 'Mind you, two of them have been killed in the war. I tried to join up but I was turned down on account of my asthma and my adenoids. The army doctor at Aldershot said that if I was in a gas attack it would do for me straight off.'

'I'm sorry, Mr Salter,' said Marriott, looking up again, 'but did you say that Daisy was friendly with a young man?' He too realized that he and Hardcastle were dealing with a sensitive situation and pretended that he had missed part of the conversation.

'She was always out with some wretched boy or other.' Rose Salter suddenly intervened with that bitter statement. 'If I told her once that she'd finish up getting herself into trouble, I must've told her a dozen times.' She grimaced, but it was more like a lopsided grin that gave the impression that one side of her face was paralysed.

'Now, now, Rose, that's a bit hard,' said Alfred Salter. 'She was only doing what young girls do. After all, we were courting when you were only just turned sixteen.' He glanced at Hardcastle. 'That's how old our Daisy was, sir.'

'Yes, but I only ever walked out with you, Alfred Salter. Never anyone else,' said Rose. 'Daisy always seemed to be out with some different boy.'

'Do you know the names of any of them, Mrs Salter?' asked Marriott.

'Huh! Names? She never went out with any of 'em long enough for us to find out, even if she knew herself. Most of the boys in the village they were, I shouldn't wonder. Them as how ain't been taken for the war, and half of them won't be coming back. She was out with one of them young gentlemen from up the college one time an' all. But that was only the once as far as I know, although it wouldn't surprise me to find out there'd been more. And then another time she was the cause of some rumpus at the Thresham Arms. Something to do with soldiers. I've never set foot in the Thresham Arms and don't ever intend to.' Rose paused.

'Only the good Lord knows what got into the girl. Possessed by the devil, if you ask me. It's this wretched war that's to blame.'

'Don't take on so, Rose.' Alfred, who had remained standing ever since the arrival of the police, moved closer to his wife and put a hand on her shoulder in a protective gesture. 'She's gone and there's nowt we can do about it except tell Mr Hardcastle here as much as we know.'

Rose Salter shook her husband's hand away. 'It would've helped if you'd spoken to her a bit sharp from time to time, Alfred Salter, instead of always having your nose in a book or being out doing your bird-watching half the night.'

'It's possible that I may have to see you again, Mr Salter.' Hardcastle had come to the conclusion that little of a useful nature was to be learned about Daisy Salter or her boyfriends from the girl's parents.

'Where's her crucifix?' asked Rose Salter suddenly.

'Crucifix, madam?' Hardcastle's interest was immediately aroused. He knew that attention to minor details of that nature would very often produce results.

'She wouldn't go anywhere without that crucifix. We bought it for her for her first birthday from a jeweller's shop in Winchester. Two guineas, it cost.'

'The price doesn't matter, Rose.' Alfred turned to Hardcastle. 'Was it found, Inspector?'

'Not as far as I know, Mr Salter, but I'll have enquiries made. Perhaps you could describe it.'

'It was gold,' said Rose, 'and was engraved with the letters INRI. That stands for Jesus of Nazareth, King of the Jews, in Latin. It's been taken, I know it has. It's God's will for her wickedness.'

'Did your daughter usually wear face powder, Mrs Salter?' asked Hardcastle. 'Or kohl on her eyes?'

Rose Salter tapped the floor several times with her walking stick in her frustration to get the words out. 'No, never, never,' she said eventually. 'That's what painted harlots wear up London.'

Alfred Salter escorted the detectives to the front door. 'You'll have to forgive Rose, sir, but she's not been herself since this terrible thing happened. She's sort of thrashing around looking for someone to blame and I happen to be the nearest. It's not been helped by her having a stroke last year that left some of her left side paralysed. She thinks it's all been visited on her by God for having sinned, but I think it was more likely our Leslie getting drowned that brought it on.'

'I quite understand, Mr Salter.'

'Can you tell me when we'll be allowed to have Daisy's body so we can give her a decent Christian burial, sir?'

'I'll let you know as soon as I can, Mr Salter, but there are certain procedures that have to be carried out.' Hardcastle was loath to tell Daisy Salter's distressed father that Dr Bernard Spilsbury, the distinguished London pathologist, was at this very moment carving up Daisy's body.

'I wonder if I could beg a favour of you, sir?' asked Salter.

'If I can help, I will.'

'I wonder if you'd be so good as to have a word with the vicar and explain what's happening. I wouldn't like him to think that we're delaying the funeral, or even having Daisy buried somewhere else because of the scandal.'

'I'll certainly do that, Mr Salter,' said Hardcastle, thinking that a word with the local clergyman could be informative. 'But I don't understand why you should think that the death of your daughter is a scandal.'

'Well, sir, she's been murdered and there's always a reason for such happenings. Like Rose always says, it's God's will.'

'Quite possibly,' said Hardcastle, and led the way down the path of the Salters' house. 'I think it's time we went back to Alton, Yardley. Perhaps the good doctor has some news for us.'

No less a person than the tail-coated manager was hovering in the foyer of the Swan Hotel in Alton High Street.

'Doctor Spilsbury warned me to expect you, gentlemen. If you follow me, I'll show you to his table.' The manager led the way into the hotel's restaurant.

'Ah, there you are, Hardcastle, my dear chap.' Spilsbury, a crisp white table napkin tucked into his starched wing collar, rose from the table and shook hands with each of the police officers. 'I've just been taking the edge off my hunger with a bread roll.'

'I hope we've not kept you waiting, sir,' said Hardcastle.

'Not at all, not at all.' Spilsbury beckoned to a waiter and invited the detectives to order drinks. 'I thought I'd tell you what I discovered in the post-mortem examination, Hardcastle, and then we can get down to the serious business.'

'The serious business, sir?' asked Yardley innocently.

Spilsbury roared with laughter. 'Eating lunch, my dear fellow. That's the serious business.'

The detectives each ordered beer and it arrived within seconds.

Putting his hand into an inside pocket, Spilsbury withdrew a bill from his tailor, on the back of which he had made a few notes. 'It'll come as no surprise to you,' he began, placing the bill on the table and smoothing it out, 'that the unfortunate Miss Salter was the victim of manual strangulation and I would estimate that she had been dead about twelve or thirteen hours when she was found by . . .?' He tapped the table in frustration.

'Joshua Blunden, sir, the owner of the farm where she was found,' said Yardley.

'Quite so. The name had slipped my mind. But that's not all. The girl was about two months' pregnant.'

'It looks as though we have a motive, then,' said Hardcastle mildly. 'All we have to do now is find the father of the unborn child and we might have our man.'

'Could it be that easy, sir?' asked Yardley, who was becoming increasingly impressed by the London DDI's approach to the investigation of murder.

'Oh, by no means, Yardley,' said Hardcastle airily, and took a goodly draught of his beer. 'The assembly of all the facts in the case is the only course of action that will lead you to the murderer. The important thing to remember is that you must never jump to conclusions.'

Sitting on the opposite side of the table, Marriott found it difficult not to laugh at Hardcastle's pompous little homily. In his experience the DDI frequently leaped to unwarranted conclusions or steered the enquiry in an unjustified direction. The irony was that he very often arrived at the right result for the wrong reasons.

'I think we'll have a few words with Master Charlie Snapper this afternoon,' continued Hardcastle as he tucked into roast beef and Yorkshire pudding.

'Snapper, sir?' queried Yardley, who was having a job keeping up with Hardcastle's mercurial changes of direction.

'Good heavens, Yardley, Mr Blunden found him in a haystack
with our murder victim about two weeks ago or thereabouts. You
took a statement from Blunden about it. D'you know where this
here Snapper lives?'

'No, sir, but I'm sure that Ted Jessop will be able to tell us.'

'In that case we'll go back to Thresham Parva straight after
lunch,' said Hardcastle. 'It's time we had a few more words with
the village constable now that we're starting to put things together,
and then we'll speak to the vicar and see what he's got to say.
Logical assembly of facts, you see, Yardley,' he added as he speared
another roast potato.

'I'll let you have my written report in due course, my dear
Hardcastle,' said Spilsbury once the meal was over. 'In the meantime, I shall make my way back to London.'

'Thank you for lunch, sir,' said Hardcastle. 'Most generous.
Young Yardley here will arrange for his taxi to take you to the
railway station. When the driver returns,' he continued, turning
to Yardley, 'Sergeant Marriott and I will get out to Thresham
Parva and I'll leave you here to organize your Boy Scouts. Once
we've had a talk with Jessop and his wife, we'll come and join
you.'

Sidney Bennett, the Scoutmaster of the Alton troop of Boy Scouts,
greeted Yardley's request with enthusiasm.

'I'm sure the lads will be more than willing, Mr Yardley. As
you know, they're helping to guard the local railway lines and the
German sailors at Alton Abbey up in Beech, but I daresay they
can be released for a few hours. How many d'you think will be
needed?'

'Half a dozen should do it, Mr Bennett,' said Yardley. 'But
there's just the question of how we're to get them to Joshua
Blunden's farm at Thresham Parva.'

'That's no problem. I'll pick the six who've got bicycles, but
how are you getting up there?'

'I'll have to get a taxi, I suppose,' said Yardley. 'The Scotland
Yard inspector has taken the one we've been using.'

'I'll give you a lift. I'm still entitled to some petrol for supervising
the prisoners up at the Abbey.' The sixty-five-year-old Bennett, a
land agent, had taken the place of the original Scoutmaster who had

volunteered for the army in 1914. Regrettably he would not be returning.

'I want you to form a line in front of that haystack, lads, with a space of about two yards between each of you,' said Yardley. 'Then I want you to move slowly forward until you reach the hedge.'

'Are we looking for clues, sir?' asked the patrol leader enthusiastically.

'No, lad, you're looking for evidence,' said Yardley, who would himself have called them clues until Hardcastle had arrived in Thresham Parva. 'Keep your eyes on the ground all the time and if you see anything out of the ordinary raise a hand and the rest of you stop until I've had a look at what you've found. But don't touch it.'

The six Boy Scouts began to inch their way forward. It took about eight minutes for them to cover the thirty yards between the haystack and the hedge, but they found nothing.

'What do we do now, sir?' The patrol leader sounded disappointed that their search had not revealed anything.

'You turn round and make your way back to the haystack, searching all the way,' said Yardley. 'You'd be surprised just how easy it is to miss something when you're searching grassland like this in a murder case.' He spoke with all the confidence of a detective with vast experience of murder investigations.

It was not until the Scouts reached the hedge a second time that one of them saw the bag.

'Sir,' said the Scout. 'There's something under there.'

Yardley bent down and retrieved what proved to be Daisy Salter's handbag. 'I wonder how that got there. It was pushed right underneath the hedge.'

'Perhaps the murderer threw it there, sir,' said the Scout. 'That'll be evidence, won't it?' he asked enthusiastically.

'From what I remember of my days as a Boy Scout there isn't a detective badge.' Yardley smiled as he stood up and brushed the knees of his trousers. 'I'll have to show it to Mr Hardcastle.'

'Is he the famous detective from Scotland Yard, sir?' asked one of the Scouts.

Yardley grinned. 'Yes, that's him, lad.'

SIX

Once the two detectives were settled in the parlour at the police house, Hardcastle wasted no time in finding out what the village policeman and his wife knew about Daisy Salter's parents.

'How well d'you know Alfred and Rose Salter, Mr Jessop? They made a point of letting me know that they were a God-fearing couple.'

'They like to give that impression, sir, but as far as I know it's only Rose Salter who's the true churchgoer. To be honest I think Alfred's so terrified of her that he'll do anything not to upset her, including going to church with her. From what I've seen of him, I don't think he's all that religious. She's a right harridan is Rose Salter, and I've heard she gives him a right tongue padding from time to time. As for the two men who work for Alfred, well, she scares the living daylights out of 'em.'

'I was going to ask you about those two,' said Hardcastle. 'They were filling sacks when we arrived at the Salters' house and didn't even glance up. Most people do so just out of curiosity.'

'No, they wouldn't, sir. They'd be scared that Rose was looking out of the window and might dock their pay for slacking. Make no mistake, sir, she's the one who wears the breeches in that household. As I said, she's a right harridan.'

'Is there a reason that those two lads aren't in the army, Ted?' asked Marriott.

'Oh, they will be, Sergeant. They've been caught up by the Derby law and they're just waiting to go. I reckon it'll be a relief for the pair of 'em. I'd think fighting the Hun is better than working for Rose Salter any day.'

'Rose Salter let slip that Alfred spends a lot of his time bird-watching. And he seemed a very strait-laced sort of chap. Strictly teetotal, I gathered.'

'Rose might have sworn off the strong liquor, sir,' said PC Jessop with a laugh, 'but Alf Salter likes a drop to drink and, as for bird-watching, he wouldn't know a nighthawk from a nuthatch. As a matter of fact, he uses a place up on Stoke Hill. An old abandoned barn, it is, though Alf calls it a hide. I was having a prowl round one night on account of we'd had a few poachers in the area when I saw a light in this old barn, so I made my way up there. And there was Alf having a one-man party. Drunk as a fiddler's bitch, he was. I reckon he goes up there to get away from his missus and he tells her he's bird-watching. I don't blame him.'

'No wonder their son ran away to the navy,' said Hardcastle. 'I'll bet he couldn't wait to get his hands on a tot of rum.'

'It was a great shame he was drowned when the *Hampshire* went down, sir,' said Jessop. 'He had the makings, that lad did. I think it was him dying that made Rose worse. To be honest, I think she's gone a bit gaga since it happened, what with that and the stroke she had a few months back. She doted on the boy, but I think he felt stifled and that's why he joined the navy as soon as he could. I should think that Daisy getting killed as well will just about turn her mind altogether.'

'I suppose you didn't happen to see Alfred Salter at his bird-watching last Monday night, did you, Mr Jessop?' enquired Hardcastle.

'No, sir, I wasn't out and about that night.'

'I'm just wondering where he was when his daughter was getting murdered, that's all. Perhaps you'd ask him when next you see him.'

'I will that, sir,' said Jessop, 'but surely you don't suspect Alfred Salter of murdering his own daughter, do you, sir?'

'It wouldn't be the first time that such a thing has happened, Mr Jessop,' said Hardcastle and, as a thought crossed his mind, he asked, 'I suppose Alfred *is* the girl's father, isn't he?'

'To the best of my knowledge, sir,' said Jessop, 'although I've not had occasion to see the birth certificate.'

'That wouldn't necessarily tell us the truth,' said Hardcastle wryly.

'We've got the result of the post-mortem on Daisy Salter, Ted,' said Marriott. 'Doctor Spilsbury did it this morning.'

'Was it manual strangulation, Sergeant?'

'Yes, it was.'

'I thought as much.'

'But,' said Hardcastle, 'young Daisy Salter was two months' pregnant.'

'I can't say as how that comes as any surprise, sir,' said Jessop. 'She had quite a reputation, did Daisy. A cheeky young hussy, she was.'

Annie Jessop appeared in the doorway from the kitchen bearing a tray. 'I've brought you some tea, gentlemen.'

Marriott leaped up to assist her, but she had put the tray down on the table before he reached her.

'I can manage a tea tray, Mr Marriott, but thanks anyway. You should know a copper's wife can do most things. It's a case of having to,' she added, shooting a glance at her husband.

'D'you mind telling Annie what you just told me, sir?' asked Jessop.

'Not at all. I was just saying to your husband, Mrs Jessop, that the post-mortem examination on Daisy Salter revealed that she was about two months' pregnant.'

'I'd have been very surprised to learn she wasn't, Mr Hardcastle,' said Annie. 'I'd have put money on her not being a virgin and I can't think of a better reason for some man murdering a young trollop like Daisy Salter than because he'd put her in the family way and didn't want to take the responsibility. Or he was married already. But if you're going to ask me who was responsible, well, I'd suggest you start in the centre of Thresham Parva and work your way outwards.' She paused and chuckled. 'For at least five miles in each direction.'

Hardcastle threw back his head and laughed. 'I think you're probably right, Mrs Jessop. Anyway, we must go and see the vicar: he might be able to help. What's his name, Mr Jessop?'

'He's the Reverend Cyril Creed, sir, and his wife's called Esmé.'

'And a more stuck-up madam would be difficult to find,' said Annie Jessop, demonstrating once again that although her husband may have to be reserved in his opinions, she was not. As she would say to friends who were hesitating about giving her a snippet of the latest gossip, 'My Ted might be in the police force, my dear, but I'm not.'

Hardcastle stood up, but then paused. 'On second thoughts, I think we'll have a word with this here Maisie Watts first. According to the Salters, she and Daisy were as thick as thieves and she might be able to throw some light on this business.'

Lavender Cottage, where Maisie Watts lived, was only a short walk from the police house and was next door to the dairy owned by Jack Watts, her father.

'Good afternoon, gentlemen.' The full-figured, attractive woman who answered the door to the cottage had flame-red hair piled untidily on top of her head. She smiled when she saw the two men on the doorstep.

'I'm Divisional Detective Inspector Hardcastle of Scotland Yard, madam, and this is Detective Sergeant Marriott.'

'I thought you might be. I'm Annabel Watts. What can I do for you?'

'Are you Maisie's *mother*?' Hardcastle did not believe that Annabel Watts looked old enough to have a sixteen-year-old daughter. He actually thought that maybe she was the girl's sister, and his expression betrayed his doubt.

'Why, Inspector, I do believe you're trying to flatter me.' Annabel Watts laughed and wagged a finger of mock admonition. 'Of course I'm Maisie's mother. But instead of standing on the doorstep paying me compliments, why don't you come inside?'

'Thank you, Mrs Watts,' said Hardcastle, hurriedly removing his bowler hat as he stepped over the threshold. Marriott followed, trying not to smile; it was not often Hardcastle was caught wrong-footed, but he had obviously been embarrassed by Annabel Watts' brazen teasing.

'Do take a seat, gentlemen.' Annabel sat demurely in an armchair, still with a mocking smile on her face, and waited until Hardcastle and Marriott were seated. 'Now then, how can I help you? I suppose you want to talk to me about this awful murder.'

'It's your daughter Maisie I'd like to talk to, Mrs Watts. I understand that she was a close friend of Daisy Salter. Is she here?'

'As a matter of fact, she's next door helping Jack in the dairy.' Annabel stood up and the two policemen began to struggle to their feet. 'Please don't get up,' she said, waving them down. 'I'll give her a shout.'

Hardcastle glanced around the room until his gaze lighted on a sepia photograph on the mantelshelf. It was of a young man in army uniform. 'I suppose that's Harry Watts,' he said.

Marriott stood up and crossed the room to study the photograph more closely. 'Hampshire Regiment,' he commented. 'Alfred Salter said he was killed in Flanders earlier this year, sir.'

'That's what everyone thought but, thank God, he's still alive.' The girl who had spoken stood in the doorway. She could have been her mother's twin had it not been for the age difference; she had the same complexion, the same build, the same red hair and the same winsome smile.

'We heard the good news only yesterday, Inspector,' said Annabel Watts as she followed her daughter into the room. 'An officer came over from Aldershot and told us that Harry had been taken prisoner at somewhere called Neuve Chapelle some months ago, but had managed to escape a week ago. It seems that after an attack they found a badly mutilated body without any identification discs and wrongly identified it as being my son, Harry. It wasn't until he escaped that they found out their mistake. The officer said it's happening all the time. And now I suppose some other poor family will be getting one of those awful telegrams.'

'I'm very pleased to hear that he's safe,' said Hardcastle as they all sat down.

'Ma said it was me you wanted to talk to, sir,' said Maisie Watts.

'We spoke to Mr and Mrs Salter, Daisy's parents, earlier today,' said Hardcastle, 'and they told us that you were too upset to carry on working there after you heard about Daisy's murder.'

Maisie Watts was unable to restrain her laughter. 'Is that what they said?'

'Isn't it true, then?' asked Marriott.

'No, it's not. To tell you the truth, sir, I couldn't abide Daisy Salter,' said Maisie. 'She was boy-crazy. When we were at school she'd even make eyes at old Booth the teacher, and he must've been sixty if he was a day. If I happened to be walking down the street talking to her and she suddenly saw some lad she knew, she'd start parading herself. And it wasn't only lads either,' she said, after giving the matter some thought. 'It was *any* man. After that I might just as well not have been there. No, mister, she was no friend of mine. She was a bad influence was that Daisy Salter. I told her that she'd get herself into trouble one day.'

'Yes, and she did, too,' said Marriott.

'Oh, I'm not talking about her getting killed,' said Maisie. 'I'm talking about her getting pregnant.'

'You knew about that?' asked Hardcastle.

'She told me. It was about two months ago that she found out, and she said that she was going to get herself a husband as a result. Even if it killed her, is what she said. And it looks as though it did.'

'Did she say who the father was, Maisie?' asked Hardcastle.

'She wouldn't tell me. She was so secretive about it, and knowing what she was like, I don't think she even *knew* who the father was. The way she carried on it could've been anyone.'

'Why did the Salters give you the day off, then, Maisie?' asked Marriott.

'They didn't. I left. Once they got the news about Daisy they started their praying. I went into the sitting room and there they were on their knees, hands together, heads bowed. They wanted me to join in. Well, I go to church, but that was too much.' Maisie lowered her voice as if fearful of being overheard. 'To be honest, I think Rose Salter's stark staring mad.' But then she negated the confidence by laughing loudly. 'D'you know, sir, I think they were almost enjoying their grief, as if a great weight had been lifted off their minds.'

'Thank you, Maisie,' said Hardcastle as he and Marriott stood up. 'You've been very helpful.'

'I'll see you out,' said Annabel Watts, and escorted the two policemen to the front door. 'You're more than welcome to come and see me again, Inspector,' she said, and afforded Hardcastle another of her wicked smiles. 'You too, Sergeant Marriott.'

'That young Maisie has got her head screwed on the right way, Marriott,' said Hardcastle as they walked the short distance to the police house.

The taxi was waiting, and the moment that Hardcastle and Marriott appeared, Jed Young, the driver, leaped out to open the rear doors.

'South Farm, driver,' said Hardcastle as he and Marriott got in, 'but you can stop at the entrance to Mr Blunden's five-acre field.'

'Ah, that'll be where young Daisy's body were found, sir,' said Young.

'How old are you, Young?' asked Hardcastle, ignoring the taxi-driver's comment.

'Twenty-six, sir.'

'Why haven't you been conscripted, then?' Hardcastle posed the question in an almost accusatory way; he knew that since Lord Derby's Military Service Act of last year few men between eighteen and forty-one years of age had been able to claim exemption. Certainly cab drivers were unlikely to qualify for preferential treatment.

'I've no idea, sir,' said Young as he started the car. 'I suppose the papers must've got lost.'

'Very convenient,' muttered Hardcastle. 'Are you married?'

'No, sir.'

'Did you know Daisy Salter?' Hardcastle posed the question suddenly.

'What, me, sir? No, sir,' said Young, a little too quickly for the DDI's liking as he brought the taxi to a standstill at the gate to Blunden's five-acre field.

'How are you getting on, Dick?' asked Marriott as the Hampshire officer approached the two Yard detectives.

'I think we might have had a bit of luck, Sergeant,' said Yardley cautiously. 'One of the lads found this.' The Hampshire DC held out a bead bag about six inches square, to which was attached a long chain. 'And I suppose this gold chain is to put over the shoulder. I've never seen one like it before.'

'Are you a qualified assayer, Yardley?' asked Hardcastle.

'A what, sir?'

'Someone who values precious metals. Because if you ain't, don't call it gold. Call it yellow metal when it's entered in the property register. If it ain't gold and whoever claims it says that's what you called it, then you could end up paying the difference.'

'Oh, I see.' Yardley did not see at all, mainly because the DDI had not explained the point very clearly, but he thought it politic to agree. 'Very good, sir.' He made a mental note to ask Sergeant Marriott later on what the DDI had meant.

'What's in the bag?' asked Hardcastle.

'I've listed the contents in my pocketbook, sir. There's a lace handkerchief with the initial D on it, a small mirror, a comb, a button and a photograph of a sailor, sir. The back of the photo has a message written on it. It says: "For my sister Daisy from your loving brother, Leslie." And there are a couple of crosses, sir.'

'That's her brother who was lost at sea in HMS *Hampshire*,' said Marriott.

'What sort of button is it, Yardley?' asked Hardcastle.

'It's a brass button marked GWR, sir,' said Yardley, handing it over.

'GWR!' exclaimed Hardcastle, savouring the letters. 'Unless I'm much mistaken that stands for Great Western Railway.'

'I can't think of anything else those letters could stand for, sir,' said Marriott.

'But what on earth is a button belonging to the Great Western Railway doing in Daisy Salter's handbag in a field in Thresham Parva, eh, Marriott? If it is the Great Western. There are dozens of women who've got buttons from an army officer's tunic that they reckon they pinched the night Mafeking was relieved by Colonel Mahon in the Boer War, but I've never heard of a railway button being grabbed in the same way. If it is a railway button.'

'Could it belong to Daisy Salter's murderer, sir?' Yardley asked tentatively.

'It's a possibility, lad, but it still don't explain what it's doing in Daisy's handbag.' Hardcastle spoke thoughtfully as he examined the button again before returning it to the Hampshire detective. 'There's no point in having that examined for fingerprints,' he said. 'Even Mr Collins wouldn't have any success with an object that small.'

'Who's Mr Collins, sir?' asked Yardley.

'Detective Inspector Charles Stockley Collins is the head of the Fingerprint Bureau at New Scotland Yard, lad, and I doubt that anyone knows more about fingerprints than he does. Anyway, I daresay that Daisy put her dabs all over it.' Although sounding like an expert, the DDI was only just beginning to grasp the technicalities of fingerprint evidence, even though the first occasion it had been accepted in court was twelve years ago when the new science had been instrumental in securing the conviction of the Stratton brothers for what became known as the Deptford oil shop murders. 'Who found it?'

'Young Freddie King, sir. He's one of the Boy Scouts.'

'Fetch him over here, Yardley.'

A somewhat apprehensive fourteen-year-old Freddie King stood to attention in front of the DDI and saluted. 'You wanted me, sir?' he asked, peering at Hardcastle through wire-framed spectacles.

'You were the lad who found the handbag, were you?' asked Hardcastle sternly.

'Yes, sir.'

'Well done, lad.' To Marriott's amazement, Hardcastle shook the young boy's hand. The DDI rarely complimented anyone and that included Marriott himself, but he supposed that being a civilian, and a youthful one at that, the boy deserved a word of praise.

'Thank you, sir.' Freddie King would remember for the rest of his life the day he helped a famous Scotland Yard detective to solve a murder. But even Freddie could see that perhaps that was assuming a little too much.

'If that proves to be useful in solving this crime, young man,' Hardcastle continued, 'you might have to attend Winchester Assizes to give evidence. Detective Sergeant Marriott here will show you how to make a note of what you did today so that you'll know what to say in perhaps six months' time, or even later.' He turned to the Hampshire detective. 'And now we'll have a word with this here vicar, Yardley.'

The Reverend Cyril Creed's appearance and demeanour was such that even without his clerical collar, frock coat and gaiters there would have been little doubt as to his calling. Probably in his early forties, he had a pink, clean-shaven, cherubic face that was slightly fleshy and appeared to have been freshly scrubbed. Even before the vicar of Thresham Parva spoke, Hardcastle knew that he would have a highfalutin, holier-than-thou voice.

'I anticipated that you would be calling on me at some stage, Inspector,' Creed said once Hardcastle had introduced himself and his two colleagues. He led them into the comfortable sitting room of the vicarage. 'Allow me to present my wife, Esmé. This is Detective Inspector Hardcastle and his colleagues, my dear.'

Esmé Creed, attired in a mauve satin frock, was seated in a chair near the fireplace. Even though she could have been no older than thirty-two or thirty-three, she extended an elegant hand towards Hardcastle in the manner of a dowager duchess who expected a social inferior such as a policeman to take it gently and bow.

Instead, Hardcastle remained upright, gripped her hand firmly and shook it. 'How d'you do, Mrs Creed.'

'Do sit down, gentlemen.' With the merest trace of a grimace, Esmé Creed gently massaged her hand. As the menfolk sat down, she rang a small bell on a side table. 'I'm sure you would all appreciate a cup of tea,' she said, and gave instructions to a maid who had appeared promptly in the doorway and bobbed a curtsy.

'No, thank you, Mrs Creed. We had tea with the village constable not too long ago, but thank you for the offer.'

'Oh, very well. If you're quite sure.' Disappointed that she would not be able to display her best china tea service, Esmé Creed turned to the maid. 'We shall not be requiring tea after all, thank you, Violet.'

'Very good, ma'am.' Once again the maid bobbed briefly and disappeared.

'Well, gentlemen, how may I be of assistance to the constabulary?' Cyril Creed stood in front of the empty fireplace, legs apart and hands behind his back. His condescending tone seemed to imply that the police could not possibly do *without* his help.

'We're investigating the murder of Daisy Salter, Mr Creed.'

'It was murder, then?'

'Quite definitely.'

'How was she killed?'

'I'm not prepared to say at this stage.' Apart from the police and those others who were actually involved in the investigation, Hardcastle had no intention of revealing the precise details to anyone else. When eventually he arrested the murderer, as he was confident he would, he wanted him to be in possession of as little information as possible about what the police knew.

'A dreadful thing to have happened and I shall say prayers for the poor girl in church this coming Sunday.' Creed raised his eyebrows. 'May I expect to see you there, Inspector?'

'No,' said Hardcastle bluntly. 'This murder will be taking up all my time. But perhaps you can tell me what you know of the girl.'

'Ah!' Creed put his fingertips together, placed them against his pursed lips and gazed at the ceiling before looking back at the DDI. 'I fear that she had strayed from the path of righteousness, Inspector. Her parents must have been terribly distressed about her comportment. I did what I could, but alas, to no avail. There are times when even a man of God finds himself helpless. We even employed her for a while.'

'In what capacity?' asked Marriott, opening his pocketbook.

'To do general cleaning about the house, but we were obliged to let her go.'

'You mean you sacked her?' asked Hardcastle, who was fast becoming irritated with the vicar and his wife.

'Yes, that's one way of putting it.'

'It's the only way as far as I know. But why did you sack her?'

'She was a thief,' said Esmé Creed.

'What did she steal?' asked Hardcastle.

'Oh, it was petty pilfering. I caught her putting a small ornament in the pocket of her apron one day and that's when I told her to go. But we're still finding the occasional small piece of bijouterie missing and I can only suppose that Daisy Salter was responsible. My husband is far too charitable at times, but I tend to be more downright than he, Inspector,' continued Mrs Creed. 'The down-to-earth truth of the matter is that Daisy Salter was a thoroughly bad girl. In fact, I would go further: she was a tart.'

Creed raised a staying hand. 'One must always err on the side of Christian charity, Esmé, my dear,' he said in tones so sepulchral that Hardcastle wanted to laugh.

'What sort of bad girl, Mrs Creed?' asked Marriott.

'She didn't mind being seen around the village with a man. Alone! By which I mean without a chaperone. Well, I ask you! Really!' Esmé Creed shook her head slowly. 'I also heard tell that on one occasion she was seen in the Thresham Arms.'

'By you?' asked Marriott, more out of devilment than a need to know.

'Certainly not.' Esmé Creed sounded outraged at the mere implication that she might have entered a public house. 'That place is nothing more than a den of iniquity.'

Hardcastle laughed aloud at the woman's posturing; a ludicrous attitude in a woman still the right side of forty. 'You don't honestly expect young women to wait for a chaperone before they speak to a man these days, do you, Mrs Creed? This is the twentieth century.'

'I don't know what goes on in London, my good man,' said Esmé haughtily, 'but loose behaviour of that sort does not go down well in a close-knit community like this. People talk, you know.'

Hardcastle was having difficulty in believing that this woman was being serious. In a village less than fifty miles from London, she was talking as though Queen Victoria was still on the throne and presiding over the sort of prim and proper behaviour that most of her subjects believed she had practised.

'In London there are women sweeping chimneys now, Mrs Creed,' the DDI said. 'And working in munitions factories, on the trams and buses, and even delivering coal, and they don't seem to have come to any harm. In fact, they are praised for their patriotism in releasing men to fight and will doubtless be granted the vote when the war is over.' Hardcastle spoke from experience: his daughter Kitty was working on the buses, albeit against his wishes, but he had no intention of telling Mrs Creed that.

'This war is precisely the cause of this lax and licentious behaviour, Inspector, and I imagine that the lying-in hospitals are overflowing with illegitimate births. And as far as I can see, the police are doing little to stem the flow of wickedness that seems to pervade our everyday life.'

Hardcastle stood up. 'Thank you for agreeing to see us, Mrs Creed, and you too, Mr Creed. We'll not take up any more of your valuable time.' His statement was bordering on the sarcastic. 'Good day to you.'

'I'll see you out, gentlemen.' Cyril Creed rushed towards the door of the sitting room, but Hardcastle got there first.

'We'll see ourselves out, thank you,' said Hardcastle.

'I do hope you catch this man, Inspector.'

'You may rest assured I shall,' said Hardcastle. 'I'll happily see his neck being stretched at eight o'clock one fine morning in Winchester Prison.' He paused. 'I suppose you'll say a prayer for him, too. And while you're about it, you might as well include one for John Ellis, the hangman. By the way, Vicar,' he continued, 'Mr Salter will be contacting you to arrange a funeral for his daughter, but he has to wait for the coroner to release her body.'

'I quite understand,' said Creed. 'Daisy may have been a sinner, but God's mercy is bountiful and she deserves a Christian burial. Please tell Mr Salter that I shall be delighted to preside over the service when the time comes.'

'Very well.' Leaving Creed to return to his sitting room, Hardcastle, accompanied by the other two detectives, strode the length of the long hallway, but deliberately paused at the end. It was long enough for him to overhear the conversation between the vicar and his obnoxious wife.

'What an incredibly rude man that inspector was, Cyril,' she exclaimed heatedly and loudly. 'Did you notice that he never once addressed me as "madam"? And you said nothing about it.'

As Hardcastle yanked open the front door, it creaked noisily. Once the three policemen were outside, he slammed it as hard as he could.

'Where to now, sir?' asked Yardley when the three police officers were in the taxi once again. He was still reeling from the shock of hearing Hardcastle's forthright condemnation of Esmé Creed's bigoted views, and his blunt suggestion that Creed should pray for the murderer *and* his hangman. In Yardley's world one did not speak to someone as important locally as the vicar or his wife with other than a respectful deference. But a further outburst was to come.

'Back to the Thresham Arms, Yardley,' said Hardcastle. 'I need a couple of pints to wash the taste of that bloody woman's patronizing, sermonizing claptrap out of my mouth. I've met some stuck-up bitches in my life, but she really does take the biscuit. Thank God I'll not have to listen to one of the vicar's sermons if he spouts the sort of rubbish his wife comes out with. And who does he think he is, wearing bishop's gaiters and a frock coat to which he ain't entitled. It's no different from you pretending to be me, Marriott.'

'Quite, sir.' Marriott had long ago decided that monosyllabic replies were all that should be made in response to Hardcastle's diatribes.

SEVEN

The saloon bar of the village inn was fairly crowded, and as the three detectives entered Hardcastle and Marriott were greeted affably by the locals, even though they had only arrived in the village yesterday.

'What can I get you, gents?' Tom Hooker, the landlord, wiped the top of the bar with a cloth.

Hardcastle ordered beer for himself and the other two and as Hooker served them, the DDI noticed a man in the public bar which was separated from the saloon bar by a windowed partition. The man appeared to be in his early twenties, roughly dressed and with black hair parted in the centre and plastered to his head with some sort of grease. He had an overall appearance of furtiveness about him, and the moment he spotted Hardcastle he finished his beer at a gulp and left the pub.

'Who was that fellow who just left in a hurry, Tom?' asked Hardcastle.

'That was Charlie Snapper, guv'nor,' said Hooker promptly. Combining self-interest with nosiness, it was a trait of all pub landlords to learn as much as they could about their customers.

'Local lad, is he?' Hardcastle posed the question in a disinterested way almost as if he was making idle conversation, as though the name meant nothing to him.

'No, he's only been in the village about a month, if that. He's a bit vague about his background when you chat to him, sir, but he reckons he comes from down Exeter way and he's up here looking for work on a farm. He said that there wasn't much work in Devon at the moment, but I think he'll find that there's not much here either. I know that Josh Blunden's got some of them girls from the Women's Land Army working at his place along with one or two German prisoners of war so he won't be needing any spare hands.'

'Where's this Snapper living, then, Tom?'

'He's taken digs with George and Lydia Booth, although I don't know how he's paying the rent, not having a job. Or how he's paying for his beer either, and he's in here most nights. I refused to let him put anything on the slate. Bit shifty, if you ask me.'

'Very wise of you, Tom,' said Hardcastle. 'And I daresay he'll move on when he can't find any work here, or when he gets conscripted.' He decided not to ask any more questions about Snapper, or at least not to pose them to Hooker. Pub landlords had a habit of gossiping – it was part of their stock-in-trade – and although very useful to detectives, it did not help when they passed on anything they had learned *from* the police.

Hardcastle led the way to a table near the window where they were able to observe and talk without being overheard.

'I had a word with Ted Jessop this morning, sir,' said Yardley. 'He passed by as we were searching Mr Blunden's field and I asked him what he knew about Charlie Snapper, seeing as how Josh Blunden had mentioned finding him and Daisy Salter in one of his haystacks.'

'What did he have to say?' asked Hardcastle.

'Pretty much what Tom Hooker said just now, that he'd come up from the Devon area looking for work.'

'Who are these people he's lodging with, Dick?' asked Marriott. 'George and Lydia Booth.'

'I asked Ted about them, Sergeant,' said Yardley. 'I understand that they're the local schoolteachers and they live in a cottage next to the schoolhouse. By all accounts the cottage belongs to the council and goes with the job of teaching.'

'I wonder if the council knows that they let rooms to out-of-work farmhands,' said Hardcastle, thinking aloud. 'Anyway, that's not my problem. This is the plan for tomorrow, then: we'll pay a visit to Charlie Snapper and see what he has to say for himself, and then we'll go up to this school that has all these hot-blooded well-to-do young gentlemen living there. Know anything about it, Yardley?'

'No, sir, but I'll soon find out.'

'Good. And then tomorrow afternoon Sergeant Marriott and me will go back up to the Smoke and have a word with the railway people about this here GWR button. I'm interested to know what that button was doing in a murder victim's handbag in a field in Thresham Parva when the Great Western Railway don't go anywhere near here.'

'Is there anything you want me to do while you're in London, sir?' asked Yardley.

'No, there isn't, Yardley, but I'll probably think of something before I go.'

'Where d'you live, Dick?' asked Marriott.

'I've got lodgings in Alton, Sergeant.'

'If we don't need Dick any more, sir, can we send him home?' Marriott knew from his own experience that Hardcastle gave no more thought to the welfare or family life of the officers working for him than he did to his own.

Hardcastle glanced up at the clock over the bar. 'Eight o'clock. Yes, you might as well have an early night, Yardley. The days could get longer as this enquiry goes on.'

'Thank you, sir.' Eight o'clock was not exactly an early night by Yardley's standards.

'See you here at eight o'clock tomorrow morning,' said Hardcastle, and waved a hand of dismissal.

'You'll soon learn, Dick,' said Marriott as the Hampshire detective stood up to leave.

When Richard Yardley arrived at the Thresham Arms at eight o'clock the following morning he found the London DDI and his detective sergeant in the dining room still enjoying breakfast. It caused Yardley to wonder why he had been told to report to Hardcastle that early, but he had yet to learn that the DDI always told officers to report to him at that time whether it was necessary or not. And Hardcastle picked that time because, as a young detective, that was the time *his* DDI had always told him to report.

'Ah, Yardley,' exclaimed Hardcastle, 'you're bright and early. Sit yourself down and have a cup of tea, and then it'll be time for us to go and have words with Snapper. Remind me where he lives.'

'At the schoolhouse, sir, with the Booths.'

'So he does, Yardley, so he does,' said Hardcastle, buttering another piece of toast. 'I must say this is splendid marmalade that Mrs Hooker serves. I think it must be homemade, Marriott.'

'Yes, I imagine it is, sir.' Marriott wondered whether the next few minutes would be taken up with a discussion about marmalade, one of the DDI's pet subjects. In fact, so taken with marmalade was the DDI that he would always complain to Marriott on the rare occasions that Mrs Hardcastle had been unable to obtain any. Naturally, Hardcastle blamed the Kaiser for the shortage.

'One thing you can do, Yardley,' said Hardcastle, taking a bite of toast. 'Find out why our taxi driver hasn't been conscripted. He's the right age and he looks fit enough.'

'Very good, sir.' Somewhat mystified by the request, Yardley made a note in his pocketbook.

The house occupied by George and Lydia Booth was next door to the single-storey stone building that housed Thresham Parva village school. Being August, however, the children were on their summer holidays and the school was closed.

'I'm Divisional Detective Inspector Hardcastle of New Scotland Yard. Are you Mr Booth?'

'Yes, I'm George Booth.' Tall and thin with a bald head and a wispy moustache, the elderly man who answered the door peered at Hardcastle through a pair of gold-rimmed pince-nez. He had a permanently stooped posture, as though his whole life had been spent ducking through doorways that were too low, and his clothes hung on him as though made for a person with a much larger frame.

'I understand that a Mr Snapper is lodging with you, Mr Booth.'

'Oh, you'd better come in, Inspector.' Booth showed the three detectives into the parlour where they were joined by a woman who at that moment emerged from the kitchen. 'This is my wife, Lydia. These gentlemen are from the police, my dear.' The Booths appeared to be about sixty years of age and, in Hardcastle's view, seemed to possess all the characteristics of typical schoolteachers. Mrs Booth particularly so: her hair was dressed into two buns – one over each ear – that Hardcastle had been told by his eldest daughter was known as an earphone style. It certainly reminded him of several of the teachers at the school he had attended over thirty years ago.

'Well, *is* Snapper here, Mr Booth?' asked Hardcastle impatiently. He was intent on wasting as little time as possible, but he had yet to accept that life in village communities was lived at a much slower pace than in London.

'No, I'm afraid you've missed him, Inspector. He left last night.'

'Left? What d'you mean by left, Mr Booth?'

'He came in from the pub at about seven o'clock last evening—' Booth broke off. 'It was at about that time he came in, wasn't it, my dear?'

'Do sit down, gentlemen,' said Lydia Booth pointedly, irritated at her husband's lack of courtesy. 'Yes, I'm sure it was about then.'

'He said that he had to leave, Inspector,' Booth continued. 'He mentioned vaguely about having spoken to somebody in the pub – that's the Thresham Arms – and that this person had told him that there was a farm down near Waterlooville that was taking on extra farmhands.'

'Where's Waterlooville?'

'It's about twenty-five miles south of here, sir,' said Yardley. 'The other side of Petersfield.'

'Did he say how he was getting there, Mr Booth?' asked Marriott.

'No, he didn't. I thought it was rather sudden, him taking off like that. Perhaps he intended to hitchhike. I can't think of any other way of getting there at that time of night.'

'I understand that he didn't have a job here in Thresham Parva, Mr Booth,' said Marriott. 'Is that correct?'

'Yes, he'd been here for almost five weeks looking for work, but without any success.'

'Can you recall exactly when he arrived?' Marriott asked.

'Yes, it was Friday the sixth of July.' Lydia Booth quoted the date without hesitation.

'Is there a particular reason you remember the date, Mrs Booth?'

'Yes. It would have been Alan's twentieth birthday.'

'Alan was our son, Sergeant Marriott,' said George Booth. 'He was killed at Arras last year.'

'I'm sorry to hear that.'

'How did Snapper pay the rent if he didn't have a job?' Hardcastle took out his pipe. 'D'you mind?' he asked.

'Not at all.' Booth withdrew a gunmetal case from the inside pocket of his jacket and took out a cigarette. 'Er, he didn't pay any rent,' he said, applying a match to his cigarette.

'Didn't pay any rent?' Hardcastle finished lighting his pipe, waved out the match and placed it in a nearby ashtray. 'That was very charitable of you.'

'Not intentionally. To be perfectly honest, we thought that he'd be able to get work and I told him that he could settle up when he was in funds. Mind you, he did clean the schoolhouse every day after Daisy left which saved my wife having to do it.'

'Daisy? Are you talking about Daisy Salter?' Hardcastle was suddenly interested.

'Yes,' said Lydia Booth. 'I had to tell her to go. I discovered that she was pilfering. Nothing very important; in fact, just silly little things, like pencils and blotting paper and that sort of thing.'

'Was this before or after she was working for the vicar and his wife, Mrs Booth?' asked Marriott.

'Before, I think,' said Lydia Booth. 'Yes, I'm sure it was before.' She paused and returned her gaze to Hardcastle. 'I suppose you think we've been rather foolish, Inspector. And I suppose we were, but it was nice to have a young man about the house again after our Alan was killed.'

'Yes, I suppose so,' said Hardcastle gruffly, avoiding any attempt at condolence.

'Did he ever mention working on the railways, Mr Booth?' asked Marriott.

'What a strange question,' said Booth. 'No, he didn't. He never mentioned anything about his life before he arrived in Thresham Parva. And now he's gone again. I don't suppose we'll ever see our rent money. Schoolteachers aren't exactly well paid, you know, Mr Marriott.'

'Did he take all his belongings with him?' asked Hardcastle.

'Yes, as far as I know.'

'Perhaps we could have a look at his room, just in case he left anything behind.'

'Yes, of course.' Booth stood up, walked to the door and then paused. 'May I ask why you're so interested in Charlie, Inspector?'

'He was known to have associated with Daisy Salter and now she's dead,' said Hardcastle. 'Murdered.'

'Oh, good heavens!' Lydia Booth put a hand to her mouth. 'Are you suggesting that we've been harbouring a murderer in our house, Inspector?'

'Not necessarily, Mrs Booth,' said Marriott. 'We just want to speak to him. He might have some information that could be useful to us.' He thought it unwise to suggest that right now

Snapper was beginning to look like a strong suspect for Daisy's murder.

The three detectives followed George Booth upstairs to the room that had been occupied by Snapper until last evening. Situated at the back of the house, it afforded a pleasant view across verdant countryside. In the distance was a large country house at the top of a gentle slope. The room contained a single bed, a washstand with a bowl and ewer, and a wardrobe. Next to the washstand was a chest of drawers, upon which stood a mirror.

'It was our Alan's room until he joined the army,' said Booth sadly.

'See if there's anything of interest, Marriott,' said Hardcastle. 'You too, Yardley.' Turning to Booth, he asked, 'Who lives in that large house you can just see on the hill, Mr Booth?'

'No one now, sir. It's Thresham College.'

It did not take long for Marriott and Yardley to conduct their search, for there was little to find. The wardrobe contained a pair of white flannels and a cricket bat, both of which George Booth said had belonged to his late son and which he had forgotten were there.

'Thought they might be, Mr Booth,' said Hardcastle. 'We don't want to hold you up, so there's no need for you to wait. We'll come down with any questions we might have when we've finished.' It was not the thought that he might be inconveniencing Booth that prompted the remark, but rather that he did not want him to be privy to anything that was found. He would prefer that the schoolteacher and his wife did not learn that Snapper was being regarded a suspect for Daisy Salter's murder, even though Marriott had more or less denied it. But it must have been obvious.

Yardley, proving that he was a thorough detective, examined not only the inside of each of the three drawers in the chest, but removed them and ran a hand along the wooden shelves that separated them.

'What's that you've found, Dick?' asked Marriott as Yardley stood up, clutching an envelope.

'I think it must have gone over the back of the drawer and finished up underneath, Sergeant,' said the Hampshire officer as he handed over his find.

'It's a letter, sir,' Marriott said to Hardcastle as he withdrew the missive from the envelope.

'Well, don't keep me in suspense, Marriott. What does it say?'

'It's dated Monday, sir, but it doesn't say which Monday. It reads: *I have to see you tonight as I've got something important to tell you. Usual place. Love, Daisy.*'

'I wonder what the hell that's all about,' said Hardcastle.

'Perhaps she wanted to tell him that she was pregnant, sir,' ventured Marriott.

'Maybe,' said Hardcastle cautiously, 'but why wait that long? Doctor Spilsbury said that she'd been pregnant for two months. If the child was Snapper's she'd have told him long before last Monday.'

'Perhaps she did, sir,' said Marriott. 'Yardley found that letter tucked away underneath a drawer, not in it. It could have been there for some time. Anyway, we don't know it was Daisy Salter who wrote it. Daisy is quite a common name.'

'If Snapper only arrived here five weeks ago, sir,' Yardley began tentatively, 'he couldn't have been responsible for Daisy Salter having been pregnant for two months.'

For a second or two, Hardcastle stared at Yardley. To the young policeman it seemed like an eternity, but then Hardcastle roared with laughter. 'I told you we'd make a detective of him, Marriott. But that aside, Yardley, in my book Snapper is still a strong suspect for the murder of the Salter girl. What other reason could he have had for disappearing like a rat up a drainpipe when he saw us in the pub?'

'Can you get a message to the police in Waterlooville, Dick,' said Marriott, 'and request that they keep a lookout for Snapper?'

'Put a notice in the *Police Gazette*, too, Marriott,' said Hardcastle. 'You can do that when we get to the Yard this afternoon.'

'Ought we to ask Mr and Mrs Salter if the letter was written by Daisy, sir?' said Yardley. 'Sergeant Marriott said it was a common name.'

'I've got a better idea,' said Hardcastle, and led the other two downstairs to the sitting room. 'Was Daisy Salter a pupil here, Mrs Booth?' he asked.

'Yes, she was. It was only two years ago that she left.'

'We've found a letter and I was wondering if you still have a sample of her handwriting anywhere that we could compare it with.'

'If you care to let me have a look at it, I can probably tell you if Daisy wrote it, Inspector.'

'Show Mrs Booth the letter, Marriott.'

Lydia Booth needed only a glance to confirm the handwriting as that of Daisy Salter. 'That's Daisy's writing all right, Inspector. D'you see how the tail of the "g" is straight? I was always telling her off about it, but d'you think she would finish it with a curl. No, that's Daisy Salter's hand, all right. In fact, if you'd like to come along to the schoolroom I'm sure there are still some of her exercise books in the storeroom. Then you could see for yourself.'

'That won't be necessary, Mrs Booth, but as you taught the girl perhaps you can tell me what you remember of her.'

'She was actually a sweet girl and very, very clever, Inspector. In fact, it would be no exaggeration to say that she was probably the brightest girl I ever taught. I had high hopes that she might even go on to university – Girton College at Cambridge, for example – but it was not to be. Her mother was against the idea. She said that women didn't need an education just to get married and have children. Very short-sighted in my view. Women are looking to break into all sorts of professions these days, but poor Daisy left school at fourteen and became a cleaner up at Thresham College. As far as I know that was all she ever did. Such a waste.'

'But she also worked for the vicar at one time.'

'Yes, of course. So she did. I even mentioned it just now.' Lydia Booth passed a hand across her forehead as though she had briefly suffered a loss of memory.

'I wonder what made her go off the rails,' said Hardcastle, half to himself.

'I think one of the factors was the loss of her brother last year,' said Lydia Booth. 'She and Leslie were very close. He always looked out for her at school and I think that his death hit her very hard.'

Hardcastle thanked the Booths for their assistance. 'I doubt that I'll have to trouble you further, but if Snapper returns perhaps you'd let me know. I'm at the Thresham Arms, Mr Booth, or you can tell PC Jessop. But I doubt you'll see Snapper again.'

'I don't think he'll come back just to pay me what he owes me,' said Booth.

'I'll give him a gentle reminder when I catch up with him, Mr Booth,' said Hardcastle.

Behind Hardcastle's back, Marriott smiled. He knew all about the DDI's 'gentle reminders'.

'If Daisy Salter was a cleaner up at this here college for the well-to-do, Marriott, we might be getting somewhere. I daresay one of the young blades up there turned her head.'

'Yes, maybe, sir.' Marriott had much experience of Hardcastle's whims and he knew that a visit to the college would probably be a waste of time. Ironically, though, Hardcastle's flights of fancy very often turned out to be successful.

EIGHT

Although called Thresham College, the school was in fact about a mile outside the centre of the village at the top of the gentle rise that Hardcastle had seen from the window at the schoolteachers' house. The college building had the imposing edifice of a large, expensively built country house set in substantial grounds. It had, in fact, been the country seat of a duke until he had been obliged to sell it, just before the turn of the century, because of a habit of betting on losing horses, and the increasing costs of maintenance and staff.

According to PC Jessop, the sixth-form boys were allowed to visit the village shops in order to make purchases – for the most part cakes and pastries from the bakery owned by Mr Pearce – but were forbidden to enter the Thresham Arms. It was the fact that the more mature students were allowed into the village that had interested Hardcastle.

As the taxi drew to a halt in front of the main entrance to the college and the three detectives alighted, a man stood up from tending one of the flower beds that ran the length of the building's facade.

'The college is closed until the beginning of next month,' said the man, 'but if you're enquiring about admissions you'd best see the secretary.'

Hardcastle assumed the man to be a college gardener, although he spoke with a refined accent. He was certainly dressed in old, worn clothing and wore a battered tweed hat that had undoubtedly seen better days.

'I'm not enquiring about admissions, my man,' said Hardcastle tersely. 'I'm Divisional Detective Inspector Hardcastle of New Scotland Yard, together with Detective Sergeant Marriott, also from the Yard, and Detective Constable Yardley of the Hampshire force. Perhaps you'd be so good as to tell me where I can find the headmaster.'

'You're talking to him,' said the man, raising his battered hat in mock salute and laughing outright at Hardcastle's obvious discomfiture. 'Doctor Arnold Mallory at your service.'

'I do beg your pardon, Doctor,' said Hardcastle. 'I'm afraid I mistook you for the gardener.'

Mallory laughed again. 'Understandable. I'm deadheading the geraniums at the moment and trimming the lavender, and it's a continuing battle against the weeds.' He waved a trowel vaguely at the candytuft. 'One of our gardeners got taken off to the war last month, which left me with just old Arthur. He's getting on a bit and he's off sick at the moment with some frightful ague, but even when he is here he suffers terribly from the rheumatics. I did have some young fellow from the village looking for work a few days ago, but I didn't much like the look of him. One has to be careful at a place like this, Inspector. However, I mustn't keep you here chatting. Come into my study and we can talk there.' The headmaster took off the gardening gloves he had been wearing and dropped them and the trowel into a trug.

'As a matter of interest, Doctor Mallory, do you recall the name of this chap who came looking for work?' asked Marriott as they walked towards the main door.

'Yes. He was called Snapper. Didn't much care for him or his name. A silly reason I know, but I didn't consider that a man called Snapper would be trustworthy. There's a lot more in a name than most people realize.'

Mallory led them along several stone-flagged corridors until he reached a door bearing a polished brass plate that simply read: HEADMASTER.

The floor of Doctor Mallory's spacious oak-lined study was covered with a Wilton carpet so large that it almost touched the walls. A huge 'partner's' desk stood across one corner of the room close to the window so that the headmaster had a view of the playing fields. The walls were adorned with pictures, many of them group photographs, and one or two that depicted military scenes. Mallory noticed Hardcastle studying them.

'I'm a schoolmaster by trade, but I served briefly in the Boer Wars and seriously considered making a career of the army. However, an injury put paid to that so I returned to the classroom.' Mallory did not elaborate, although Hardcastle had noticed that he walked with a slight limp and assumed that the headmaster had suffered a war wound. 'Do sit down, gentlemen,' he said as he took a seat behind his desk.

'We're enquiring into the murder of Daisy Salter, Doctor Mallory.'

'Miss Salter has been murdered?' The shocked expression on Mallory's face made it plain that he knew nothing of the killing. 'When did this happen?'

'Last Monday night, sir,' said Marriott. 'Her body was discovered early on Tuesday morning at South Farm.'

'Have you any idea who was responsible for this terrible crime?'

'Not yet,' said Hardcastle.

'Well, thank you for coming to tell me, Inspector.' Mallory placed his hands flat on the desk and began to stand up. 'It was most kind of you. You obviously knew that she was once employed here as a cleaner, but she no longer works here.'

'That was not the purpose of our visit,' said Hardcastle.

'It wasn't? What then?' The headmaster sat down again, his head to one side in an enquiring pose.

'I've been told that on one occasion Daisy Salter was keeping company with a young man from this college.'

'I'm afraid that's true, Inspector.' Mallory slowly shook his head. 'In fact, the young fool even talked of marriage. I find it difficult to think of any other way in which to ruin a promising career. I wrote to the boy's father and suggested that he be removed from the college and thus from the temptation that, I'm sure, was little more than an adolescent infatuation. The rules are quite explicit on the matter. No boy will consort with any female member of the staff; neither will they make the acquaintance of any young ladies in the village. Thus he had incurred what in tennis I suppose is called a double fault. Our boys are here to learn and to prepare themselves for a professional career.'

'And was the boy removed, Doctor Mallory?' asked Marriott.

'No; his father and I reached a compromise. Sir Robert is with the Indian Civil Service and I hadn't realized that he was on extended leave and would shortly be returning to India. So the upshot was that the lad got a severe dressing down from his father and another from me, and was allowed to stay until he took the army examination for the Royal Military College at Sandhurst which, I'm pleased to say, he passed in eleventh place: a good result.' Mallory paused. 'However, it turned out to be a waste of time; the normal entry requirements have been suspended due to the war and they're pushing young men through as though it were a sausage machine in order to get them to the Front as fast as possible.'

'And he'll probably be dead within weeks if this war continues,' said Hardcastle.

'I fear you may be right, Inspector.' Mallory shook his head despairingly. 'I sometimes wonder if I'm wasting my time. We've lost seventeen former pupils already, one of whom was awarded a posthumous Victoria Cross, for what good that'll do him. It might be some comfort to his parents, I suppose.'

'Where is Sir Robert's boy now, Doctor Mallory?' asked Hardcastle. 'At Sandhurst?'

'No, he's still here in college.' A thought struck Mallory. 'Oh my God! You don't suspect him of this awful crime, surely, Inspector?'

'I thought that all the pupils would be away for the summer holidays,' said Hardcastle, declining to rise to the headmaster's hoped-for denial.

'Some boys are permitted to remain in college during the long vacation,' said Mallory. 'In young Elliott's case it's because both his parents are now back in Calcutta and he has no relatives in this country. Sadly, we have another lad here, sixteen years of age, whose father, a captain in the Royal Fusiliers, was killed during the debacle of the Gallipoli landings, and the boy's mother committed suicide as a result. In an act of charity the board of governors have waived his fees for the duration of his stay here.'

'I'll have to interview young Elliott, Doctor Mallory,' said Hardcastle, fearing that the headmaster was about to recite a catalogue of the hardships of the college's pupils.

'Yes, of course. I quite understand that you would need to. I'll send for him.'

'How old is he?'

'Just turned eighteen.'

'Perhaps you would remain, Doctor. As he's a minor I'd rather that there was an independent adult present.'

Laurence Elliott was a handsome, foppish, six-foot tall young man, casually dressed in a colourful blazer, grey flannel trousers and an open-necked cricket shirt. His blond hair was longer than was customary and, coupled with his general appearance, made him more suited, Hardcastle thought, to someone with an artistic bent rather than to a future army officer.

'This is Detective Inspector Hardcastle of Scotland Yard, Elliott,' said Mallory. 'He wishes to ask you some questions.'

'Good morning, sir.' Elliott nodded in the DDI's direction and glanced at the other two detectives more with curiosity than apprehension.

'Sit down, lad,' said Hardcastle. 'I've just been telling Doctor Mallory that I'm investigating the murder of Daisy Salter.' The DDI waited to see what reaction this bald statement would bring.

'I didn't know she'd been murdered, sir.' Elliott coloured slightly and ran a hand through his hair, but otherwise appeared to be quite unmoved by the news.

'You knew her, of course.'

'Yes, sir. She was employed here as a cleaner.' Still Elliott remained composed.

'But you knew her better than just being a cleaner here.' Hardcastle sensed that this young man was about to prevaricate.

Elliott realized that this inspector would already have learned of his conduct from the headmaster. 'We had a mild flirtation a few months ago and it got me into a lot of hot water,' admitted Elliott ruefully, and shot a glance in the headmaster's direction. 'Not only with Doctor Mallory, but with the guv'nor too.'

'The guv'nor?' queried Hardcastle.

'My father. He took a rather poor view of my consorting with a servant girl.'

Hardcastle had always called his own father 'Pa', a form of address that Hardcastle's own son used to him. 'Yes, I suppose he would've done,' he said, imagining that Sir Robert Elliott would likely have become apoplectic at the thought of his son marrying a domestic servant. 'And when did this flirtation, as you call it, begin?'

'About a month ago, sir.'

'How long did it last?'

'No more than a couple of weeks, sir.'

'But long enough for you to consider marriage,' suggested Marriott mildly.

Elliott turned slightly to face the sergeant. 'It wasn't my idea, sir. It was Daisy not me who was talking about getting married and that was what made me decide to break it off. It'll be some years before I consider getting married.'

This was not what Mallory had told Hardcastle, and the head-master was about to interrupt the questioning to put the record straight when the DDI raised a hand. 'How often did you have sexual intercourse with Daisy Salter, Elliott?' asked Hardcastle.

'Never, sir,' replied Elliott vehemently and blushed to the roots of his blond hair.

'Really? I find that hard to believe. How old are you?'

'Eighteen, sir.'

'Eighteen?' Hardcastle savoured the word as though just learning that the boy was that old, rather than it being information the headmaster had given him just before Elliott had entered the study. 'You're eighteen and you're telling me that when you and Daisy Salter were rolling about in Farmer Blunden's haystack at South Farm you didn't have a bit of jig-a-jig.' He took a guess that Elliott and Daisy had been in the haystack at some time or another and Elliott did not deny it. 'Just the sort of girl to sow your wild oats with, I'd have thought.'

'We didn't become intimate, sir.' Elliott spoke adamantly and raised his chin slightly, as though finding Hardcastle's coarseness abhorrent.

'You didn't become intimate. That's a nice turn of phrase, Elliott, but did you screw the tart?'

'No, I did not.' Elliott struggled to get the words out; he had never before had to deal with someone as coarse as this rough diamond of a policeman.

Apparently satisfied with Elliott's reply, Hardcastle leaned back in his chair and then glanced in Marriott's direction.

'Are you sure you're telling the truth, Laurence?' asked Marriott. 'You see, Daisy Salter was pregnant.'

'I didn't know that, sir.' The reply was bland and showed no signs of guilt.

'Oh, but I think you did and I suggest that when she told you she was expecting your child, you panicked. You could see that any future career in the army would be in jeopardy and that your father would probably disinherit you. So you took hold of her with the intention of shaking some sense into her because you thought she was lying in order to trap you into marriage. But you grabbed her more forcefully than you thought. The next thing you knew she was dead. But it was an accident, wasn't it, Laurence? It happens more often than you might think, so why don't you tell us exactly how it happened?'

Sitting beside Marriott, Detective Constable Yardley was astonished at Marriott's forceful and devious line of questioning. He had to admit that he was learning more about the investigation of murder since the arrival of the Scotland Yard officers than he thought possible in so short a period of time.

'Oh my God!' Elliott looked at the headmaster and then at Hardcastle, and then back at Marriott. 'It's not true. None of it's true,' he protested, shaking visibly and his face now as white as a sheet; he thought he was about to be sick. He had read lurid crime novels – penny dreadfuls, they were called – that described how the author believed the police interrogated suspects and bullied them or even beat them into making a confession. Not only had Elliott believed it, but he was convinced that he was now experiencing it first hand. What he didn't know was that a coerced false confession was useless to the police, and would quickly be destroyed by defending counsel, particularly one of the calibre of Edward Marshall Hall. He stared at Marriott, his face distraught, tears only just held in check. He knew that he was old enough to go to the gallows and the thought terrified him. 'I swear I know nothing about her murder, sir. We were just having a bit of fun and anyway, she was older than me. I couldn't possibly have married her.'

Hardcastle did not bother to point out that Daisy Salter had been sixteen. Instead he imagined that she had falsified her age to young Elliott, and with the application of face powder and a little kohl had made herself appear more mature. She had certainly been wearing similar make-up when her body was found. 'Where were you last Monday night, Elliott?' he demanded suddenly.

The change in direction of the questioning momentarily disconcerted the boy. 'Er, here, in college, sir. I was in my room, reading.'

'Does anyone know that you were there?'

'No, sir. I was alone all evening.'

'Are you a collector, Elliott?' asked Hardcastle, once again changing the subject with disturbing effect.

'A collector, sir?' Elliott looked suitably mystified.

'Yes. In my experience, most young men collect things as a hobby.'

'Oh, I see. You mean like butterflies, or something of that sort.'

'I was thinking more of mementoes of the railways, like signs or flags, or even uniform buttons.'

'No, sir. I only collect books about the army. Oh, and I've one or two regimental cap badges.'

'All right, lad, you can go,' said Hardcastle.

A surprised Elliott, who thought he was about to be arrested, got unsteadily to his feet and made for the door. The room was spinning and he was not quite sure that he would make it. But he did, and once there, nodded in the headmaster's direction, mouthed the word 'sir' and left.

'Well, Inspector?' Mallory gave Hardcastle a quizzical glance.

'He didn't do it,' said Hardcastle firmly.

'But how can you be so sure?' Mallory leaned forward, arms folded on his desk, as intrigued as Yardley was to learn more about how the police investigated cases of murder.

'That lad's too naive to have committed a brutal murder, and anyway he had no alibi. Any killer worth his salt would have made sure he had an alibi before the police came anywhere near him asking questions.' Hardcastle stood up and leaned across the desk to shake hands with the headmaster. 'Thank you for your assistance, Doctor Mallory. We'll find our own way out.'

When the trio reached the main entrance to the college and Hardcastle had stopped on the steps to admire the view, Yardley asked the same question. 'How can you be so certain that Elliott wasn't the murderer, sir?'

'I'm not, Yardley. Not by any means. It's quite possible that he did do it, but at the moment I've no evidence and so I keep my suspicions to myself. What do you think?'

'I don't think he did it either, sir. If he met Daisy a month ago and broke off seeing her after two weeks, he couldn't be responsible for her pregnancy.'

'Well, he would say that, wouldn't he, Dick,' said Marriott. 'Particularly if he *knew* she was two months' pregnant.'

'He's been picked to be an officer in the army, Sergeant, so I suppose he must have some strength of character.'

'Maybe,' said Hardcastle doubtfully. 'But according to Colonel Frobisher, the assistant provost marshal of London District, the army is so desperately short of subalterns that these days they're commissioning almost anyone. After all,' he added with chilling cynicism, 'they're only expected to last six weeks before they're killed. But all that aside, if I'd told Doctor Mallory that I thought Elliott was guilty of murdering Daisy Salter but couldn't prove it, there's no telling what young Elliott might do. He might even top himself.'

'Surely Doctor Mallory wouldn't tell Elliott if you'd said you suspected him, would he, sir?'

'Oh Yardley, Yardley!' said Hardcastle, shaking his head. 'For all I know, Mallory might be one of those people who thinks that a girl like Daisy Salter is just a common tart and that a well set-up young gentleman like Laurence Elliott shouldn't have his army career blown away just because he put some slut in the family way and then strangled her to solve the problem.'

Hardcastle did not think that for a moment, but there was another reason for not confiding in the headmaster. 'I don't want Mallory suggesting to Sir Robert Elliott that it might be politic to whisk the lad off to India where he could not easily be reached by the arm of the law, Yardley. Even though, when it comes to arresting murderers, it's a very long arm. Sir Robert's probably the sort who thinks that, given time, it might all blow over.'

'Do you think Sir Robert might think that, sir?' Yardley, in his naiveté, had always believed that anyone with a title was beyond reproach.

'It don't bother me one way or the other, Yardley. It doesn't matter what Daisy Salter got up to or whether people thought she was a slut,' continued Hardcastle as he got into the taxi. 'She deserves to receive justice the same as if she was a duke's daughter. And now you can drop Sergeant Marriott and me at the railway station and we'll see what we can learn about that there button you found in Daisy Salter's handbag.'

NINE

'Scotland Yard, cabbie,' said Hardcastle as he clambered into a taxi at Waterloo railway station. Turning to Marriott, he added, 'Tell 'em Cannon Row, Marriott, and half the time you'll finish up at Cannon Street in the City of London.'

'So I understand, sir.' Marriott attempted to disguise his exasperation; he had been offered this advice on almost every occasion that he and the DDI had taken a cab to Cannon Row.

Once back at their police station, Hardcastle threw open the heavy wooden flap in the counter and allowed it to fall with a crash before marching through the front office.

The station officer who was writing busily in the Occurrence Book had not noticed Hardcastle's arrival and leaped to his feet somewhat belatedly. 'I'm sorry, sir. All correct, sir.'

'I'm glad to see you're awake, Sergeant,' snapped Hardcastle acidly. He was always irritated by the requirement for officers to report thus whether all was correct or not, but, perversely, annoyed that the sergeant had failed to do so immediately.

Taking the stairs two at a time, despite his bulky figure, he opened the door of his office and was further irritated to find Detective Inspector Edgar Rhodes seated behind the desk.

'Good afternoon, sir.' Rhodes rose to his feet and, seeing the DDI's obvious displeasure, said, 'Mr Hudson suggested that I used your office while I was acting-up for you, sir.' Although Rhodes was now acting divisional detective inspector, and therefore on a par with Hardcastle, he had no intention of calling him by his first name. He knew that Hardcastle would resume his former role once his current enquiry was resolved.

'Yes, very wise.' Had Hardcastle been in the same position as Superintendent Arthur Hudson, the officer in charge of A Division, he would probably have made the same suggestion. 'Anything happening, Mr Rhodes?' Hardcastle was not really interested and knew perfectly well that Rhodes was capable of doing the job of a DDI, but at the same time felt that he should not relinquish all responsibility for A Division's CID.

'A couple of burglaries near Vincent Square last night, sir. Looks like the same method in each case. Mr Collins is checking the fingerprints that were found at the scene against his index. And the usual crop of dips at Buck House guard change.'

'There's nothing new about that.' Hardcastle was always instructing his junior detectives to mingle with the crowds at the Buckingham Palace guard change and make the lives of pickpockets a misery. He was surprised that so many people turned out to watch the ceremony on the forecourt of the palace; the event had taken on a sombre character since khaki had been substituted for the traditional scarlet tunics of the Guards Brigade. Turning to Marriott, he asked, 'Have you found out where the head office of the Great Western Railway is?'

'Yes, sir,' said Marriott, who knew the question would be asked sooner or later. 'Paddington railway station.'

'Yes,' said Hardcastle. 'It would be, I suppose.'

The concourse of what was still called by some the *new* Paddington railway station had been opened in 1854, and was dominated by an iron and glass roof on cast-iron pillars. But this afternoon Hardcastle had no time to admire Isambard Kingdom Brunel's architecture.

'I'm DDI Hardcastle, Metropolitan, lad,' said Hardcastle, stopping in front of a railway policeman. He always called constables 'lad', regardless of their age, and this one was probably as old as the DDI. 'I need to talk to someone at the head office of the Great Western Railway who knows about uniforms.'

'Follow me, sir, and I'll see if I can find the right man for you.'

After several enquiries and one or two wrong turnings in the railway's labyrinthine offices, Hardcastle and Marriott were eventually shown into the office of a man whose door plate stated that he was called Hubert Merryweather and bestowed upon him the splendid title of 'Departmental Head of Purchasing (Uniform and Accoutrements)'.

'I'm told you're the man who deals with railway uniform, Mr Merryweather,' said Hardcastle as he entered the office.

'If you're trade representatives, you must make an appointment,' replied Merryweather crossly as he looked up from the file in front of him. He was a rotund little man with heavy eyebrows, horn-rimmed spectacles and a waistcoat that appeared to be having difficulty containing his well-fed figure. Rising from behind his desk, an aggressive expression on his face, he was obviously a man plagued by itinerant commercial travellers intent upon selling their wares.

'I'm a police officer, Mr Merryweather. Detective Inspector Hardcastle of Scotland Yard.'

'How do I know that?' Merryweather's experience clearly led him to believe that salesmen would employ all manner of ruses in order to get an interview with a buyer, and this portly visitor, accompanied by a younger man obviously learning the tricks of the trade, was clearly one of them.

'Perhaps this will satisfy you,' said Hardcastle with a restraint that surprised even Marriott, and produced his warrant card.

'Oh, I do beg your pardon, gentlemen,' said Merryweather, pushing his spectacles up to the bridge of his nose, 'but you'd be amazed at the stories some individuals come out with in order to get into my office. The clothing and equipment budget for the Great Western Railway is quite substantial and those manufacturers unlucky enough not to have secured army clothing contracts are hungry for any business they can get, including ours.'

'Yes, I quite understand,' said Hardcastle, and introduced Marriott.

'Please take a seat and tell me how I can help you, Inspector.' After his initial gaffe, Merryweather became suddenly solicitous.

'I'm investigating a murder that took place in Thresham Parva, Mr Merryweather.'

'Thresham Parva, Thresham Parva,' muttered Merryweather, and turned in his chair to consult a large diagrammatic wall chart of the Great Western Railway's operations. 'Not one of our ports of call, so to speak,' he said, turning back again.

'No, it wouldn't be, Mr Merryweather,' said Marriott. 'It's in Hampshire.'

'Well, what can I do for you?' Merryweather seemed to be mystified that the police were seeking his advice about a murder in Hampshire.

'It's a question of a button, Mr Merryweather.' Hardcastle was showing remarkable patience with this fussy little man, but he needed his help. 'Show Mr Merryweather the button, Marriott.'

Marriott took the button from the tissue paper in which it had been wrapped and placed it on the desk in front of Merryweather. 'It's quite all right if you want to pick it up, Mr Merryweather,' he said. 'There are no identifiable fingerprints on it.'

Merryweather opened a drawer in his desk and without looking inside took out a magnifying glass. It was an act that caused Hardcastle to conclude that the pedantic little buyer would easily be able to lay hands on anything he wanted because it would always be in its allotted place.

Examining the button closely, Merryweather eventually looked up. 'I shall inspect the reverse, Sergeant,' he said unnecessarily. 'Unfortunately the obverse does not tell the whole story.' Again bringing his magnifying glass to bear, he finally leaned back in his chair with a satisfied smile on his face. 'Nineteen-oh-five,' he announced.

'What is?' asked Hardcastle.

'That button was introduced in 1899 when the Great Western Railway acquired the Golden Valley Railway. But when in 1905 the Wye Valley Railway was acquired this button was declared obsolete.'

'What has the button to do with the buying up of railways?' asked a bemused Hardcastle.

'Nothing whatever, Inspector,' said Merryweather, 'but in the railway world we tend to mark dates by acquisitions of companies, locomotives or rolling stock.' Lowering his voice and adopting a suitable grave expression, he added, 'And railway accidents.'

'So what happened to all the obsolete buttons, sir?' asked Marriott.

'Sold to metal dealers, I suppose. I'm only the buyer, not the seller, you see,' said Merryweather airily as he pushed his glasses up to the bridge of his nose yet again. 'No doubt some were snapped up by people who collect such things. There are a great number of people who accumulate all manner of railway paraphernalia, whether it be buttons, old signs, signal lanterns, red flags, green flags, or guards' hats and whistles, and even station-masters' top hats. The list is endless. I even read in the *Railway Magazine* the other day that a sign bearing the legend "Gentlemen" was sold for thirty shillings. It's outrageous; a new one would cost less.'

'Thank you for your assistance, Mr Merryweather,' said Hardcastle. 'You've been extremely helpful.'

'Only too pleased to be of help, Inspector. But tell me, was the victim of this murder a servant of the railway?'

'No,' said Hardcastle. 'She was a sixteen-year-old girl, but the button was found with the body. Of course, it may have nothing whatever to do with the murder.'

'How very strange,' said Merryweather, rushing across his office to open the door for the detectives. 'How very strange.'

'Well, that don't get us any further forward, Marriott,' said Hardcastle when the two of them were in a taxi on the way back to the police station. 'Apart from learning a lot about miscellaneous railway bits and pieces that we didn't need to know.'

'It could be as you said, sir, that the button has nothing to do with Daisy Salter's topping.'

'Maybe, Marriott, but there again maybe not. I wonder if Snapper ever worked for the Great Western.'

'I suppose we could have asked someone in their staff department while we were there, sir,' suggested Marriott.

Hardcastle shot Marriott a doleful look. 'You could have mentioned that before we left, Marriott. That's what sergeants were created for.'

'Yes, sir, but then I thought that you wouldn't want to advertise the fact that we suspected Snapper. Someone would be bound to let him know that we were anxious to talk to him.'

'Yes, you're quite right, Marriott. I can see you can read my mind.'

Only very rarely, thought Marriott, as the cab turned into the forecourt of New Scotland Yard.

'You don't mind if I use my office for a few minutes, do you, Mr Rhodes?'

'Of course not, sir.' DI Rhodes, hardly in a position to refuse Hardcastle's request, gathered up a few papers and made for the door.

Hardcastle sat down behind his desk, took out his pipe and lit it. 'Now then, Marriott, what have you done about Snapper?' he asked, emitting a plume of tobacco smoke towards the ceiling. 'Apart from advising me not to talk to the Great Western Railway about him.'

'I've arranged for a notice to be published in the *Police Gazette* asking that his whereabouts be discreetly ascertained and that you be informed, sir, but that he's not to be arrested or alerted to our interest. I also had them put in that he was lately of Thresham Parva in Hampshire.'

'Did you mention that he might be in Waterlooville?'

'Yes, sir, but I also added that he had probably moved on by now.'

'That'll do for the time being. It would be very satisfactory if his fingerprints turned out to be in Mr Collins's collection and it would have been even better if they'd been on that there button that young Yardley's Peewit Patrol found for us.'

'There is another possibility, sir,' suggested Marriott tentatively. 'It was mentioned that Daisy Salter was known to have frequented the Thresham Arms and that there was some trouble with soldiers. I suppose it's possible that it was a tommy who put young Daisy up the duff.'

'Yes, that had occurred to me,' said Hardcastle, to whom it had not occurred at all until Marriott had raised the possibility. 'But the chances are that if some soldier *was* responsible he's now lying dead somewhere in Flanders or in any other place where our army is being slaughtered.'

'Supposing she knew that, sir, or knew that there was no chance of him putting a ring on her finger, might she have tried to talk Snapper into believing that the baby was his? Or even that it was young Elliott's?'

'It's just possible she could've sweet-talked them into believing anything, I suppose. After all, it was only Doctor Spilsbury who knew that the girl was *two months'* pregnant,' said Hardcastle. 'I doubt that even Daisy knew, especially if she'd been screwed by more than one of the local blades.' He took out his half-hunter, noted the time and slipped it back into his waistcoat pocket. 'For all young Elliott's la-di-dah accent and having a "sir" for a father, he's still a naive youngster. Anyway, we can think about that tomorrow. Get off home and spend the night with your family,

Marriott. Meet me at Waterloo station at eight o'clock tomorrow morning.'

'Thank you very much, sir.' Marriott was taken aback by the DDI's decision. He had never before known him to be so considerate, and was firmly convinced that it had been Hardcastle's intention to return to Hampshire that evening.

'Give my regards to Mrs Marriott,' said Hardcastle.

'And mine to Mrs H, sir.'

'But before you go, Marriott, get a message to young Yardley.'

'Very good, sir. He's probably wondering where we are.'

'I'm not bothered about what he's wondering about, Marriott, but I want to make sure he's at the station to meet us with his taxi tomorrow morning.'

'Is that you, Ernie?' Alice Hardcastle's voice came from the direction of the kitchen.

'Yes, it's me, love.' Hardcastle glanced at the clock in the hall and compared the time it showed with his half-hunter. Muttering to himself, he opened the glass screen of the hall clock and moved the minute hand to show the correct time: ten minutes past seven.

'I suppose you'll be wanting some supper.' Alice turned from the gas stove as Hardcastle joined her in the kitchen. 'I don't know, Ernest. You might've let me know you were coming.' The use of her husband's full name was an indication of her irritation at his unheralded arrival.

'I wasn't sure myself until about half an hour ago, Alice, love.' Hardcastle was intent on not upsetting his long-suffering wife, who often said that there was only one thing worse than being a policeman and that was being a policeman's wife.

'Isn't it about time we had a telephone installed?'

'*A telephone!*' exclaimed Hardcastle, almost choking over the word. 'I'll not have one of those damn things in the house.'

'Language, Ernest,' said Alice sternly. 'Maud's in the parlour.'

'She's home early,' said Hardcastle.

'She's early shift this week,' replied Alice. For some time now, Maud, the Hardcastles' youngest daughter, had been working as a nurse at Dorchester House, Colonel Sir George Holford's mansion in Park Lane, which had been converted into a hospital for wounded officers. 'Anyway, if we had a telephone the station could just ring you up when they wanted you, instead of one of those poor PCs having to walk round from Kennington Road every time you are called out. And often in the pouring rain.'

'That's what PCs are for,' muttered Hardcastle unsympathetically. 'I had to do it often enough when I was a PC *and* we walked a beat in all weathers. As far as I know that hasn't changed, although the Job's getting a bit slipshod since I was a PC.' The prospect of his police station being able to telephone him whenever they felt so inclined horrified him; he could foresee a host of calls about matters of little importance. He would be nearly in as bad a situation as the superintendent at Alton who was obliged to live at the police station.

But any further discussion on the subject was stilled by the noise of maroons being set off from Renfrew Road fire station a few hundred yards away.

Hardcastle took out his half-hunter. 'It's twenty past seven,' he announced. 'They always set off the maroons when the bombers are crossing the coast so it'll be getting on for an hour before they're anywhere near us.'

Although the giant Gotha bombers were capable of a top speed of about eighty-six miles per hour and Hardcastle's estimate was usually correct, he was wrong on this occasion. He was not to know of the dense low cloud prevailing where the enemy aircraft had crossed into England seventy miles away, and he was not to know that although the observers had heard the aircraft engines, they were unable to identify them with any degree of accuracy. Consequently it was only when the deadly German bombers were spotted flying above the River Thames, which they used as their guide into London, that the alarm was sounded.

Ten minutes after Hardcastle had assured Alice and Maud that there was no need to take shelter just yet, a terrifying and thunderous explosion shook the house. All the front windows blew out with a crash of breaking glass as they fell to the pavement outside; the curtains, torn in places, billowed in and then out, and the front door crashed open and then slammed shut again. At the same time came the nearby sound of cascading brickwork.

'Christ Almighty!' exclaimed Hardcastle, and this time there were no recriminations from Alice about his bad language. 'Are you all right, love?'

'Yes, Ernie. So's Maud, aren't you, dear?'

'Yes, I'm OK, Ma.'

Such was the shock at having a bomb fall so close that Hardcastle did not admonish Maud for her use of slang, as he usually did. 'That was near,' he said, making one of his customary understatements. 'Better have a look.' He stepped out of his front door and peered across the road through a fog of descending dust. Overhead, one of the huge white Gothas with the sinister Maltese crosses on the wings was descending in a slow dive towards Westminster, smoke issuing from its port engine. 'At least they got one of the buggers,' he said. 'I just hope it doesn't hit my police station.'

'What's happened, Pa?' asked Maud as she joined her father.

'Arthur Hogg's house has got a direct hit by the look of it, love.' Concerned neighbours were already pulling at baulks of timber and tossing bricks out of the way in an attempt to rescue anyone who was still alive in the debris. Dashing across the road, Hardcastle joined the would-be rescuers.

A policeman, his uniform torn and covered in dirt, was coordinating the rescue. As Hardcastle appeared, he said, 'Give us a hand with this beam, mate.' And then, recognizing the DDI, said, 'Oh, I'm terribly sorry, sir, I didn't realize it was you.' He turned to another bystander and repeated his request.

'Don't be bloody daft, lad. I'm still a copper.' Hardcastle grabbed hold of the length of timber and, with the PC at the other end of it, lifted. Beneath it was a woman, her face covered in blood and moaning. 'That's Bertha Hogg, lad. Give me a hand to get her out.'

Together the two police officers gently lifted the woman from among the debris of what had once been her home and laid her on a mattress that had been pulled from the ruined house.

'We'll soon get you to hospital, Mrs Hogg,' said Maud, appearing at her father's side.

'Bugger the bleedin' Kaiser,' said Bertha Hogg, and lapsed into unconsciousness.

'Get back indoors, Maud,' ordered Hardcastle sternly. 'This sort of situation is no place for a young woman.'

'Oh, for Christ's sake, don't be so bloody stupid, Pa,' shouted Maud angrily as she flicked a lock of hair out of her eyes. 'I'm a nurse. I see worse than this every day.'

Utterly amazed, and stunned into silence at being sworn at by his young daughter, Hardcastle stared at her for some seconds before speaking. 'All right, girl. We'll get her across to our house and you can do what you can for her while we're waiting for the ambulance.' He turned to a man standing nearby. 'Give me a hand, will you.'

'Leave it to us, guv'nor.' Effortlessly, or so it seemed, a couple of men gently lifted the mattress bearing the small figure of Bertha Hogg on to an abandoned door, and together with two other volunteers carried her across the road.

'I've put some cushions on the parlour floor, Ernie,' said Alice, who had been standing at her front door watching what was occurring opposite. 'Just in case.'

Having moved Bertha Hogg on to the cushions, the men picked up their makeshift stretcher and took their leave.

'Hot water and a flannel. And I shall need towels.' Having given those orders to her parents, with a certain measure of impatience, Maud immediately set to work dealing with her patient. The ward sister at Dorchester House would have been proud of her.

Ten minutes later an ambulance attendant, accompanied by a woman driver, entered the room. 'The copper over the road said as how you'd got a casualty in here, guv'nor.' The attendant addressed Hardcastle.

'Yes, we have.' Maud stood up, holding her bloodstained hands at her sides and away from her dress. 'Compound fracture of the left tibia, simple fracture of the left fibula and a four-inch laceration on the right side of the head behind the ear. There's obviously a possibility of concussion and the patient is lapsing into unconsciousness at about twenty-second intervals, but recovering after five or so. But I didn't have time to splint up before you arrived.'

'Are you a nurse, then, love?' asked the attendant, clearly impressed by Maud's concise diagnosis.

'You blokes catch on quickly,' said Maud, grinning at the man. 'Dorchester House.'

'Ah, that explains it. I've been there a few times, although we usually do the run from Victoria to Charing Cross collecting the wounded off the trains and taking them to the hospital.'

The attendant and his driver lifted Bertha Hogg on to a stretcher and carried her out to the waiting ambulance.

As the vehicle departed, Hardcastle crossed the road to where the PC was standing. 'Did they manage to get Arthur Hogg out of there, lad?'

'Yes, sir, but he was dead.' The PC acknowledged Hardcastle with a salute. 'Bloody marvellous, isn't it? He lost a leg at Neuve Chapelle a couple of years back, got invalided out and then goes and gets himself killed in an air raid in Blighty.'

'What about the two children?'

'Both gone, I'm afraid, sir. They was upstairs in their beds. Never stood a chance.'

'Bloody war,' muttered Hardcastle, and returned to his front room. 'Arthur Hogg was killed, Alice,' he said. 'And the two bairns.'

'Oh, poor Bertha. It's unbelievable, isn't it? And Arthur too. How can a man be so unlucky?'

'What are you talking about, Ma?' asked Maud.

Alice Hardcastle repeated what the local PC had just told Hardcastle, news of which had rapidly travelled the length and breadth of Kennington Road.

'It happens,' said Maud phlegmatically. 'I'll just get this blood off my hands, Ma, and then I'll help you to clear up.'

'We'll have supper first,' said Alice.

As Maud left the room, Hardcastle looked at his wife and shook his head. 'I do believe our little girl has grown up, Alice,' he said eventually. 'D'you know she actually swore at me across the road because I told her that dealing with the injured was no job for a young woman.'

'Serves you right, Ernie,' said Alice. 'It's time someone swore at you. You have it too easy at work. Everyone jumps when you say jump.'

When Maud returned to the parlour, her father was waiting with a glass in his hand. 'There you are, girl. I reckon you've earned that. It's Scotch so take it slowly.'

'Cheers!' Maud promptly downed the whisky in a single gulp and held out the glass for a refill.

'Have you had whisky before, then?' asked a dumbfounded Hardcastle.

'Yes, of course I have. We've got a ward sister who comes from Inverness and she reckons it's the best way to round off a shift.'

Maud drank her second whisky, a little more slowly, and handed the glass to her father. 'I'll go and get changed now,' she said.

Hardcastle shook his head unbelievingly as Maud left the room. 'I've learned more about Maud in the last hour, Alice, than I learned in the whole of last year,' he said.

'You're never here to find out, are you, Ernie? And I suppose you'll be off again tomorrow.'

'I'm afraid so, but what are we going to do about all this?' Hardcastle waved a hand at the broken windows. 'And there's the lock to fix on the front door.'

'Good heavens, Ernest, use a bit of common sense. If you haven't got a sergeant to run about doing things for you, you're completely lost. Go down to Frank Meakin's place on the corner. Being an ironmonger, he's bound to know a glazier and a lock-smith.' Alice shook her head. 'If we had a telephone, you could do all that without moving and that would suit you down to the ground, wouldn't it, Ernest Hardcastle?' And with that parting shot she went into the kitchen to try to salvage what she had been cooking for supper before the bomb fell.

Crunching his way over broken glass, Hardcastle found his way to Frank Meakin's ironmonger's shop.

'Ah, Mr Hardcastle.' Meakin looked up and nodded.

Hardcastle did not much care for Meakin and liked his shop even less. It was a complete hotchpotch and how Meakin managed to trade was a complete mystery to the DDI's ordered detective's mind. And yet, to Hardcastle's irritation, one had only to ask for a specific item and Meakin would disappear into the chaos and lay hands on it within seconds.

'I'm in need of a glazier and a locksmith urgently, Mr Meakin.'

'Thought you might be, sir. Seeing as how you're in an important job, I'll get them on to it straight away.' Meakin grinned owlishly, believing himself now to be in this senior policeman's good books, thus proving that Meakin did not know DDI Hardcastle as well as he thought.

TEN

Hardcastle, peering about impatiently, was already at Waterloo railway station when Marriott arrived.

'Ah, there you are, Marriott.'

'Are you all right, sir?' Marriott was surprised to see the DDI. 'My next-door neighbour, Sid Lewington, a station sergeant on B Division, told me that a bomb fell in Kennington Road last evening.'

'I don't know how a skipper on the other side of the river knew that,' said Hardcastle, 'but he's right. One of my neighbours was killed and his wife was injured. And their two children were killed as well. What time is the train?' The DDI's succinct response was similar to that of many other people who had become inured to the carnage brought about by total war: seemingly callous, it was in fact a defence mechanism.

Marriott pointed to an entry on the departures board. 'I think we'll be in time to catch that one, sir,' he said. 'It's a Winchester train that stops at Alton, and I've bought the tickets.'

'You did get second-class tickets, I hope.'

'Of course, sir,' replied Marriott. Hardcastle had frequently reminded him that as a divisional detective inspector he was entitled to second-class train travel, and so was Marriott when he was accompanying the DDI. Had Marriott been travelling alone, he would have been obliged to go third class, such was the rank-conscious parsimony of the police hierarchy. 'I got you a copy of the *Daily Mail* as well, sir.'

'Very thoughtful.' Hardcastle took the newspaper but made no attempt to reimburse Marriott. For his part, Marriott had purchased a copy of *John Bull*, the overly patriotic magazine published by Horatio Bottomley, whose impassioned oratory had raised thousands of pounds to assist the war effort and brought hundreds of recruits flocking to the Colours.

'This big push of Haig's seems to be in trouble,' commented Hardcastle as the train got under way. 'It says here,' he continued, tapping the newspaper with the stem of his pipe, 'that our guns

and tanks are bogged down in mud that's waist-deep in places.'
The battle to which Hardcastle was referring was the third major
attempt by the Allies to break out of the Ypres salient. As a
preamble to the offensive, nineteen huge mines had been detonated
under the Messines-Wytschaete ridge two months previously,
killing over ten thousand Germans. It was also a memorable date
of an event closer to home. At the very moment of the explosion
two of Hardcastle's detective constables – Henry Catto and Fred
Wilmot – had arrested two murderers in the back garden of a
house in Lewisham.

When the train arrived at Alton, DC Yardley was waiting on the
platform.

'Good morning, sir. I don't know what you had in mind for
today, but there are three young ladies of the Women's Land Army
working at South Farm this morning. I took the liberty of telling
Mr Blunden that you might want to interview them.'

'I'm glad you thought of that, Yardley.' Hardcastle tossed his
newspaper into a litter bin. 'I was just about to ask you to arrange
it,' he said, but in fact had completely forgotten all about it, mainly
because he did not think that those three women would have
anything to contribute to his pitifully small pile of evidence.

'I understand that there are also a couple of German
prisoners-of-war there as well, sir. I made enquiries of Mr Blunden
and apparently they are the two who always come to him.'

'Very well,' said Hardcastle. If Yardley was expecting a word
of praise he was disappointed.

'I've checked up on Jed Young, our taxi driver, and why he's
not been conscripted, sir,' said Yardley. 'It seems the papers were
lost, so I've informed the authorities that he's available for service.
But,' he added hurriedly, 'I asked them to wait until you'd finished
with him.'

'Quite right, Yardley.'

'Good day to you, Inspector.' Joshua Blunden, smoking his clay
pipe, was leaning over the gate of his five-acre field, close to
where the body of Daisy Salter had been found. 'Mr Yardley told
me that you want to have a word with my young ladies.' He took
off his cap and scratched his head.

'If that is convenient, Mr Blunden, but I don't want to interfere with the essential work of farming,' said Hardcastle smoothly. 'It's very important in wartime.'

'You've come at just the right time, as it happens, Mr Hardcastle. They've just stopped for a cup of tea. That's 'em, over there.' Blunden took the pipe out of his mouth and pointed the stem towards three young women who were standing in a group near a haystack.

As the detectives approached the group, Hardcastle was surprised to see that rather than the baggy riding breeches issued to members of the Women's Land Army, all three women were dressed in tight-fitting khaki jodhpurs, together with riding boots. But that was not the only surprise: they were wearing what appeared to be men's shirts, their hair was bobbed in a fashion that was fast becoming popular among women who were doing men's work and none of them wore hats. But despite this casual sort of attire having become more commonplace after three years of war, Hardcastle was still having difficulty accepting it, even though it was no longer regarded as out of the ordinary by a large section of the public.

'I thought the Women's Land Army was provided with proper uniform, Mr Blunden.' Hardcastle preferred not to pose the question direct to the women.

But the farmer did not get the opportunity to reply. One of the women threw back her head and gave a tinkling laugh. 'Good heavens, Inspector, we don't want to look like frumps.' She was in her early twenties, Hardcastle surmised, and spoke in cultured tones.

'Who are you, miss?'

'Victoria Homersham, Inspector. I'm sorry that our get-up appears to have shocked you, but we weren't going to wear that awful stuff the Women's Land Army issued us with. So I got these for the girls from my brother's tailor in London. Apart from anything else, this is a far more suitable outfit for what we're doing.' She waved vaguely at her jodhpurs, but still managed to make it an elegant gesture. 'Some of the Land Army women – townies mostly – love dressing up like soldiers with their badges and armbands and all that sort of palaver. They're jolly good at supervising and they love to have parades, but they don't much care for getting their hands dirty. If you were to suggest to some of them that they muck out a pigsty they'd probably have a touch of the vapours.' She made a wry face and giggled.

'Did any of you young ladies know Daisy Salter, the girl who was murdered?' asked Marriott, determined to stem Victoria Homersham's inane chattering.

'Yes, we all did,' said Victoria, smiling and locking eyes with Marriott for longer than was necessary.

'Perhaps you'd care to introduce your friends.'

'That's Nancy Harris and she's Dolly Elwood,' said Victoria, pointing to each of her two companions in turn. She suddenly caught sight of DC Yardley. 'Oh, hello, Dickie. I didn't see you standing at the back. How are you? We must have a drink sometime.'

'Hello, Vicky,' said Yardley, rather self-consciously.

Hardcastle shot a glance in Yardley's direction but said nothing to him. Addressing himself to the three women, he asked, 'How is it that you ladies knew Daisy Salter, then?'

'We met her in the public bar of the Thresham Arms,' said Victoria Homersham, having clearly appointed herself spokeswoman for the group.

'What were you doing in the Thresham Arms?' Hardcastle tried to visualize this sophisticated young lady in the spit and sawdust part of the village pub. And he was having difficulty getting sensible answers from her too, especially as she appeared determined to do most of the talking.

'Having a drink, of course, Inspector.' Victoria deliberately misinterpreted Hardcastle's question and emitted her tinkling laugh again. 'We always go in there for a drink before going off home. What on earth did you think we'd be doing?'

'Were you there the night the military police were called to a fight? I've been told that there was a disturbance and that it was something to do with Daisy Salter and some soldiers.' Hardcastle was still struggling to converse with this girl.

'No, we weren't there that night,' said Victoria, 'but we heard all about it afterwards. Apparently Daisy got her dates in an awful stew, silly girl. Either that or the jolly young soldiers did. Anyway, two of them turned up at the same time intent on taking her out for a bit of naughtiness.' She looked directly at Marriott and smiled. 'They obviously didn't care much for the idea of sharing her and there was a bit of a set-to.' She paused. 'Anyway, that's what we heard.'

'Did you know her socially?' asked Marriott.

'Good heavens, no. She was only a kid. What, sixteen or seventeen?' Victoria glanced at the other two girls as if seeking confirmation. 'Something like that, I suppose, but we only ever sort of said hello. To be perfectly honest I could see she was riding for a fall and, lo and behold, she came a real purler.'

'It's right what Vicky said.' The speaker was the girl who had been introduced as Dolly Elwood. 'It was obvious that she was going to come a cropper, the way she was behaving.'

'Did you know her well, then, Miss Elwood?'

'Heavens, no. I live in Aldershot. My father's in the army, you see. Anyway, we heard about the kerfuffle in the pub, but we weren't Daisy's muckers. At least not Vicky and me. I think Nancy knew her a bit better, didn't you, Nancy?' she asked, turning to the third girl.

'What on earth is a mucker?' Hardcastle was starting to think that these women, Victoria in particular, were using words that were completely alien to him and talking to him in a fashion intended deliberately to rile him. But he frequently thought that people he styled the 'champagne and caviar lot' were condescending when in fact they talked to their peers in exactly the same way.

'It means a friend or colleague, sir,' said Marriott. 'My brother-in-law told me it's army slang. There are a lot of new words coming into the vocabulary as a result of the war.'

Marriott's brother-in-law was a sergeant-major serving with the Middlesex Regiment in Flanders, and Marriott's wife was constantly concerned that she might one day hear that her brother had been killed.

Hardcastle grunted, something he frequently did when put in the unsought position of having things explained to him by his sergeant, particularly in public. 'How well did you know Daisy Salter, then, Miss Harris?' he asked.

'We were at school together,' said Nancy Harris. 'Well, not exactly together because Daisy was two years younger than me, but we were there at the same time.' She paused. 'Some of the time, I should say.'

'So you live locally.'

'Yes, I do.'

'Do you know of anyone Daisy was particularly friendly with?'

'Most of the girls. She was a very outgoing, chummy sort of person.'

'I think my inspector is more interested to know if she was friendly with any boys.' Being nearer their age, Marriott was more at ease than Hardcastle when talking to the young women.

Nancy laughed. 'All of them, I should think. She certainly liked the boys. I think she even made eyes at Mr Booth when she was at school. He was the headteacher, but he was probably old enough to be Daisy's grandfather.' And with that comment, she dissolved into laughter, to be joined by the other two.

'I'll let you get back to work,' said Hardcastle grumpily. He had come to the conclusion that these three women had nothing to add to what he knew already about Daisy Salter and that nothing they had said got him any nearer to discovering the identity of the girl's murderer.

'Don't forget, Dickie,' shouted Victoria, giving Yardley a wave. 'Must have a drink sometime. In fact, make it this evening. Shall we say about half past six? I'm sure the nice inspector will let you off. I'm staying at the Swan in Alton pro tem.'

'The two German prisoners are back at the house if you want to speak to them, Inspector,' said Blunden, 'and I daresay you could do with a cup of tea anyway.'

'Thank you, but I doubt we'll have time for tea.' Hardcastle did not intend to stay long. So far the morning had been wasted and he did not hold out any hope that matters would improve.

'They're good lads despite being Germans,' said Blunden as the four of them walked back to the farmhouse. 'They've been working in the barn, but I daresay Martha's given them some tea and toast. Spoils 'em rotten, she does.'

The two German prisoners were indeed in the farmhouse. As Blunden and the three police officers entered the kitchen, the two men sprang to their feet.

'This gentleman is an important policeman from Scotland Yard and he wants to have a few words with you,' said Blunden. Turning to Hardcastle, he added, 'The older one speaks quite good English, Inspector, and the other lad's learning fast.'

The elder of the two soldiers clicked his heels and bowed slightly. 'I am *Feldwebel* Adolph Krämer, sir.'

'That's German for sergeant, sir,' said Marriott, turning to Hardcastle.

'*Ja*, that is so, sir, and this is *Gefreiter* Franz Albrecht,' said

Krämer, indicating his fellow prisoner. 'He is a lance-corporal, but he does not speak so good English as me.'

Albrecht also clicked his heels and bowed.

'Well, I'm glad we've got that sorted out,' said Hardcastle. 'Do you know anything about the girl who was murdered at this farm last Monday night?'

Albrecht glanced at Krämer and raised his eyebrows, and Krämer quickly translated Hardcastle's question into German.

'*Nein. Ich weiß nichts davon.*' An expression of alarm crossed Albrecht's face.

Krämer laughed and turned to Hardcastle. 'He is saying that he knows nothing of this affair, sir.'

'He looked very guilty.'

'It is unfortunate, sir, but *Gefreiter* Albrecht thinks always that the British are blaming the German prisoners for anything bad that happens. He has yet to understand that not all English think this way. But in any case, we have only just come back to *Herr* Blunden's farm after a week working in another place at the military school in Sandhurst. I would not do anything to annoy the people of this country because I hope to stay here after the war is finished.'

'Don't you want to return to Germany, then?' asked Marriott. 'Don't you have a wife?'

'No, I am not married, sir, but perhaps one day I marry a nice English girl. Anyway, Germany is finished. *Kaputt!* The war is lost and our soldiers are tired out of the fighting. We had more prisoners come to the camp last week and they are speaking to us that at home in Germany the people are starving. It is no place to go back for, sir. I want very much to stay here.'

'Three pints of your best, please, Tom,' said Hardcastle the moment that he and the other two detectives walked into the saloon bar of the Thresham Arms. 'We'll be sitting over there.' Hardcastle indicated a table near the window.

'I'll bring it across, sir.' Hooker began drawing the beer.

'Well, we didn't learn much this morning, sir,' said Marriott.

'You have to cast your net wide to get a decent catch, Marriott,' said Hardcastle enigmatically before turning to the Hampshire officer. 'And how d'you know Miss Homersham, Yardley?'

'As a matter of fact, she's Lady Victoria Homersham, sir, daughter of Earl and Countess Homersham. She lives with her parents near Henley but she borrows her brother's car while he's in the army. That's how she gets over here, but you probably heard her say that she's staying at the Swan for the time being.'

'Is that a fact?' Hardcastle put his glass of beer on the table and gazed steadily at the young detective. 'And how was it that you made the acquaintance of an earl's daughter, Yardley?'

'It was last year, sir. I was a uniformed PC at Basingstoke at the time and Lady Victoria's brother, Charles, was involved in an accident in his car. He's an officer in the Grenadier Guards and was on leave from Ypres. He wasn't hurt, but the car's steering was damaged so that it couldn't be driven and Vicky, er, Lady Victoria, drove over from Henley to pick him up. We got chatting and she told me that she was staying in Alton during the week and working on a farm in Thresham Parva. We met a few times for a drink and . . .' Yardley paused. 'Well, that's how I got to know her, sir.'

'Are you going to marry the girl?' asked Hardcastle bluntly.

Yardley's face reddened. 'Good heavens, sir, I've never even thought about marriage.'

'You should, lad. Marrying an earl's daughter can't be a bad thing. What d'you think, Marriott?'

'Quite possibly, sir,' said Marriott diplomatically, but in reality he thought it unlikely that the Earl Homersham would be much impressed with the idea that his daughter may be contemplating marriage to a policeman. The social mores of the period dictated that she marry someone who was her social equal, if not of even higher status.

'Go and have a drink with her, Yardley,' said Hardcastle thoughtfully. 'I've got a feeling she knows more than she's telling. On the one hand she told us that she only said hello to Daisy, but the next minute she's saying that she could see she was riding for a fall. I doubt that I could have got anything out of her because I occasionally tend to have an effect on people so that they don't open up. But it don't often happen, does it, Marriott?'

'No, sir,' said Marriott tactfully. In his view the DDI had that effect on most people most of the time.

'Must I, sir?' Yardley looked doubtful. 'It's not quite the thing, is it, sir, to take advantage of the friendship of a young lady to obtain information?'

'What the hell are you talking about, Yardley?' Hardcastle put down his beer glass for a second time and stared at the young detective. 'When you're a police officer only one thing counts: getting the job done. And if you want to be a success as a detective, don't ever forget that golden rule.'

'Of course, sir,' stammered Yardley, his face reddening. This was a side of the London DDI he had not seen before, but he was rapidly learning that Hardcastle was a man who put duty before all else, and it seemed that he did not care what he had to sacrifice to achieve the result he wanted. He wondered briefly what sort of family life the DDI enjoyed.

'We'll go back to London, Marriott,' said Hardcastle, having suddenly made up his mind that little could be done before Monday. There were others to be interviewed in the village, but they could wait. The DDI was not altogether convinced that the murder had been perpetrated by a local man, although he was keeping his mind open. The DDI knew that Daisy Salter had been the cause of a disturbance in the Thresham Arms, and although he had been assured that no soldiers had been seen in Thresham Parva since, it was still possible that the murderer was a soldier.

'When will you be back, sir?' asked Yardley.

'Monday morning. Meet me at the station at nine o'clock, Yardley.'

'Is there anything you want me to do while you're away, sir?'

'Keep your eyes and ears open. Hang about in the pub; that's where the gossip is. And take the opportunity to have a drink with Lady Victoria. I heard her suggest this evening.'

ELEVEN

Yardley reluctantly followed Hardcastle's advice that he should accept Lady Victoria Homersham's invitation to meet her for a drink that evening, and the taxi dropped him at the Swan Hotel in Alton High Street. A pearl grey forty-horsepower Lanchester tourer that he recognized as belonging to Victoria's brother Charles was parked outside the hotel. Yardley thought it too powerful a car for a girl to drive, but he knew that she was an accomplished horsewoman who could control the most spirited of mounts, and assumed naively that such abilities could also be applied to driving a motor car.

'Good evening, Dick, and how's my favourite policeman?' The hotel receptionist smiled brightly at the Hampshire detective, a handsome young man whom she knew but would like to know a great deal better.

'I'm very well, and how is the prettiest girl in Alton?' Although displaying an element of shyness in the presence of sophisticated, well-connected young women like Victoria Homersham, Yardley was very much the gallant with girls of his own social class.

Bridget fluttered her eyelashes, blushed and said nothing.

'Is Lady Victoria Homersham in her room, Bridget?'

'I'll enquire.' Bridget turned to the switchboard with a sigh, plugged in a line and wound a handle. She had to face the fact that she stood little chance of attracting Dick Yardley when she was competing against a woman who was not only a real lady and a beauty, but drove a motor car as well. 'Mr Yardley is in reception, M'lady,' she said when Victoria Homersham replied. 'One moment, M'lady.' She turned to Yardley and put a hand over the mouthpiece of her headset. 'Her Ladyship asked if you would care to join her in her room, Dick,' she whispered, raising her eyebrows and giving him a wicked smile that was full of hidden meaning.

'I don't think so,' said Yardley regrettably, and shook his head. 'Tell her I'll meet her in the lounge.' Hotel receptionists were notorious gossips and if word reached the superintendent, or worse still the Chief Constable, that Yardley had visited a lady in her hotel room his career would probably be over; at best he would be back walking a beat. Such a meeting may well be quite innocent, but it would never be seen in that way.

There was also another consideration: Victoria Homersham had a reputation for being somewhat avant-garde in her approach to life, and was forever 'kicking over the traces', as she herself put it. She had once told Yardley that her father had forbidden her to ride to hounds unless she rode sidesaddle, a posture she dismissed as matronly, but she had continued to ride astride nevertheless. The earl had also barred his wayward daughter from driving her brother's powerful motor car, but she had smiled sweetly and carried on driving it just the same. On one occasion her father had caught sight of her in her tight-fitting jodhpurs and white shirt and almost suffered an apoplectic fit. Victoria had laughed and skipped out of the room before the earl had recovered sufficiently to administer a rebuke.

Lady Victoria descended the imposing staircase almost as if she were floating. Clad in a silk confection that was a daring few inches shorter than the socially acceptable length, it would have been evident to the practised eye that the dress had cost a substantial amount of money.

'Dickie, you came. How lovely,' gushed Victoria Homersham. She kissed Yardley lightly on the cheek and led the way into the lounge.

'How could I possibly resist?' said Yardley with a lame attempt at flattery. But in fact he was overawed by Victoria's confidence and the cultured tones that were indicative of an aristocratic background and an expensive education.

'M'lady.' A waiter, moving as fast as his advanced years would allow, approached the couple and half bowed as they sat down in the comfortable armchairs with which the lounge was furnished. He presented Yardley with a list of the drinks available, but it proved to be unnecessary. Victoria ordered a cocktail that Yardley had never heard of, and he settled for a pint of beer.

Once the drinks had been served, Victoria took out a cigarette case and offered it to Yardley. 'Do you smoke these yet, or are you still stuck with that pipe of yours?' she asked as she put a cigarette into a long cigarette holder.

'No, thanks, I'll stick to my pipe,' said Yardley, lighting a match and applying it to Victoria's cigarette, even though he had been brought up to believe that a lady should never smoke in public, if at all. 'Now,' he asked, once his pipe was alight to his satisfaction, 'why were you so keen to have a drink with me? It's Saturday evening and by now you're usually at home in Henley and getting changed for dinner.'

'Is it so unusual for a girl to want to have a drink with a hand-some, eligible young bachelor?' Victoria fixed Yardley with the sort of level gaze that defied him to argue. 'Anyway, dinner at home is quite the most awfully stuffy thing imaginable. I daresay my father will have asked some dreadful bores like the chairman of the magistrates and the master of the local hunt and their unspeakable wives.' She took a sip of her cocktail. 'That inspector who spoke to me this morning is an awful man,' she said. 'So uncouth. I didn't like him at all. Mind you, I could quite take to that sergeant who was with him.'

'The inspector's very good at his job, Vicky.' Yardley felt impelled to defend Hardcastle, regarding a criticism of the Metropolitan detective as a slight on the police force as a whole.

'Well, all I can say is that if he's as rude as that all the time, I'm surprised he gets anyone to tell him anything.'

'He's solved an awful lot of murders,' said Yardley, signalling to the waiter for another cocktail for Victoria and hoping that he had enough cash with him to pay the bill.

But his fears on that score were negated when Victoria told the waiter to put the cost of the drinks on her account.

'Oh, no, Vicky, I can't let you pay for my drinks; it's just not done.'

'Don't be so ridiculously old fashioned, Dickie. You can't afford it on the pittance they pay you. Anyway, women are becoming emancipated. Hadn't you heard that they're doing all sorts of things now? And once this war is over we're not going to be put back into our little boxes and be made to embroider samplers and do good works.' She smiled impishly over the rim of her glass. 'However, Dickie, the real reason I asked you to have a drink with me is that I think I might be able to help you with this murder you're investigating. And I thought that if I told you what I know, you could tell that awful inspector and he'd think that you'd been ever so clever in finding out all by yourself.'

Yardley had anticipated that his meeting with Victoria Homersham would merely comprise social chitchat, but now he realized that she had something important to say.

'There is someone you really ought to speak to, Dickie.' Suddenly the flippancy and the light-hearted banter vanished and for the first time since meeting her months ago, Yardley realized that there was a serious side to Victoria Homersham. 'I'm sure that you'll learn something quite interesting.' And with that enigmatic statement, she leaned across and whispered a name in Yardley's ear.

'Where did you hear that, Vicky?'

'In the Thresham Arms last Wednesday evening, Dickie.'

'Was it that girl who told you? The one whose name you've just given me?'

'No. The person I was speaking to didn't know where she'd gone.'

Hardcastle was strangely quiet during the journey back to London and Marriott had been surprised by his decision to return to the capital for the second day running. Usually when the DDI was engaged on a murder enquiry he was quite relentless in his pursuit of the killer and would make the life of his subordinates unbearable with his constant and sometimes impossible demands until he achieved a result. But for some reason that Marriott was unable to fathom, Hardcastle's approach to this particular murder appeared to be more casual.

He did not appreciate, however, that Hardcastle was tired of being treated like a dogsbody. Cannon Row police station, being just across the road from New Scotland Yard, made A Division's divisional detective inspector a natural choice whenever a senior officer was required for an out-of-town investigation and one was not available at the Yard.

Hardcastle's wife, Alice, had often said that his police station was too close to what policemen call Commissioner's Office, and that he should seek a posting to another division, preferably somewhere quieter. But Hardcastle, with his usual perversity, decided that he did not want to be moved. There was, after all, a certain cachet in having Buckingham Palace within one's bailiwick.

But this feeling of being put upon was not the only reason for his discontent. Of late he had become frustrated with constabularies that did not have the resources to investigate their own murders and expected the Metropolitan Police to do it for them – often, it seemed, in the shape of DDI Hardcastle.

He was so obsessed with his own negative thoughts that he did not say a word until they reached Waterloo.

'See you here at eight o'clock on Monday morning, Marriott, and my regards to Mrs Marriott,' said Hardcastle once he and Marriott had passed through the ticket barrier.

'Very good, sir, and my regards to Mrs H.'

Without a backward glance, Hardcastle strode towards the cab rank. Unable to afford the luxury of a taxi fare, Marriott walked out to York Road in search of a bus that would take him to Vauxhall Bridge Road, whence he would walk to his police quarter in Regency Street, Victoria.

'Is that you, Charlie?' The tone of Lorna Marriott's voice betrayed surprise at the unexpected arrival of her husband.

'Yes, it's me, Lorna, pet.' Marriott hung his hat and coat on the hook in the small hall and walked through to the parlour. His wife was relaxing in an armchair and reading a copy of *Woman's Own*. For a moment or two he gazed at her, still unable to believe his good fortune, even after ten years of marriage, at having persuaded such a tall and slender, strikingly good-looking blonde to become his wife. They had met when Marriott, then walking a beat on D Division, had been called to deal with a persistent – and drunken – pedlar who had called at her father's house in Bentinck Street and refused to leave until he had made a sale. She was nineteen and Marriott was twenty-four. A year later they were married, despite her bank-manager father's mild objection that they were too young. At first she had been hesitant about marrying a policeman, but when the war had started she was grateful that he was in an occupation that kept him out of the fighting. It was a fact brought more painfully into focus after the boy who had been courting her when she met Marriott had been commissioned into the Rifle Brigade and was killed at Mons within days of the outbreak of war.

The Marriotts' two children were playing on the floor. The six-year-old Doreen abandoned her doll's makeshift cot – in fact, a cardboard shoebox – ran towards her father and threw her arms around his legs. James, the eight-year-old, oblivious to his father's arrival, was lost in a game of make-believe with a tinplate model of a tank and a wooden field gun. Nearby lay several model German soldiers that had been knocked over.

'Jimmy, your father's here,' said Lorna. And then in a light-hearted remark aimed at her husband, she added, 'Although you may be forgiven for not recognizing him.' It was one of her complaints that the children rarely saw their father. The lot of a CID officer was such that Marriott was rarely home before the children's bedtime and even the weekends were occasionally lost to Hardcastle's demands. She sometimes wished that her husband had remained the uniformed constable he had been when they first met.

Young James looked up. 'Hello, Daddy,' he said, and resumed his 'battle'.

'This is unusual, love,' said Lorna. 'Don't tell me you've solved the case.'

'Not yet. The guv'nor decided to spend the weekend at home.'

Lorna put down her magazine and crossed the room to embrace her husband. Having kissed him, she leaned back, still held by his encircling arms. 'Is Ernie Hardcastle going soft in the head or has he suddenly developed a concern for his officers and their families?' she asked with an impish smile.

'To be perfectly honest, pet, I think he's got fed up with the Job. His heart certainly doesn't seem to be in this murder we're dealing with. He's got his pensionable time in already and it wouldn't surprise me if he retired as soon as the war's over.'

'What's to stop him from going now, then?' Lorna asked. In common with most policemen's wives, she knew that a retirement of one officer would mean a promotion for another, and Charles Marriott's next step up would be to detective inspector, albeit third-class.

'No one's allowed to retire until the war's over unless they're suffering from ill health, pet,' said Marriott. 'And Ernie Hardcastle's as fit as a flea.'

'I'll make some tea,' said Lorna. She waved at the table next to the chair in which she had been sitting. 'There's a letter from Frank there if you want to read it.'

'How is he?' Marriott was always keen to hear news of his brother-in-law.

'I don't like the sound of it, love,' said Lorna. 'Reading between the lines, it seems that his battalion is advancing towards Westhoek, and he mentioned a place called Passchendaele.' She stumbled over the pronunciation of the tiny Belgian town.

'How on earth do you know all that? I thought letters from the Front were censored.'

'Yes, they are,' said Lorna, 'but last time he was on leave he had a rough idea where they were going when they broke out of Ypres and I suggested we drew up a sort of code. He listed the names of some Belgian villages and towns with the name of a London pub next to each of them. The idea was that when he mentioned in his letter how he'd like to visit one of the pubs, I'd know which village he was writing about.'

'You're a bright girl, Lorna, my love.'

'Ah, you've noticed.' Lorna gave a gay little laugh. 'Anyway, Frank says that the weather is awful. The mud is so deep that the wagons just get stuck and apparently they're having to use pack horses to get supplies up to the front line.'

Hardcastle's arrival at his house in Kennington Road was hardly a surprise to Alice Hardcastle. She had been a policeman's wife for so many years that little would catch her unawares these days, least of all the unexpected appearance of her husband.

'Got him, then, Ernie?' Alice's terse enquiry was an indication that the couple had been together for so long now that they were able to converse in a form of verbal shorthand.

'Not by a long chalk,' said Hardcastle, pouring himself a whisky. 'Glass of sherry, love?'

'Please. What's happened then? The enquiry suddenly switched back to London?' Alice licked her finger and touched the sole of the flat iron. Satisfied that it was still hot enough, she carried on ironing shirts.

'I'm in no hurry, Alice. There are loads of people still to interview and the weekend's no good for seeing the sort who live down there. You wouldn't think there was a war on. They're all out hunting at the weekends and as tomorrow's the Glorious Twelfth they'll be off shooting defenceless birds out of the sky. They'd be better off trying to shoot down these blasted Gotha bombers.'

'They can't all be landed gentry, Ernie, surely?'

'No, but them as ain't are being employed as beaters or to hold their horses for 'em.'

'Changing the subject,' said Alice, fearing that her husband was embarking on another of his critical commentaries on the state of the nation, 'Arthur Hogg and the two children are being buried next Tuesday at St Mark's in Kennington Park Road. Will you be able to go?'

'No, I'll be back in Hampshire. Are you going to be there?'

'Yes. I think it's only proper, and I've arranged for flowers to be sent.'

'How's Bertha Hogg? Have you heard?'

'She's not too good, Ernie.' Alice put down the iron and sat down on a kitchen chair. 'They don't seem to think she'll survive.'

'It wasn't that serious, though, was it?' Hardcastle handed his wife a glass of Amontillado before taking a sip of his Scotch. 'Maud said it was a compound fracture of the leg.'

'So it was,' said Alice, 'but it was the shock that set her back. When she asked after Arthur and the two children they had to tell her they were dead. I reckon it'll finish her off.'

'It'll probably be for the best, if you think about it,' said Hardcastle. Then, realizing that his wife had been in the house alone when he had arrived, asked, 'Where are the children this evening?'

'Kitty's on the back shift. She's got a new route apparently. Her bus takes her up Park Lane and she even had Maud as a passenger the other day. Maud's working late at the hospital, but Wally should be in shortly, unless there's been another sheaf of telegrams to deliver. Last week he delivered seventeen just in this area, telling women that their husband had either been killed or wounded.'

'The bloody Kaiser has a lot to answer for,' grumbled Hardcastle. 'Talking of which, I see that Meakin's people did a good job on the windows and the front door.' He glanced around. 'You wouldn't think there'd been any damage at all.'

'The bill's on the mantelshelf, Ernie,' said Alice.

Hardcastle opened the buff envelope and extracted Frank Meakin's invoice. 'Ye gods!' he exclaimed. 'It's downright profiteering. And I suppose we'll have to wait until the war's over before the government pays out.'

On Sunday morning, Hardcastle walked down to the corner shop owned by Horace Boxall. Barriers were still around the ruins of the Hoggs' house in Kennington Road and a policeman stood guard against the possibility of looters.

'Dreadful business, Arthur Hogg getting killed like that, Mr Hardcastle,' said Boxall as Hardcastle entered his shop.

'They were obviously out to get him, Horace,' replied Hardcastle phlegmatically. 'Ounce of St Bruno and a box of Swan Vestas, please.'

'Yes, rotten luck that, being invalided out of the army with a war wound and then copping it over here. Things have come to a pretty pass when nobody's safe in his own home any more.' Boxall slid a copy of the *News of the World* across the counter, knowing that that was the Sunday paper that Hardcastle always read. 'Nothing but gloom in that an' all,' he added. 'There's a bit about Captain Chavasse getting killed. It happened on the fourth of August apparently, three years to the day after war broke out, but it's only just been reported.'

'He was the medical officer who won the Victoria Cross a year ago at Guillemont.' Hardcastle was an avid reader of newspaper accounts of such bravery. 'Where did this happen?'

'Some place called Wieltje according to the paper, but I've no idea where that is,' said Boxall.

'It's just outside Wipers,' said Hardcastle, using the soldiers' pronunciation of Ypres that had now become commonplace even among civilians.

'Some of the papers are saying that he ought to get another VC to go with the first one.'

'That don't often happen,' commented Hardcastle as he picked up his tobacco, matches and newspaper.

'Only once before,' said Boxall.

TWELVE

Richard Yardley was uncertain whether to pass on the information that Victoria Homersham had given him on Saturday. She was an attractive and lively girl and he enjoyed being in her company, but he was not wholly convinced that what she had told him was based on anything other than gossip. There again, even in his short career as a CID officer, he had learned that gossip could sometimes result in solving a crime.

Although Yardley had known DDI Hardcastle for a matter of only six days, he had already discovered that the London detective was an irascible and impatient individual. He was certainly not a man who would relish acting on information that proved to be without foundation and therefore time-wasting. Yardley thought that his best course of action would be to have a quiet word with Detective Sergeant Marriott when the opportunity presented itself.

Yardley continued to ponder the problem as he waited at Alton railway station for the arrival of the London train on Monday morning.

There was, however, something even more pressing than wondering what to do about the name that Vicky had passed on to him. Yardley had called at Alton police station on his way to meet Hardcastle's train, and the station sergeant had told him that Charlie Snapper had been sighted late the previous evening in a public house in Waterlooville by an alert off-duty constable. Having read the entry in the *Police Gazette* directing that Snapper should not be arrested or questioned, the officer had merely followed the suspect at a discreet distance until he had discovered where he was living.

'Ah, there you are, Yardley.' Hardcastle emerged from the booking office, followed by Marriott.

'Snapper's been spotted in Waterlooville, sir,' said the Hampshire detective enthusiastically.

'Who in hell's name is Snapper?' demanded Hardcastle as he handed his overnight bag to the taxi driver.

'Charlie Snapper's the man who was lodging with the school-teachers, Mr and Mrs Booth, sir, and he skedaddled after he'd seen us in the Thresham Arms last Wednesday evening.'

'Good God, Yardley, I can't be expected to remember the names of everyone who's come up in this enquiry.' Hardcastle knew exactly who Snapper was, but he was in one of his more cantankerous moods this morning. Yardley was not to know that Hardcastle was still fuming about the bill he had received from the ironmonger for the repairs to his front door and windows.

'I'm very sorry, sir.' A contrite Yardley glanced at Marriott and was surprised to see the sergeant wink. In Marriott's view, Hardcastle was always cantankerous; the only difference was the level of cantankerousness.

'Well, now, Yardley, we'd better get down to this place called Waterlooville a bit *tout de suite*,' said Hardcastle, ignoring the young officer's apology.

'As I said the other day, sir, it's about twenty-five miles from here, just north of Portsmouth. However, the police station for Waterlooville is at Fareham.'

'How far is Waterlooville from Fareham?'

'About eight or nine miles, sir,' said Yardley, taking a wild guess which, in the event, turned out to be accurate.

'Then I suppose we'd better start there,' grumbled Hardcastle, who much preferred the density of London, where police stations were mostly near enough to be reached easily and quickly.

'I'm Divisional Detective Inspector Hardcastle of New Scotland Yard,' announced the DDI as he swept into the front office of Fareham police station in Osborn Road.

'We've been expecting you, sir.' The station sergeant stood up and took a sheet of paper from a tray on his desk. 'All the details are on there, sir.' He handed Hardcastle the report and indicated a uniformed constable of mature years. 'This is Yates, sir, the officer who's responsible for Waterlooville. It was him what spotted your man Snapper. I daresay you'd like him to show you the way to the address.'

'That would be very helpful, Sergeant. This here is DC Yardley of your force and he's had the foresight to charter a taxi for the duration of our investigation.'

'PC Yates came here on his bicycle, sir,' said the station sergeant, immediately foreseeing logistical difficulties if PC Yates ended up in Waterlooville while his bicycle was still in Fareham.

'That'll be all right, Sergeant,' said Yardley. 'I'll make sure Yates gets back here.'

'We took the precaution of obtaining a search warrant from the local beak this morning, sir, just in case you wanted to turn the place over,' said the station sergeant, turning to Hardcastle.

'Excellent!' said Hardcastle, rapidly warming to the Hampshire County Constabulary's efficiency. 'What sort of place is it?'

'A newsagent and tobacconist, sir,' said PC Yates, speaking for the first time since Hardcastle's arrival, 'and it's run by a couple called Stanley and Nellie Dawson who let rooms over the shop. They're decent enough folk, and I daresay they took pity on the lad.'

'More than I will,' growled Hardcastle. 'Has this Snapper come to the notice of police since he turned up here?'

'No, sir,' said Yates. 'I read the notice in the *Police Gazette*, of course, but the first I knew of his arrival was when I saw him in a pub called The Heroes of Waterloo in Wait End Lane. If you don't mind my saying so, sir, your description of Snapper was very good. I was able to pick him out the moment I set eyes on him.'

'We're very good at drawing up descriptions in the Metropolitan Police,' said Hardcastle airily, glossing over the fact that it was Marriott who had been responsible for obtaining it from the schoolteachers. 'Well, Yardley, get your taxi driver to take us to this here newsagents.'

Stanley Dawson had just finished serving a customer when the group of police officers entered the shop.

'Good morning, Mr Yates.' Dawson looked at the three other officers with an expression of curiosity mixed with an element of nervousness. 'Is there something wrong?'

'These gentlemen are CID officers, Mr Dawson, and they're investigating a crime that took place in Thresham Parva last Monday.'

'Ah, I suppose that'll be the murder of that young lass whose body was found in a field,' said Dawson. 'I saw a piece about it in the *Hampshire Chronicle*, and it said that Scotland Yard had been called in.' He paused, an expression of alarm on his face caused by the fact that four police officers had suddenly appeared in his shop talking about a murder that had occurred some twenty-five miles away. 'But what's that got to do with me? I don't know anything about that murder.'

'I'm Divisional Detective Inspector Hardcastle of New Scotland Yard, and this is Detective Sergeant Marriott and DC Yardley,' Hardcastle announced, indicating the other two. 'D'you have a man staying here by the name of Snapper, Mr Dawson? Charles Snapper.'

'Yes, I do, sir. Why, what's Charlie done?' The colour drained from Dawson's face. 'Oh my God! D'you think he done that murder, then? And he's been living here these last three days.' He began to wring his hands. 'Oh my God!' he said again, concerned that he might have been harbouring a murderer, but at once pleased that the police did not appear to be suspecting him of any involvement. Secretly, however, he was hoping that the police would arrest Snapper for something. Dawson felt threatened by the man who had turned out to be nothing more than a layabout and who flew into a rage when asked about paying the rent. He also made it plain that he expected to be fed while he was under the Dawsons' roof.

'Is he here now?' asked Hardcastle, declining to answer the newsagent's question.

'No, sir, he stepped out about half an hour ago. He said he was going out to look for work.' Dawson turned his head to glance at a clock on the wall behind the counter. 'But I daresay he'll be back before long. My Nellie usually gives him a bite to eat about half past twelve.'

'How much rent does he pay for board and lodging, Mr Dawson?' asked Marriott.

'Well, nothing at the moment, sir. I let him have the room on tick as you might say, and I agreed he could settle up once he'd found hisself a job.'

'I think you can forget about your money,' said Hardcastle tersely.

'D'you need me any more, sir?' asked PC Yates.

'No, Yates, that'll be all,' said Hardcastle.

'Good piece of work, Yates, recognizing Snapper on description,' said Marriott quietly, knowing that the officer would get no word of praise from the DDI. 'Well done. I'll make sure my inspector mentions it in his final report to the Chief Constable.'

'Thank you, Sergeant.' Yates nodded and left the shop.

'I have a warrant to search these premises, Mr Dawson,' said Hardcastle. 'Be so good as to show us to Snapper's room.'

'A warrant?' Dawson looked aghast. 'I can assure you that I've done nothing wrong, Inspector.'

'I'm not suggesting you have,' said Hardcastle, but judging from Dawson's expression it crossed the DDI's mind that the newsagent might have contravened the Defence of the Realm Act in some way or other. Not that it was too difficult to do so unwittingly. That, however, was none of Hardcastle's concern; in fact, he had often contravened DORA himself. 'It's Snapper we're interested in. We'll remain in his room until he gets back, but you're not to tell him that we're there. Is that clearly understood?'

'Yes, of course. I'll just get Nellie to mind the shop and then I'll show you up to his room.'

'You stay down here, Marriott,' said Hardcastle, 'until Snapper gets back. Then you can follow him up.' But it was more a case of the DDI not wanting Dawson to warn his lodger that the police were upstairs searching his room. Snapper had run once and was likely to do so again. 'And you, Yardley, come with me.'

'This is my wife Nellie, Inspector,' said Dawson as he returned from the back room accompanied by a buxom woman in a floral apron. She fussed at her hair as she sighted the three policemen.

'Mrs Dawson.' Hardcastle raised his bowler hat.

'Charmed, I'm sure,' said Nellie, who had been told by her husband that the visitor was a famous Scotland Yard detective. But people like the Dawsons believed that all Scotland Yard detectives were 'famous'.

'Follow me, gentlemen,' said Dawson, and led the way through to the back of the shop and up a flight of stairs. 'This is Charlie's room, Inspector. It used to be our Jim's before he went to the war. Unfortunately he was in the battle of the Somme, you see.'

'I'm sorry to hear that. My sympathies,' muttered Hardcastle, making his usual lame attempt to express condolences.

'Oh, he's not dead,' said Stanley Dawson.

'I thought from the way you said it that he was one of the thousands who were killed that morning.'

'No, he got took prisoner on the second of July last year, and he's in a prisoner-of-war camp in some place called Bad Fallingbostel. It's somewhere between Hanover and Hamburg, so they say.'

'That's bad luck,' said Yardley.

'Not really,' said Dawson. 'At least he's safe now and out of the fighting. And another thing . . .' It sounded as though the newsagent was intending to go on at some length.

'That'll be all, thank you, Mr Dawson,' said Hardcastle curtly. 'You can leave us to have a look round.'

'If you're sure.' Denied the novelty of watching detectives at work, Dawson somewhat reluctantly made his way back down the stairs.

The room contained an iron-framed bed, a wardrobe, a pine chest of drawers and a washstand with washbowl and ewer. A small, worn carpet completed the sparsely furnished accommodation. And it was spotlessly clean.

'Very well, Yardley. Let's see what we can find.' Hardcastle made for the chest of drawers while the Hampshire DC began a search of the wardrobe.

'I think most of this stuff probably belongs to Mr Dawson's son, sir.' Yardley glanced across at the DDI. 'I've been through the pockets and they're all empty.'

'See if there's anything in that suitcase on top of the wardrobe, then.'

'It's empty, sir,' said Yardley as he replaced the suitcase. 'Snapper seems to be the sort of man who travels light.'

'Hah!' Hardcastle gave a shout of triumph as he found a small metal object secreted in one of the drawers.

'Is it another Great Western Railway button, sir?' asked Yardley, and crossed the room to where Hardcastle was displaying the object in the palm of his hand.

'No, it's not. It's a sight more significant than that.' Hardcastle chuckled and sat down on the only chair in the room. 'They can't resist it, Yardley. They've always got to hang on to a souvenir. Take the weight off your feet, m'boy.' The DDI waved at the bed. Yardley had never seen him so affable. Certainly none of his own inspectors would speak to him in that way.

Downstairs, Marriott was standing in the corner of the newsagent's shop, out of sight of anyone approaching the door.

'He's coming across the road now, Sergeant,' said Dawson from his place behind the counter, 'and he's making straight for the door.'

'Don't forget, Mr Dawson, not a word about us being here.' Marriott picked up a copy of *Fishing News* and made a pretence of reading it, not that he had any interest in angling.

The shop door opened, ringing the bell that was attached to the top of the jamb.

'Hello, Charlie,' said Dawson. 'Any luck?'

'Not yet, Stanley old cock. No one seems to be taking on labour at the moment, but I'll keep trying.' In truth, Snapper had made no attempt to find work but, having become quite skilled at picking pockets, he had spent an hour in a pub spending the money he had just stolen. 'I'll just go up to my room for a quick rinse and then I'll be ready for one of Mrs D's dinners.' He lifted the flap in the counter and opened the door at the rear that led to the staircase. He did not see Marriott.

Waiting until he knew that Snapper would be at the top of the stairs, Marriott sprinted after him, reaching the top just as Snapper opened the door to his room and took a couple of steps inside.

'What the hell?' Snapper stared at Hardcastle and Yardley. 'Oh, Christ!' Suddenly recognizing them, he turned with the intention of fleeing but came face-to-face with Marriott.

'Not so fast, Snapper, my lad,' said Marriott, 'and just so you'll be under no illusion, I'm a police officer and there are two more officers behind you. But you knew that. If you attempt to escape, my inspector will undoubtedly shoot you. If I don't manage to do so first.'

Snapper, his face draining of blood, immediately threw his hands in the air. He had always believed that the British police were unarmed, but he was not prepared to take any chances. The fact that the country was at war may have changed that, but he need not have worried. Hardcastle not only abhorred firearms, but had enjoyed a reputation during his four years as a foot-duty constable of never having used his truncheon. And Marriott would readily confess that he was completely unfamiliar with firearms.

'We'll start with your date of birth, Snapper,' said Hardcastle.

'What d'you want that for?' demanded Snapper truculently, but something in Hardcastle's stony expression made him acquiesce. 'Seventeenth of July 1895.'

'When did you work for the Great Western Railway?'

'I've never worked on the railways, never.' Snapper's expression of surprise was so obviously genuine that Hardcastle believed him.

'How many times did you have it up with Daisy Salter?' The DDI posed the question almost conversationally.

'What? Who you talking about?'

'I'm talking about the young woman who was found strangled in Joshua Blunden's five-acre field at South Farm in Thresham Parva last Tuesday morning, Snapper. That's who I'm talking about.' Hardcastle took out his pipe and began slowly to fill it with tobacco. He lit it and put the match back in the matchbox. 'Perhaps you can persuade me that you had nothing to do with it.'

'I never, I swear.' Beads of sweat began to run down Snapper's face and his hands started to twitch uncontrollably. 'Is it all right if I smoke?'

'No,' said Hardcastle, expelling a plume of pipe smoke towards the ceiling.

'But you were in Thresham Parva,' said Marriott. 'I saw you in the Thresham Arms.'

'All right, so I was there.'

'Then why did you run the moment you saw us?'

'I don't remember seeing you in there.'

Marriott produced the note that Yardley had found behind a drawer at the Booths' house. 'When did Daisy send you this note, Snapper?'

'I've never seen that before, mister. It weren't sent to me. But old Booth told me that his son was in that room before I had it. Perhaps it was meant for the boy, but he got killed at Arras, so Mrs Booth told me.'

Hardcastle emitted a sigh and stood up. 'Oh, well, we needn't waste any more time talking to you, Snapper.'

'Is that it, then? I'll go down and have me dinner,' said Snapper, believing that he was in the clear. But his optimism proved to be short-lived.

'Charles Snapper, I'm arresting you on suspicion of murdering Daisy Salter on or about Monday the sixth of August.' Hardcastle turned to the Hampshire detective. 'Put the darbies on him, Yardley. I don't want him running again.'

'I never touched her, I swear. I never,' protested the white-faced, struggling Snapper as he was taken downstairs.

'What on earth's happening?' asked Stanley Dawson as the handcuffed Snapper was escorted through his shop.

'Mr Snapper's volunteered to have a chat with us at Fareham police station, Mr Dawson, but I doubt that you'll be seeing him again,' said Hardcastle as he donned his bowler hat and followed his prisoner down to the waiting taxi.

'This here is Snapper, and you can lock him up in a cell for a bit while I think what to do with him,' said Hardcastle to the station sergeant.

'Very good, sir.' The station sergeant took a large bunch of keys from a hook on the back wall. 'All right to take the cuffs off him, sir?' he asked.

Hardcastle gave the impression of giving that query some thought before nodding. 'Yes, I suppose so,' he said eventually.

'Are you charging him with anything, sir?' asked the station sergeant, once Snapper had been escorted to a cell by a constable.

'Not at the moment, Sergeant, but I would like an enquiry to be made by telegraph. Can you do that for me?'

'Certainly, sir. If you care to write down what you want done, I'll see it gets sent off immediately.' The sergeant handed Hardcastle a pad of message forms.

It took Hardcastle a mere three minutes to pen his request and hand it to the sergeant. All he had to do now was to wait for the reply. 'Be so good as to stress the urgency, Sergeant.' He was not greatly concerned at how long he kept Snapper locked up, even if it were a week, but he did not want to waste too much of his own time in Fareham. He glanced at Marriott and Yardley. 'That looked like a decent pub just down the road. I think it's time we had some lunch and then I'll be in a better mood to deal with Master Snapper.'

Once again, Yardley was amazed at the nonchalance of the London detective. Here he had a possible murderer locked up in a police station and he was calmly suggesting going for a drink. Had he known Hardcastle a little better, he would have realized that, if possible, the DDI rarely asked a suspect a question unless he already knew the answer. And the point of the message he had just arranged to have sent would, he hoped, provide him with one of those answers.

Hardcastle led the way into the saloon bar. There were a few well-dressed men at the bar, and the DDI presumed that this particular pub was a regular haunt of local professionals.

'You two can buy your own beer,' said Hardcastle. 'I don't want to be accused of breaching the Defence of the Realm Act by treating you,' he added archly.

Once they had obtained their drinks, the three detectives moved to a table near the window, out of earshot of the men at the bar, several of whom were clearly wondering who the newcomers were.

'D'you think he's our man, sir?' asked Marriott.

'I don't know,' said Hardcastle, 'but if my telegraph message gets the answer I'm hoping for, Master Snapper won't be leaving the police station yet awhile.'

THIRTEEN

I t was two o'clock by the time that Hardcastle and the other two detectives returned to Fareham police station.

'I've just this minute had a reply to your telegraph, sir,' said the station sergeant, and handed Hardcastle a message form.

'That was quick.' Rapidly scanning the contents of the form, the DDI emitted a shout of triumph. 'I bloody thought so,' he said. 'Fetch him up, Sergeant.'

The room in which Charles Snapper had been placed by the sergeant was small and windowless. There was a table and three chairs, all of which had been bolted to the floor to prevent recalcitrant prisoners from throwing them at police officers. When Hardcastle, Marriott and Yardley entered, Snapper was already seated in the single chair that was furthest from the door. He was a stocky individual with a foxy expression that seemed never to leave his face, a pointed nose and deep brown eyes that were constantly darting in all directions.

'What's this all about?'

'You're about to tell me.' Hardcastle, dismissed the attendant constable, took a seat and began to fill his pipe. Marriott sat next to him, but Yardley was obliged to stand with his back to the door. 'Now you've had time to think about Daisy Salter, Snapper, you can answer my questions. For a start, how often did you see her, and how often did you get across her?'

'Who says I did?' Some of Snapper's original truculence had returned, even though the directness of Hardcastle's questions had momentarily disconcerted him.

Hardcastle slammed the top of the table with the flat of his hand. Marriott was accustomed to the DDI doing that – it was a habit of his – but Yardley jumped at the loud noise and so did Snapper.

'I don't intend to waste any time on you, Snapper, so you'd better give me an answer pretty bloody *tout de suite.*' It was obvious that Hardcastle was losing his temper, or at least giving that impression.

Scared by the DDI's sudden aggression, Snapper was quick to reply; he had heard tales of what could happen to uncooperative prisoners in police stations. 'All right, so I went out with her a couple of times and we had some fun in one of Blunden's haystacks, until he caught us. He threatened to run me in to the law and so I dropped her like a hot potato. But I never screwed her, I swear.'

'Run you in?' Hardcastle scoffed. 'Why d'you think the law would have wasted time on the two of you messing about in a haystack, then, eh? It goes on all the time, and it ain't against the law.' But the DDI now knew the real reason why Snapper so desperately wanted to avoid any contact with the police.

'Blunden reckoned it was. He said something about it being against the law because Daisy was under age. That's why I never saw her again. I never wanted to get into no trouble.'

'And how old was Daisy Salter?'

'I don't know for sure, but I never had nothing to do with her murder, and that's the God's honest truth.'

'Well, Snapper, if it ain't the truth I'll come and get you, my lad.'

'You'll have to find me first,' sneered Snapper, now firmly believing that he had been exonerated and was about to be released.

'I wouldn't be too sure about that if I were you. I'll know exactly where to find you.' Hardcastle took the telegraph message from his pocket and handed it Marriott. 'Read that to our Mr Snapper, Marriott.'

'It comes from His Majesty's Dockyard, Portsmouth, and it reads: "On the thirteenth of November 1916, Ordinary Seaman Charles Edison Snapper, Royal Navy, born the seventeenth of July 1895, of Drake Battalion, attached to the 63rd (Royal Naval) Division of the British Expeditionary Force, was found to be absent from duty when his battalion was about to go into action near the river Ancre. He has since been officially posted as a deserter."'

'It's a lie,' exclaimed Snapper, but the fact that the blood drained from his face contradicted his denial. In truth he had known, the moment His Majesty's Dockyard, Portsmouth was mentioned, that he had been tracked down.

'Oh, it's true all right, Snapper,' said Marriott mildly. 'It was signed by the Port Admiral who seems to be a very efficient officer, and it would appear that he keeps a list of Royal Navy deserters close at hand.'

Snapper looked around the stark room with a hunted expression on his weaselly face, as though seeking an escape. 'How did you find out?'

'First of all, the fact that you scarpered the moment you saw us in the Thresham Arms, and then we found this in your chest of drawers. You shouldn't have kept a souvenir, Snapper. You'd be surprised how many deserters have been caught just because they hung on to their cap badges.' Hardcastle produced the small metal object he had found in Snapper's room. 'That's the cap badge of Drake Battalion and I was helped out by what it said on the bottom,' he added and chuckled. He put on his spectacles and peered closely at the Latin maxim at the bottom of the badge. '*Auxilio Divino*. What's it mean again, Marriott?'

'By Divine Aid, sir.'

'Ah, yes, that's it. It'd quite slipped me memory for a moment.' Hardcastle put his glasses back in his pocket. 'Now then, very shortly an escort of . . . What did the message call those chaps, Marriott?'

'Regulating petty officers, sir.'

'That's it, yes. They're coming to collect you and take you back to the Navy, Snapper. So I *will* know where to find you.' Hardcastle turned to his sergeant. 'I think it'd be a good idea to ask the Navy not to execute Snapper before we've finished our enquiries, don't you, Marriott?'

'Yes, sir, a very good idea. I'll see if I can find out who we ought to talk to about it.'

'I'll just tell the station sergeant to hold on to him until the Navy comes for him. And then we'll go back to Thresham Parva and see if we can find ourselves a murderer who's a better spec than Ordinary Seaman Snapper here. Otherwise we'll have to make do with him. I'll see you in the taxi, Marriott.'

Snapper gripped the sides of the table as perspiration poured from his face, and for a second it appeared that he was about to faint. It had suddenly struck him that his life was likely to end very soon. The only difference would be whether it would be on the scaffold or in front of a firing squad.

Detective Constable Yardley had remained silent throughout Hardcastle's interrogation of Snapper, mainly because he was so impressed by the way in which the DDI had gone about it. But the final comment that in the absence of someone more suitable the DDI might 'make do' with Snapper for the murder utterly astounded him. In his innocence he had believed that the DDI had been serious, but only because he had yet to get the measure of Hardcastle's black humour.

'That was the most amazing interview I've ever seen, Sergeant,' he said, allowing his enthusiasm to get the better of him. 'We haven't got anyone who's anything like Mr Hardcastle in the Hampshire County Constabulary.'

'You can learn a lot from Mr Hardcastle, Dick; he's a very good detective. But he has to work the way he does because we've got a collection of hard villains in London and we have to play by different rules.' Trying hard not to smile when faced with Yardley's ebullient naiveté, Marriott did not want to enlarge on Hardcastle's methods, methods that were deemed unconventional even in certain quarters of Scotland Yard. Neither did he wish to reveal that the DDI had been joking when he suggested that Snapper would be charged with the murder in the absence of anyone else. 'I must admit that we Metropolitan chaps would be lost trying to solve some of the crimes you have down here in the countryside.'

'I doubt that, Sergeant,' said Yardley, 'but can I ask you something?'

'Fire away.'

'I saw Victoria Homersham on Saturday.'

'Did you indeed? That's an attractive girlfriend you've got there, young man.'

'Oh, she's not my girlfriend, Sergeant,' said Yardley hurriedly. 'No, what I wanted to ask you was whether I should pass on to Mr Hardcastle what she told me.'

'Depends what it was.'

'Vicky gave me the name of a girl who lives in the village who, she said, could tell us something important that might be connected to the murder of Daisy Salter.'

'Did Lady Victoria know what this "something" was?'

'No, she didn't. Well, not exactly. Apparently this girl—'

'Wait a minute. You're obviously duty-bound to tell the DDI, but you may as well wait, otherwise you'll have to repeat it. But a word of warning, and it's one I give to all my young detectives in London: don't reveal the name of your informant.'

'Victoria's hardly an informant, Sergeant,' said Yardley.

'She's given you information that may be connected with this murder we're investigating and that makes her an informant. But the moment you reveal her identity to another detective, Dick, your snout becomes his snout and you'll lose her. If Mr Hardcastle tries to bully it out of you, stand your ground. He'll respect you for it. He'd never reveal the names of any of his informants, even to me. Nor would I give him the names of any of mine, and he wouldn't expect me to.'

'Thanks, Sergeant, I'll remember that.' Yardley did wonder, however, whether he had now lost his informant to Marriott.

'That's that dealt with,' said Hardcastle, appearing on the steps of the police station.

'Yardley's got something to tell you, sir,' said Marriott.

'Oh, and what's that?'

'It's some information I've received, sir,' said Yardley. 'Shall I tell you on the journey back?'

'Certainly not,' said Hardcastle sharply. 'We don't want your taxi driver cocking an ear or it'll be all over Hampshire before you can say Jack the Ripper. What is it? And keep your voice down.'

'I've been told that there is a girl in Thresham Parva who had an encounter with a man my informant thinks tried to have sexual intercourse with her, and when she refused he made threats.'

'Who is the girl, Yardley? Did your informant tell you that?'

'Yes, sir. She's called Marjorie Tindall and she's sixteen years of age.'

'I see. And who was this man?'

'My informant didn't know, sir. Apparently Miss Tindall wouldn't say any more, fearing that she'd said too much already, but apparently she'd had a little too much to drink, otherwise she'd likely not have said anything. It seems that she's extremely frightened of the man.'

'What's the name of your informant, Yardley?' asked Hardcastle.

The young Hampshire detective hesitated before answering. 'I'm sorry, sir; I'm not prepared to reveal the informant's name.'

'Oh? Then how d'you expect me to assess whether this information's worth anything if I can't talk to your snout, eh?'

'The information was given to me in good faith, sir, and I'm satisfied that it's reliable.' Yardley was finding it hard to stand up to the DDI and almost yielded. He certainly would not have spoken like that to a senior officer in his own force, and imagined that Hardcastle was about to send him back to Alton with a request that he be replaced by another officer.

'That's good enough for me, lad,' said Hardcastle, and got into the taxi.

Marriott glanced at Yardley and nodded, but Yardley did not see Hardcastle wink at Marriott.

Yardley had been unable to tell Hardcastle exactly where Marjorie Tindall lived in Thresham Parva simply because Victoria Homersham had not known. In fact, Victoria knew very little about the girl at all, other than the brief conversation she'd had with her in the Thresham Arms. And that conversation had only arisen because the murder of Daisy Salter had been a topic of conversation – and speculation – in the pub.

Consequently, Hardcastle decided that he would start by speaking to PC Jessop.

'Good afternoon, sir.' Annie Jessop was seated at the desk inside the front door of the police house, busy filing some reports. In the remoter parts of the county constabularies, wives were expected to be unpaid assistants to their husbands and accepted it as part of being a country copper's wife. Consequently, an unmarried constable was unlikely to be posted to a village beat.

'Good afternoon, Mrs Jessop.' Hardcastle doffed his hat. 'Is your husband in?'

'Not at the moment, sir, but I don't think he'll be that long. He's around the village making sure as those who should have gun licences have renewed 'em. You see, sir, under the Gun Licences Act of 1870, licences always expire on the thirty-first of July. But you'd know that, being an inspector.'

'Yes, of course,' said Hardcastle confidently, but in fact he knew nothing of that particular legislation. Secretly he was amazed at the extent of legal knowledge possessed by some policemen's wives. His own wife, Alice, had learned quite a lot about the law when she had tested her husband in preparation for the several promotion interviews he had been obliged to face in order to reach his present rank.

Mrs Jessop glanced at a calendar on the wall. 'And it's the thirteenth of August now. That's a fortnight's grace, so Ted's making sure that everyone is properly licenced. Being the countryside there are quite a few gun-owners hereabouts.'

'Perhaps you can help me, then, Mrs Jessop.' Hardcastle had come rapidly to the conclusion that Ted Jessop's wife was every bit as knowledgeable about local matters as her husband. Possibly even more so.

'If I can, sir. Perhaps you'd like to come into the parlour and I'll make some tea. Ted will probably be in shortly anyway.' Mrs Jessop removed the pencil that was tucked into her hair and put it down on the desk.

Once the three detectives were settled in the back room of the police house and Annie Jessop had served tea, Hardcastle posed his question.

'We've heard that a girl by the name of Marjorie Tindall has some information that might help us, Mrs Jessop. We were told that she lives in the village. Can you tell us where?'

Annie Jessop replaced her teacup in the saucer and considered the question carefully. 'I can tell you where she *did* live, Mr Hardcastle, but there's a bit of a mystery attached to that young hussy.'

'Perhaps we could start with the address, Mrs Jessop,' said Marriott, his pocketbook at the ready.

'Barn Cottage, Mr Marriott, next door to Reg Tapp the chandler, who happens to be the girl's grandfather. As I said, she did live there, but she's gone.'

'Gone? What's the story behind that?' asked Hardcastle.

'It's a rather sad tale really. But to begin at the beginning, Marjorie's father Frank was a carpenter and joiner. Born and bred in the village, he were, same as his future bride, Elsie Tapp. He was twenty-one when he was wed to Elsie and she gave birth to Marjorie four months later.' Annie Jessop raised her eyebrows and then laughed. 'I don't have to do the sums for you, do I, Mr Hardcastle?'

'No, you don't,' replied Hardcastle with a chuckle. 'D'you think they would have got married if she hadn't been expecting?'

'Difficult to say, sir, but I can say this: it wasn't a happy marriage. Like I said just now, her father, Reg Tapp, was the chandler. Well, he owned Barn Cottage and let his new son-in-law have it on a peppercorn rent. The trouble was that Reg's wife Hilda was a busybody who was always ready to put her oar in, and living right next door she'd go beetling in to see her daughter practically every day and, generally speaking, always interfering. Of course, Frank Tindall didn't care too much for that. The upshot was one great big bust-up between Frank and his mother-in-law, which turned into a sort of feud. Of course, it caused a bit of a rift between Frank and Elsie, and Hilda and Elsie, and even between Reg and Hilda. Anyway, it all dragged on for years until Frank got conscripted under the Derby Act at the end of last year. Six weeks later, he was dead.'

'I know the army's short of men, but I didn't think they went into action that quickly,' said Marriott. 'They usually have longer than that in training.'

'Oh, he wasn't killed in action, Mr Marriott. He got run over by one of them Army Service Corps steam wagons right there in Aldershot.'

'So, what happened to Marjorie?' Hardcastle was getting a little impatient, but realized that it would be counterproductive to hurry the village policeman's wife, who was obviously a mine of local information. He took out his pipe and held it up. 'D'you mind if I smoke, Mrs Jessop?'

'Lord, no, you go ahead, sir.' Annie Jessop leaned across, picked up an ashtray and placed it in front of the DDI. 'The real trouble was that Marjorie was the apple of her father's eye and he ruined her rotten. She went completely off the rails after he was killed.' Annie Jessop poured more tea without asking if the three detectives wanted a second cup. 'From that day forward, poor Elsie couldn't do a thing with her and the day before yesterday Marjorie upped sticks and left. No one knows where she's gone. Poor Elsie's beside herself with worry because someone told her that Marjorie had run off with a soldier.'

'Just now you described her as a young hussy, Mrs Jessop,' said Marriott.

'Like mother like daughter, I suppose you'd say. Elsie Tapp, as was, had quite a reputation before she was married, and there's been tittle-tattle about her and one or two men even since she was wed. So it comes as no surprise that young Marjorie has an eye for the boys, and once her father died she's more or less done as she pleased. Her mum certainly couldn't control her. How she never finished up being pregnant Lord alone knows. Pure luck, I reckon.'

'D'you think there's anything in this story of her running off with a soldier?' asked Hardcastle.

Annie Jessop shook her head. 'Your guess would be as good as mine, sir. Mind you, it's possible. She had a job as a cleaner and washer-up in the Thresham Arms for a bit, round about the time they had the trouble with soldiers. I s'pose one of them might've taken a fancy to her. She got the sack from the pub on the day of the riot, but that was nothing new. I think she's worked for just about everyone in the village as how can afford servants and the like, but she never lasted long anywhere.'

'I think the best thing would be for me to have a word with Mrs Tindall.' Hardcastle and the other two stood up just as PC Jessop entered the room.

'Good afternoon, sir.' Jessop took off his helmet and placed it on top of the bookcase. 'Anything I can help you with?'

'I don't think so, Mr Jessop. Your good lady here has told us all we need to know.' Hardcastle glanced at Annie. 'You can tell your husband what we've been talking about, Mrs Jessop,' he said, well knowing that she would anyway. 'By the way, Mr Jessop, we arrested Charlie Snapper.'

'For the murder, sir?' Jessop sounded surprised.

'No, he was on the run from the Royal Navy. But I haven't crossed him off my list of suspects yet. At least I'll know where to find him if I need to.' Hardcastle picked up his bowler hat and thrust his pipe into his pocket. 'Thank you for the tea, Mrs Jessop.'

'That's all right, sir. It's a pleasure to have someone to have a chat with.'

Hardcastle hid a smile; Annie Jessop had been the one doing most of the talking.

FOURTEEN

Reginald Tapp's chandler's store was on one side of Barn Cottage and a gunsmith's shop was on the other. Both had originally been private dwellings, but curiously it was now Barn Cottage that looked out of place between those two commercial properties. Furthermore, the cottage had clearly been neglected: the doorstep had not been whitened for some considerable time and the windows had remained unwashed for many a long week.

The moment that Hardcastle knocked on the door of the cottage, a window on the upper floor of the chandler's store flew open and a woman's head appeared.

'You someone else come to poke yer nose in, then?' she bellowed in a rasping voice that was probably heard the length and breadth of the village.

Hardcastle took a step back and looked up. 'I'm a police officer, missus. Mind your own business and get back inside before I arrest you for a breach of the peace,' he shouted in response to the woman he was certain was Hilda Tapp, Elsie Tindall's mother.

'Well, I never did,' said the woman. 'I ain't been spoken to like that in all my life,' she muttered half to herself, but in the face of Hardcastle's threat withdrew her head and slammed the window shut. At that precise moment the door of Barn Cottage was opened.

'Mrs Tindall?' Hardcastle raised his bowler hat.

'Yes,' said the woman listlessly. Her clothes, although appearing to be of reasonably good quality, hung on her as if they had been purchased when she was a larger size which, on reflection, they probably had. Her long black skirt was stained in places and her once-white blouse now had a slightly greyish tinge from lack of thorough and frequent washing.

She could not be described as slender or slim, and she was certainly not attractive; in fact, she was just plain thin; thin and haggard. Her long titian hair lacked lustre and was unwashed and unkempt. Hardcastle knew, from what Mrs Jessop had told him, that Elsie Tindall was thirty-six years old, but she looked nearer fifty.

'We're police officers, Mrs Tindall. May we come in?'

'I s'pose you've come about Marjorie?' Without waiting for confirmation, the woman turned and walked back inside the cottage, leaving the three policemen to follow.

The parlour into which the detectives were shown was a cheer-less room. Cheap curtains hung at the windows, the few ornaments on the mantel and the windowsills were in need of dusting and there was fluff in the corners of the room. An armchair and a sofa, both worn and stained, were positioned on a near-threadbare carpet as though they had just arrived and no decision had been made as to their final location. The grate still contained the ashes of last year's fire, and the brass fire-irons were badly tarnished, even showing verdigris in places. It was apparent that housework was not among Elsie Tindall's priorities.

Hardcastle examined an upright chair, one of four, that stood next to a deal table more suited to a kitchen than a living room, and decided to remain standing.

'Have you any idea at all why your daughter should have run away, Mrs Tindall?' Hardcastle decided not to waste time on niceties or to attempt to express condolences on the loss of the woman's husband. An indefinable odour and a general mustiness pervaded the whole property, and he was anxious to escape from it as soon as possible.

'No.' Elsie Tindall's answer was unemotional and only just audible.

'None at all?'

'No.'

'I've been told that she may have run away with a soldier.'

'I s'pose she might.'

'You don't seem very concerned, Mrs Tindall,' said Marriott.

'Wouldn't do no good. Worrying, I mean. If she's gone, she's gone. It was her dad what she loved, not me, and now he's gone and so's she. And that's that.' Elsie Tindall made the statement with an air of finality, as though her daughter was dead.

'I understand that Marjorie had a job in the village,' suggested Hardcastle.

The girl's mother scoffed derisively. 'She had dozens of jobs. Never lasted in any of 'em. She got herself a job at Fortune's the grocer's one time, but Adam Fortune's wife Nina made her husband get rid of her.'

'Why was that?' asked Marriott.

'Always ogling the men what went in the shop and dropping hints so's their wives complained to Adam Fortune, and on top of that she was making eyes at Adam hisself. Well, that was enough for Nina and she threw her out.'

'What happened to Marjorie after that?'

'Adam Fortune told Roland Fallow all about our Marjorie, but Roland never took no notice and took her on at his sub-post office. He was always a soft touch for a pretty girl was Roland, but when he caught her stealing money out of the till, his wife Mavis made him give her the boot. She wanted her run in to Mr Jessop, but Roland said they ought to be lenient on account of my Frank getting killed, otherwise she'd have finished up in the police court in Alton. Mind you, I think there was more to it than that.'

'What d'you mean?' asked Marriott.

'I reckon there was something going on between Roland and my Marjorie, but I ain't saying no more than that.'

'Is that why she ran away?'

'No, least not straight off; she did have other jobs. Not that any of 'em lasted more'n a few days. A couple of weeks at best. I think her last job was cleaning up at Reverend Creed's for a week. Before that she had a spell up the college doing cleaning, but that never lasted neither. Trouble was she'd never put her back into a job like that and they sacked her for not doing it proper. Least that's what the bursar said, but if I know my Marge she was giving the glad eye to the young gents up there. Oh, and she had a spell at the Thresham Arms an' all, but she spent more time chatting to the soldiers than serving the customers. But it was after the trouble that Tom Hooker give her the elbow.'

'What trouble was that?' asked Hardcastle, feigning ignorance.

'It was her friend Daisy Salter, the one what's been killed, what caused it. But because our Marge was egging the tommies on to have a dust up over Daisy that Tom saw red and chucked the pair of 'em out the same night.'

'She was obviously a close friend of Daisy Salter,' said Marriott, 'but did she have any other close female friends?'

'Search me, mister,' said Ethel.

Looking at the woman, Marriott was glad that the invitation was not intended to be taken literally.

'We'll not bother you any further, Mrs Tindall,' said Hardcastle, and made for the door.

'She doesn't seem to care one jot, sir,' said Marriott once they were outside in the street.

Hardcastle glanced up at the window above the chandler's shop, but the face of Hilda Tapp rapidly withdrew from sight and the net curtain was hurriedly put back in place. 'I reckon Elsie Tindall will top herself before she's much older,' he said. 'What with her husband dead and her daughter running, on top of which she's living next door to that harridan of a mother-in-law, I don't reckon she's got much to live for.'

'Is there nothing we can do for her, sir?' asked Yardley, taken aback by Hardcastle's seemingly callous assessment of Elsie Tindall's predicament.

'We're a police force, not a charity, Yardley,' said Hardcastle. 'Now then, you're an up-and-coming detective, my lad. What did you notice about the parlour?'

'The parlour, sir?'

'Yes, Yardley, the room we were in. A detective's job is to notice everything, not just to listen to the replies. Take it all in. It's always a good idea to have a gander at bookcases too, not that I think you'd have found one in that house, but they'll tell you a lot about the person who owns the books in them. What did you notice?'

'It wasn't very clean, sir, and it was musty.'

'That was obvious to anyone. Anything else?'

'Ah, no photograph of her husband, sir.'

'Exactly, Yardley. It's the first house I've ever come across where a husband or son has been killed in the war and there hasn't been a picture of him. No, that was no love match.'

'What's next, sir?' asked Marriott.

Hardcastle took out his hunter, glanced at it, briefly wound it and dropped it back into his waistcoat pocket. 'Half past five. Time for glass of ale in the Thresham Arms and a word with the landlord. He might know more than he's said about Marjorie Tindall.'

Once Tom Hooker had served the detectives with beer, Hardcastle beckoned him towards one end of the bar, out of earshot of the other customers.

'Tell me more about this bit of trouble you had with the military that seemed to have something to do with Daisy Salter.'

'I'd been stupid enough to take her on as a cleaner and washer-up, Mr Hardcastle.'

'Not as a barmaid?'

'Of course not. You know better than me that I daren't employ a sixteen-year-old kid behind the bar, guv'nor.' Hooker sounded indignant that the DDI should even hint at such a thing, but at once appeared slightly guilty.

'So how come she sometimes had a drink in here, Mr Hooker?' asked Yardley, aware that Victoria Homersham had told him as much.

'I don't know anything about that,' said Hooker, a little too hurriedly. 'I don't want to lose my licence, Mr Yardley, do I now?'

'Marjorie Tindall.' Marriott floated the word to see what sort of reaction he would get from the landlord.

'Yeah, well, I was employing her at the same time to do the washing up and cleaning.'

'As well as Daisy Salter?' Marriott took out his pocketbook with a flourish, rested it on the bar and opened it. He took his pencil from his pocket and placed it beside the pocketbook. It was a piece of theatre that further discomfited Hooker.

'There's a lot to do running a pub of this size, Mr Marriott,' Hooker said plaintively, but it was clear that the questions were making him edgy. 'And it's the only pub in the village.'

'Look, Tom,' said Hardcastle confidentially, leaning over the bar so that he was closer to the landlord, 'I've got a murder to solve and quite frankly I don't give a fig if you were serving underage girls or using them to pull pints. That's something between you and PC Jessop. I won't tell him and neither will DC Yardley here.' The DDI shot a warning glance at the Hampshire detective. 'But a word of advice: if PC Jessop does catch you serving youngsters, or letting them serve behind the bar, you'll lose your licence for sure.'

'All right,' said Hooker, admitting defeat, 'so I did use the two of them behind the bar when times was busy, Mr Hardcastle, but it weren't that often. And I got rid of 'em anyway.'

'Why was that?'

'Sticky fingers. My Amy caught Daisy at it, and I caught Marjorie Tindall thieving an' all. On the same night, cheeky little bitches. So I gave 'em their marching orders.'

'How was it that they were in here the night of the trouble with the military, then?' asked Hardcastle.

'It was that same night. They were flouncing out through the public bar after I'd sacked 'em when these tommies came in. Two of 'em seemed to think they were taking Daisy out for a stroll.' Hooker scoffed. 'If you know what I mean by a "stroll". Not at the same time, of course. It turned out that there'd been a mix-up over dates; whether it was the swaddies' fault or Daisy's didn't matter in the end because the two tommies had a set-to right there in the public bar.'

'And that's what set it off,' suggested Marriott. 'A dispute over Daisy?'

'Too true,' said Hooker. 'Trouble was that the other soldiers joined in and all hell was let loose. Daisy was as pleased as Punch at having a couple of tommies fighting over her, and Marjorie Tindall was encouraging the other soldiers to join in an' all. The upshot was a load of damage, and PC Jessop called the mounted military police from Aldershot and they came over at the gallop, literally. I barred the two girls from ever coming anywhere near the place and the general in charge of the Aldershot Garrison put the whole of Thresham Parva out of bounds to the army. And of course the army paid for the damage.'

'I've been told that Marjorie Tindall was seen in here drinking *after* the incident with the army and *after* Daisy was murdered,' said Yardley, recalling what Victoria Homersham had told him.

'I don't know anything about that,' said Hooker. 'If I'd seen the young hussy, she'd have been out on her ear quicker than that.'

'My problem,' said Hardcastle as the landlord drew more pints of beer for the DDI and the other two, 'is that I've got to find Marjorie Tindall because I think she might have some information for me.'

'On the house, guv'nor,' said Hooker, pushing Hardcastle's florin back towards him. 'Isn't she with her mother at Barn Cottage, then?'

'Much obliged,' said the DDI as he lifted his pint. He had decided that Hooker was not a suspect for the murder of Daisy Salter and could safely be allowed to buy him a drink. 'No. I called there just before we came in here. Elsie Tindall hasn't any idea where the kid might have gone.'

'I think my Amy might have an idea, Mr Hardcastle. Hold on a moment.' Hooker opened the door that led to the parlour. 'Amy, love, spare a minute, will you?'

Amy Hooker appeared behind the bar. She was drying her hands on a tea towel and looking decidedly harassed. 'I'm washing up, Tom,' she said crossly, 'which I've had to do ever since you got rid of our cleaning staff.'

'The inspector's trying to find Marjorie Tindall, Amy, love, and I said I thought you might be able to help.'

'Oh, I'm sorry, Mr Hardcastle, I didn't know it was you what wanted me.' Amy Hooker dropped the tea towel on the low shelf behind the bar.

'Have you any idea where she might have gone? I spoke to Elsie Tindall this morning and she didn't know. In fact, I got the impression that she didn't really care what had happened to her daughter.'

'After her husband Frank was killed, Elsie was never able to do anything with that girl,' said Amy, echoing what Annie Jessop had said earlier that day. 'But I do know that Marjorie Tindall had a friend who worked up at the college, and I think she's still there.'

'D'you think that's where Marjorie might've gone, Mrs Hooker?' asked Marriott.

'It's a possibility. It's a big place and I reckon that if Winnie had a mind to hide her mate up there, no one would ever know.'

'Who is this Winnie, Mrs Hooker?' asked Hardcastle, at last believing that he was getting nearer to finding the elusive Marjorie Tindall.

'She's Winifred Reeves, but everyone calls her Winnie.'

'Does she live in the village?' asked Marriott.

'No, Mr Marriott, she lives-in up at the college. She doesn't come from these parts. As far as I know she came from an army family in Aldershot. Her father was a sergeant in the regular army and was killed at Mons in 1914, and soon afterwards her mother ran off with a trumpet-major from the Queen's Royal Lancers and left Winnie to her own devices.'

Just when Richard Yardley thought that Hardcastle had finished for the day, the DDI decided that they would go straight to Thresham College to follow up the information given to him by Amy Hooker. To Marriott, it was a case of the DDI going off on another of his wild goose chases.

'That must be Old Arthur, the rheumatic gardener that Doctor Mallory mentioned.' Hardcastle pointed at a man kneeling in front of a flower bed.

'Good evening, sir.' The gardener stood up and took off his cap, but remained stooped as the detectives alighted from their taxi. 'Can I help you, sir?'

'No, thanks,' said Hardcastle. 'I'm looking for Doctor Mallory and I know where to find his study.'

'I think he be playing a round of golf, sir,' said Arthur. 'It being a fine evening, like.' He pulled a 'turnip' watch out of his waistcoat pocket and stared at it. 'He'll likely not be back come eight o'clock, sir, on account of his being partial to a drop of gin at the nineteenth hole.'

'I see. Is there a bursar or a housekeeper, or someone like that, Arthur? It is Arthur, isn't it?'

'It is that, sir.' Arthur afforded the DDI a crooked grin displaying yellowing teeth. 'I can tell you're a detective, sir.'

'Yes, I am, but is there a bursar or a housekeeper?'

'The bursar's on his holidays, sir, but if you go through the main entrance and turn right, sir, you'll see a door marked "Housekeeper". Her name's Mrs Boot.'

Following Old Arthur's directions, Hardcastle and the other two found the housekeeper's office. Hardcastle tapped loudly on the door with the handle of his umbrella.

'Wait!' The voice was very loud and came from within the office. Moments later the same voice commanded, 'Come.'

Hardcastle opened the door. Seated behind a desk was a woman of at least sixty who promptly stood up when she saw that her visitors were adults. Severe of countenance and hairstyle, she wore a high-necked, full-length black dress. In place of a belt there was a chain, from which hung a large bunch of keys.

'Oh, I do beg your pardon, gentlemen. I thought it was one of the young gentlemen. I always make 'em wait as a matter of principle. We have a few of them staying on here during the vacation: them as has families serving abroad. I'm Agnes Boot. But if you're enquiring about admissions, I suggest—'

'No, it's you we've come to see, Mrs Boot. I'm Divisional Detective Inspector Hardcastle of Scotland Yard, and these are my colleagues,' said the DDI, and introduced Marriott and Yardley.

'You were here the other day talking to Doctor Mallory.' Mrs Boot made it sound like an accusation.

'Yes, we were.'

'How can I possibly help you, then?' Mrs Boot was of a class that had a high respect for learning and could not conceive that she might be able to assist where Dr Mallory had not. 'Please, take a seat,' she said, indicating a row of chairs set against the side wall of the office.

'We're investigating the murder of Daisy Salter, Mrs Boot.'

Mrs Boot nodded knowingly. 'I'm not surprised,' she said enigmatically, leaving Hardcastle wondering whether the lack of surprise was that Daisy Salter had been murdered or that he was investigating it.

'I understand that you have a girl called Winifred Reeves employed here as a cleaner, Mrs Boot.'

'Yes, we do. She's not in any sort of trouble, is she? A good worker is that lass and as honest as the day is long. Do anything for anyone.'

'We think she might have been a little too charitable, Mrs Boot,' said Marriott. 'It's been suggested to us that she is harbouring a young woman by the name of Marjorie Tindall, and it's Marjorie Tindall we wish to speak to.'

'Are you suggesting that the Tindall girl might be living here?' Agnes Boot sounded scandalized at the very idea. 'We employed her and that Daisy Salter as cleaners here at one time. Both totally unreliable, the pair of them. I was obliged to dismiss them. But the possibility that Tindall is living here without my knowledge is, quite frankly, laughable, Mr Marriott.'

'There's one way to make sure, Mrs Boot,' said Hardcastle. 'If you would be so kind as to send for Winifred Reeves, we could ask her.'

'If you think that's best, but you're wasting your time,' said Agnes Boot irritably. She pressed a bell push on her desk and seconds later a frightened young girl entered the office and bobbed. 'Go and find Reeves,' she ordered.

'Yes, ma'am.' The young girl bobbed another curtsy and fled.

'What age is Winifred Reeves, Mrs Boot?' asked Marriott.

Agnes Boot opened a large book that rested on her desk and turned a few pages. 'Seventeen last month,' she said.

FIFTEEN

I t was a matter of ten minutes before Winifred Reeves appeared in the housekeeper's office, but during that time Mrs Boot talked at great length about the progress of the war, a subject upon which she seemed particularly well informed.

'You wanted to see me, ma'am?' The girl who entered bobbed briefly before closing the door. She was tall, pretty and confident, but the moment she saw the three police officers that confidence appeared to wane.

'This gentleman is an inspector from Scotland Yard, Reeves, and he wants to ask you a few questions.'

'What about?' Winifred Reeves fiddled with her apron and glanced apprehensively at Hardcastle who, being the eldest of the three, she assumed was the inspector Mrs Boot was talking about.

'I think it would be better if we were to talk to Miss Reeves alone, Mrs Boot,' said Hardcastle. 'Perhaps there is an available room somewhere that we can use.'

'Shouldn't I be present, Inspector?' asked Agnes Boot. 'She's only a young girl, you know.' But her question was prompted more by an inveterate nosiness than concern for the girl's welfare.

'She's not a suspect, Mrs Boot, and I doubt she'll even be a witness,' said Hardcastle sharply. 'Now, unless you'd rather I took her to the police house to answer a few questions, I'd be obliged if you'd find me a room as quickly as possible where we could talk. I don't have a great deal of time, and certainly none to waste arguing with you.'

Taken aback and rendered speechless by the brusqueness of the DDI's tone of voice, Mrs Boot rose from her desk and, with a toss of her head, took a key from a board on the wall and led the way out of her office.

Once ensconced in a small room near the housekeeper's own, Hardcastle invited the young girl to sit down.

'I gather that Mrs Boot is a bit of a tartar,' he said.

Winifred Reeves smiled. 'She can be a bit hard at times, sir.'

'I'll bet she can.' Hardcastle laughed in an attempt to put the girl at her ease. 'Now then, Winnie, I'm investigating a murder, and I'm sure you know that that's a very serious crime.'

'Oh, yes, sir. That'll be poor Daisy Salter you're talking about.'

'That's right. You knew her, of course.'

'Yes, sir. She worked here as a cleaner for a while.'

'Why did she leave?' Hardcastle knew the answer, but always liked to get what the medical profession calls a second opinion.

'She got friendly with one of the young gentlemen, sir, and that's strictly forbidden,' said Winifred, lowering her voice as though fearing being overheard.

'And who was that, Winnie?'

'Laurence Elliott,' said Winnie, her voice now almost a whisper, 'but once Mrs Boot found out she reported it to Doctor Mallory, and that put an end to it.'

'It would have done, I suppose,' said Hardcastle casually, and then changed the subject. 'Now I want you to be completely honest with me, Winnie, and I can promise you that you won't get into any trouble with either Mrs Boot or Doctor Mallory. D'you understand that?'

'Yes, sir.'

'Good. How long has Marjorie Tindall been staying here with you?'

'I'm sure I don't know what you mean, sir.' Winifred Reeves was clearly taken by surprise at both the suddenness and bluntness of the DDI's question, and blushed scarlet the moment she spoke the lie.

'Let me answer the question for you, then, Winnie,' said Hardcastle gently. 'She arrived here last Wednesday evening, and probably picked that time because she knew that Mrs Boot gets the bus into Alton on Wednesday afternoons to do some shopping and doesn't get back until quite late.' It appeared to be guesswork, but Hardcastle was so experienced a detective that he had made a safe assumption.

Winifred Reeves burst into tears. 'I'm ever so sorry, sir. I never meant no harm, but poor Marjorie was scared half out of her wits and I never knew what to do. So I let her stay in my room, but only for a while. I told her she'd have to find somewhere else

because if Mrs Boot found out I'd get the sack.' She sniffed and
wiped her nose on the corner of her apron. 'And I s'pose I will
now.'

'No you won't; I promised you that you wouldn't be in any
trouble. Did Marjorie tell you why she was so scared?'

'No, sir, she wouldn't say, but it was obvious that something
had scared her. I've never seen her that frightened before.'

'Is she in your room now?'

'Yes, sir.'

'Good. Go and fetch her and tell her that she's not in any trouble,
but that I need to speak to her. Now off you go, lass.'

Winifred Reeves almost ran from the room.

Hardcastle glanced at Yardley. 'Are you learning anything,
Yardley?'

'Yes, sir. All the time.' Yardley was astounded at the gentle way
that Hardcastle had almost tricked Winifred into confirming what
the DDI had apparently known already about Marjorie Tindall's
whereabouts. He had expected him to bully and cajole, but he was
realizing, almost by the hour, that there were many facets to the
London detective's character. And, for that matter, many sides to the
art of being a successful murder investigator. 'But how did you know
that Mrs Boot goes into Alton every Wednesday afternoon, sir?'

'Because that's what women do, Yardley. What's more, I took
the trouble to find out that there are only two buses a week into
Alton from Thresham Parva: one on a Wednesday afternoon and
the other on a Saturday afternoon, but the Wednesday one returns
quite a bit later than the Saturday one. And I made a point of
finding that out because the more you know about the place where
the murder occurred, the more chance you have of solving it. You
don't just look at the obvious evidence. You find out everything
that might come in handy.'

The door opened and Winifred Reeves ushered a frightened girl
into the room.

Almost immediately, Agnes Boot, whose inquisitiveness had
compelled her to lie in wait just for this moment, burst through
the door. 'Have you been keeping this girl in college, Reeves?'
she demanded, her voice almost reaching screaming pitch. 'Well,
I can tell you this much, young woman: your employment is
terminated as of now.'

Yardley now witnessed yet another mercurial change in Hardcastle's character.

'You have just interrupted an important police interview, Mrs Boot, and I'm sorely tempted to arrest you for obstructing me in the execution of my duty.' The DDI spoke sharply and rose to his feet as though about to fulfil his threat. 'And as for dismissing this young lady, I'm afraid that once I report the matter to Doctor Mallory, you are more likely to be the one looking for a new job. And without a reference, I imagine,' he added portentously.

'I, er, I don't know what you mean, sir,' stuttered Mrs Boot, clearly unnerved by Hardcastle's threatening attitude.

'Are you responsible for all the accommodation rooms in this college, Mrs Boot?' asked Hardcastle mildly. 'Staff as well as pupils?'

'Of course, sir.' Agnes Boot preened herself slightly. 'I'm a senior staff member and answerable only to Doctor Mallory.'

'In which case,' continued the DDI, 'the fact that a trespasser spent the last five nights in a room for which you have responsibility means that the blame for the girl's presence here rests entirely with you. It's called—' He paused and turned to Marriott. 'What's the phrase, Marriott?'

'Vicarious responsibility, sir.'

'That's it. Quite slipped my mind for the moment. However, Mrs Boot, at the very least I shall suggest to Doctor Mallory that your slackness makes you guilty of lack of supervision. On the other hand, if you did know about it and did nothing, the question of criminal conspiracy may well arise, for which, I would remind you, the penalty is several years imprisonment.' Hardcastle waved a hand vaguely in the direction of the two young women as if to imply that they were guilty of some heinous crime in which Mrs Boot was complicit.

Agnes Boot crumbled, as bullies invariably do. 'I'm sure no harm's been done, sir,' she said and clutched at the doorpost for fear of fainting. Now utterly terrified, she only just managed to hold back her tears. 'I daresay I spoke a bit hasty in the heat of the moment. No, sir, it's quite all right. Young Winifred's a good worker and I couldn't really manage without her. She's the best girl I've got here.'

'I daresay you'll be thinking about promoting her to deputy housekeeper, then, Mrs Boot, and then Doctor Mallory can make her housekeeper if he decides to dismiss you.' Hardcastle paused to give effect to his unlikely forecast; in fact, he had no intention of mentioning the incident to the college principal. 'However, I mustn't interfere in the workings of the college, must I?' he added airily. 'I'll bid you good day.' He smiled at Winifred Reeves. 'Thank you for your help, Winnie.' And with that he and the other two officers escorted Marjorie Tindall out to the waiting taxi.

It was seven o'clock that evening in what had been a long day when the three detectives and Marjorie Tindall arrived at the police house in the village. Hardcastle had decided that the austere and rather intimidating surroundings of Alton police station would not be suitable for interviewing a frightened young girl.

'I'd like to use a room here in the police house to talk to Marjorie Tindall, Mr Jessop.'

'That's all right, sir,' said Jessop. 'I'll tell Annie that you'll be using the parlour for a while.'

'As a matter of fact, I'd like to have your wife present, if that's acceptable. Apart from the Tindall girl being only sixteen, to have a woman there might put her at ease. But it shouldn't take more than a couple of minutes.'

Marriott and Yardley took Marjorie Tindall into the parlour while Hardcastle went into the kitchen to talk to Annie Jessop.

'Only too happy to help, sir,' said the village policeman's wife once Hardcastle had explained what he wanted her to do. 'I take it you want to coax the truth out of her rather than putting the fear of the good Lord into her.'

'That's it exactly, Mrs Jessop.'

Hardcastle and Annie went into the parlour. Marjorie Tindall, looking very frightened, was sitting hunched up in a wheelback Windsor armchair.

'If you and Yardley go into the kitchen, Marriott,' whispered Hardcastle, ushering the two detectives towards the door, 'I'm sure you can persuade PC Jessop to make you both a cup of tea.'

'Don't you want us in here, sir?' Marriott was surprised to be excluded from what could be a vital interview.

'Not for the moment, Marriott. I don't want to frighten the girl any more than she is already. If we get to the point of writing formal statements, I'll possibly send for you.'

'While you're at it, Mr Marriott,' said Annie, 'perhaps you'd ask my Ted to bring three cups of tea in here as well. And as it's for the inspector, tell him to make ours first,' she added with a smile.

'Now Marjorie,' said Hardcastle, 'you're not in any trouble, but I've been told that a man threatened you recently. I want you to tell me exactly what happened.'

'I daren't, sir. No one would believe me.' Marjorie Tindall gripped the wooden arms of the chair until her knuckles showed white, and tears began to roll unchecked down her cheeks. This was an entirely different young woman from the drunken hussy that Tom Hooker claimed he had seen egging on soldiers to fight each other in the Thresham Arms. This was a terrified child suddenly enmeshed in the sordid reality of life.

'Try me,' said Hardcastle. 'One of the things I've learned as a policeman is that very often the most unlikely stories turn out to be true.'

'It's all right, Marjorie.' Annie Jessop leaned across and placed a reassuring hand on the young girl's arm. 'You can trust the inspector.'

The door opened and Ted Jessop appeared with three cups of tea and some slices of cake on a tin tray that he placed silently on a small table. Guessing that the interview was a delicate one, he had had the foresight to remove his tunic, knowing that a policeman in shirtsleeves did not look so authoritarian.

'Now, what happened that frightened you so much, Marjorie?'

The girl took a bite of cake and looked at Annie, but despite receiving a reassuring smile, she remained silent.

'I've got a daughter not much older than you, Marjorie,' said Hardcastle, 'and she sometimes tells me all sorts of secrets that she can't tell anyone else.'

'I can't!' Marjorie blurted out the words and dissolved into tears.

Hardcastle let her recover before speaking again. 'Would it be better if you just talked to Mrs Jessop without me being here?' His experience told him that what the girl was about to reveal was too embarrassing to relate to a man.

Marjorie raised her tear-stained face and nodded. 'Yes, sir,' she mumbled.

'Just a minute, then.' Hardcastle glanced at Annie Jessop and nodded towards the door. Once they were outside the room, the DDI said, 'Are you happy to try to get as much out of the girl as you can, Mrs Jessop?'

'You just leave it to me, sir. She's not the first young lass I've had to talk to because she didn't want to talk to my Ted. Especially where intimate matters are concerned.'

'Do you know how to take a statement from her later on if it's necessary?'

Annie Jessop laughed scornfully. 'I've been a policeman's wife for nigh-on twenty-two years, Mr Hardcastle, and I've probably taken more statements than most of the young coppers in the Hampshire County Constabulary.'

'My apologies, Mrs Jessop. The ways of the county constabularies take a bit of getting used to after London.'

Annie Jessop and Marjorie Tindall had been closeted in the parlour for almost three-quarters of an hour before the policeman's wife emerged, a grave expression on her face.

'How did you get on?' asked Hardcastle.

'Badly. At least from the girl's point of view, sir.' Annie appeared thoughtful for a moment or two. 'I don't think we should leave her alone in the parlour.'

'She won't steal anything, not from us,' said Ted Jessop.

Annie shot her husband a scathing glance. 'Of course she won't, you daft hap'orth, Ted Jessop. But we don't want her jumping out of the window and running off, or worse still doing herself some harm.'

'Perhaps you'd sit with her while your wife tells us the tale, Mr Jessop,' said Hardcastle.

'Of course, sir.'

'I think we need another cup of tea,' said Annie Jessop, and then paused. 'In fact, I reckon a drop of whisky wouldn't go amiss. What d'you say, Mr Hardcastle?'

'Much appreciated,' said the DDI.

Once Annie and each of the detectives had a Scotch in front of them, Annie began.

'Once I'd got her to open up, she was quite honest, Mr Hardcastle, and told me that she wasn't a virgin, something I'd guessed already from village gossip. However, she only went with men who were at the most a few years older than she was. But it was when she was working as a cleaner at this particular place that the man in question made an indecent suggestion to her. Not satisfied with her refusal, he then said that she'd been stealing and she could either do as he asked or be taken straight to the police. But she still refused him. At that point, he grabbed hold of her and forced himself on her.'

'Is she claiming that she was raped, Mrs Jessop?' asked Marriott.

'Yes. She was quite adamant about it, and I believed her. She described what happened in such intimate detail and was so upset while she was telling me that it's got to have been the absolute truth.'

'When did this rape occur?'

'Last Wednesday, Mr Marriott. That'd be the eighth.'

'That was the date that my informant heard about the girl, sir,' said Yardley, nearly mentioning Victoria Homersham by name, 'but she didn't mention that she'd been raped.'

'Your informant obviously doesn't know everything, Yardley,' said Hardcastle, 'but why was Marjorie Tindall so scared? Scared enough to run away and hide. Did she tell you that, Mrs Jessop?'

'The man said that if she told anyone at all he would kill her, just as he'd killed Daisy Salter. Then he went on to say that even if she did repeat it to anyone else they wouldn't believe her, and she'd be in trouble with the police for telling lies about him.'

'Did she say who the man was, Mrs Jessop?' asked Hardcastle.

'Yes, she did, sir. I took a complete statement from her and got her to sign it straight away in case she changed her mind later on. Everything's there.' Annie Jessop handed the few sheets of paper across the table to the DDI.

Hardcastle glanced at the name, but remained expressionless. He passed it across to where Marriott and Yardley were sitting.

'What do we do next, sir?' asked Marriott, having scanned the statement.

'First of all, we've got to protect our witness, Marriott.' Hardcastle turned to Annie Jessop. 'With your husband's approval, Mrs Jessop, I'd like Marjorie Tindall to stay with you until we've made the arrest. She'll be quite safe here and if things go according to plan it'll be for just one night. By tomorrow I'll have this individual locked up in Alton police station.'

'It'll be no trouble at all, sir,' said Annie Jessop. 'And I tell you this much: I'd like ten minutes alone with just him and my pinking shears.'

Hardcastle laughed. 'D'you want to ask your husband before agreeing to the girl staying here?' he asked.

Annie scoffed. 'Ted Jessop will do what he's told, Mr Hardcastle. He might lord it round the village but not in my kitchen.'

Hardcastle just nodded. The more he saw of Annie Jessop, the more she reminded him of his wife, Alice.

'How do you think she'll do in the witness box, Mrs Jessop?' asked Hardcastle.

'She'll be fine, sir. Once I'd told her that she'd got the protection of Scotland Yard behind her and they'd let nothing happen to her, she perked up immediately.' Annie Jessop laughed. 'In fact, one might say she's almost looking forward to the trial. I've never seen such a change in a young woman. Especially one who's been through what she's been through.'

'A warrant, sir?' asked the ever-practical Marriott.

'I think so. We'll start with a search warrant. Find me a magistrate who will grant a warrant this evening, Yardley.'

'*Tonight*, sir?' asked the stunned Yardley.

Hardcastle took out his half-hunter. 'Why not? It's only half past eight.'

Under Hardcastle's guidance, Yardley's confidence and resourcefulness were improving by the hour. The solution to the problem that the DDI had set him was resolved simply by asking Ted Jessop for the name of a local magistrate.

'We've got a justice living here in Thresham Parva who sits on the Alton bench, Dick,' said Jessop, running a hand round his chin as he gave the matter some thought, 'but this is a tricky one. As it's a local matter, Mr Hardcastle wouldn't want word getting to the suspect before he's had a chance to execute the warrant.'

'But a magistrate wouldn't do that, would he?' asked Yardley innocently.

'I can see you've got a lot to learn about human nature, young Dick, and they don't teach that at those new-fangled instruction classes they're giving to recruits nowadays. Your best bet is to see

Colonel Ashley Fitzroy. He lives about four miles from here and sits on the Aldershot bench. Here, I'll write down his address for you.'

Colonel Ashley Fitzroy lived in a secluded ivy-covered villa at the end of a narrow lane.

'Yes? What is it?' The man who answered the door raised a monocle to his left eye and stared at the three men on his doorstep.

'Colonel Fitzroy?'

'Yes. Who the devil are you?' Fitzroy had a guardee moustache, bushy eyebrows and a permanently fierce expression. His brown tweed suit had clearly seen better days, and the elbows bore leather patches.

'Divisional Detective Inspector Hardcastle of New Scotland Yard, sir.'

'The devil you are! What in the name of God is an inspector from Scotland Yard doing in the wilds of Hampshire at this time of night?'

'Seeking a search warrant, sir,' said Hardcastle.

'Are you, be damned? Better come in, then, and tell me all about it,' said Fitzroy. 'Don't want to disturb the memsahib,' he murmured as he led the three officers into a room that was obviously his study. 'Sit yourselves down.'

'This is Detective Sergeant Marriott, also from the Yard, and Detective Constable Yardley of the Hampshire County Constabulary.'

'That makes you the junior man, then, eh, Yardley?' bellowed Fitzroy as he allowed the monocle to drop from his eye.

'Yes, sir,' said the completely overawed Yardley. Until the arrival of Hardcastle in his life he would never have contemplated disturbing so august a figure as Colonel Fitzroy in order to get a warrant that, in his view, could have been just as easily obtained in the morning. But he also knew that Hardcastle was an impatient man.

'Splendid. In that case you can pour the whisky, Yardley.' Fitzroy pointed to a table upon which were a whisky decanter, several crystal tumblers and a jug of water. 'And don't put any water in mine. Had a veterinary officer attached to my regiment once who always put water in my damn whisky because he said it was good for me liver. D'you know the damn fella would never

wear his pith helmet because he said it gave him a headache? Of
course, the sun got to him and he went mad and resigned his
commission. After that I think he became a member of parliament.' He paused. 'Or was it a dentist? No matter. Now then,
Inspector, it was good of you to call in. Always enjoy a chat and
a glass.' The colonel stood up.

'Er, the warrant, sir?'

'Ah, of course it was. What's it all about, eh?'

Hardcastle explained about the search for Marjorie Tindall
and her credibly genuine terror at the prospect of being murdered
herself. 'I could arrest the suspect, sir, but I only have the girl's
word for it. I also have in my possession some material evidence.
However, I think I'm justified in asking for a search warrant in
the hope that I might find further evidence that would support the
girl's allegation.'

'Ah, a sort of fishing expedition, eh? Well, I can quite understand
why you didn't want to seek a warrant from that magistrate who
lives in Thresham Parva. These civilian chaps lack the discipline,
don't you know,' said Fitzroy enigmatically, and took another sip
of his whisky before crossing to his desk. Taking out an official
form, he entered a few details and scrawled his signature at the
bottom. Handing it to Hardcastle, he said, 'There you are, Inspector.
Should have got you to swear that on oath, I suppose, but we'll
take that as read, eh? I hope he's your man. Damned people ought
to be in the army. I'd be out there meself if they hadn't told me
I was too damn old. Bloody audacity. I could still show some of
those young whippersnappers a thing or two. The other day I read
of some young fella being made a brigadier-general at twenty-eight
years of age.' He shook his head. 'Don't know what the army's
coming to.'

'Thank you for the warrant and for the whisky, sir,' said
Hardcastle as he and the other two officers rose to leave.

'Yes,' said Fitzroy vaguely, and waved a hand of dismissal.

SIXTEEN

I t was seven o'clock on the following morning, a Tuesday, when Hardcastle hammered on the door. Behind him stood Marriott, Yardley and PC Jessop.

'What is the meaning of calling here at this hour of the morning, Inspector?' The ludicrous image of a barefooted man attired in a tasselled nightcap and a nightshirt short enough to reveal hirsute legs tended to undermine the indignant anger he was attempting to display.

'It's not a social call,' snapped Hardcastle. 'I have a warrant to search these premises.'

'You mean you want to search my house?' spluttered the man, disbelief apparent in his expression.

'Yes,' said Hardcastle.

'I'm sorry, but I won't allow it.' The man spread his arms wide as if to prevent the police from gaining access.

'Stand aside or I shall be obliged to arrest you for obstructing me in the execution of my duty.' At seven in the morning, Hardcastle's disposition was even less equable than usual.

'This is outrageous,' protested the Reverend Cyril Creed as Hardcastle, Marriott and Yardley pushed past the vicar. PC Jessop remained on the doorstep to prevent anyone entering or leaving the premises.

'What on earth is happening, Cyril?' Esmé Creed, attired in a cream peignoir and a pair of embroidered velvet bedroom slippers, appeared behind her husband.

'It's the police, my dear. For some reason they want to search the vicarage.'

'Search the vicarage!' screeched Esmé Creed. 'How dare you people come in here making such demands? I shall personally telephone the Chief Constable. Don't stand there, Cyril, do something. This is nothing short of sacrilege.'

'Serve the warrant, Marriott,' said Hardcastle in a tired voice, completely ignoring the vicar's wife's tirade.

'I have here a warrant signed by Colonel Ashley Fitzroy, a justice of the peace for the County of Hampshire, Mr Creed,' began Marriott. 'It authorizes Divisional Detective Inspector Hardcastle and any officers accompanying him to search the premises known as The Vicarage, Thresham Parva in the County of Hampshire.' He held up the warrant for Creed to see, but when the vicar attempted to take hold of it, Marriott stopped him. 'You may read it, but not take it,' he said. He knew of policemen who had relinquished a warrant only to see it torn up or thrown on to a fire. 'This warrant also authorizes the breaking down of doors where necessary.'

'I shall telephone the Chief Constable immediately,' announced Esmé Creed as she began to move towards the sitting-room door.

'No, you won't,' said Hardcastle, 'and as I just explained to your husband, any further obstruction will result in your arrest as well as his.'

Esmé Creed began fanning her face with a hand. 'I think I'm going to faint,' she moaned.

'In that case, I should sit down if I were you, Mrs Creed, and get your husband to fetch you a glass of water,' said Hardcastle unsympathetically. 'Right, Marriott, get on with it, and you, Yardley. You know what you're looking for.'

Marriott had a very good idea what they were seeking, but wisely Hardcastle had not specified it in the vicar's hearing.

'I'd take the weight off your feet if I were you, Vicar,' said Hardcastle. 'This could take some time.' He turned and gazed out of the window.

'Are you going to tell me why you're searching my house, Inspector, or do I have to guess?' Creed's question, addressed to the DDI's back, was larded with sarcasm.

'I am acting on information received,' said Hardcastle, without turning from the window.

'I'll have you know that as a man of the cloth, I do not expect to be treated in this cavalier way, Inspector, and I have standing and influence in this parish and beyond,' said Creed, puffing himself up with even more indignation than hitherto he had displayed. 'As my wife suggested, it's nothing short of sacrilege and when I inform the bishop of your insolent and high-handed behaviour here this morning, he will doubtless speak to the Archbishop of

Canterbury who will, in all probability, mention the matter to the Prime Minister. Furthermore, as I'm sure you know, the archbishop has right of audience with His Majesty the King. And . . . and . . .' Creed finally ran out of implied threats.

'If you're thinking about pleading benefit of clergy, Vicar, I would remind you that it was abolished in 1827,' said Hardcastle mildly, finally turning from the window.

'I think you ought to come and have a look at this, sir,' said Marriott, barely able to conceal his excitement as he came back into the sitting room.

'One moment, Marriott.' Hardcastle went to the front door. 'Be so good as to come inside, Mr Jessop, and keep an eye on the reverend and his missus. I don't want them interfering with anything or going anywhere while I'm with Sergeant Marriott.'

Creed stared angrily at Jessop as he entered the room, as though it was the constable who was to blame for Hardcastle's actions this morning. As he was on duty, Jessop did not remove his helmet. Esmé Creed imagined that to be a deliberate act of discourtesy designed to irritate her, but rather than protest she simply passed a hand across her forehead, moaned and fell back in her armchair. Curiously, though, Cyril Creed seemed unimpressed by his wife's histrionics.

'This is Creed's study by the look of it, sir,' said Marriott as he showed Hardcastle into a small room at the back of the house.

'What in particular did you want me to look at, Marriott?'

'That, sir.' Marriott pointed at a double-shelved oak bookcase. 'Young Yardley obviously took your advice about looking at people's bookshelves.'

'What so special about these here books, then, Yardley?' asked Hardcastle.

'Practically every one of them is about trains, sir. It looks to me as though the vicar is mad keen on railways. But it gets better, sir.' With all the panache of a stage magician revealing an amazing illusion, Marriott flung open a door on the far side of the study. 'This room was locked, sir, but I managed to open it with my twirler,' he said, displaying a skeleton key which he then put back into his pocket.

Hardcastle walked into the room and stared around in amazement. The walls were covered with posters and railway signs of every description. A framed collection of railway tickets hung over the fireplace. Three sides of the room bore shelves laden with signal lanterns, railwaymen's caps, whistles, signal flags and timetables.

'This room is exactly as Marjorie Tindall described it in the statement Annie Jessop took from her, Marriott.' Hardcastle smashed the fist of one hand into the palm of the other. 'We've got the bastard. There's no way she could've made this up without having seen it and as it was locked she could only have come in here if Creed let her in or, more likely, brought her in. And then there's that.' He pointed at a seven-foot-long brown velvet chaise longue set against one wall. 'I'll be very surprised if there's not some evidence of rape on it.'

'You'll be interested in this, too, sir.' Marriott pointed at a glass-topped display table. 'It contains a collection of railway uniform buttons and badges. They're all carefully labelled and doubtless catalogued somewhere, but the significant thing about it is this.' Lifting the hinged top of the cabinet, he indicated a label that stated 'GWR button 1899–1905'. But the button itself was missing.

'Well, well, if that ain't a piece of what you might call evidence by omission, Marriott, I'll eat my titfer. That is exactly how our friend Hubert Merryweather at Paddington described the button we showed him and which was found in Daisy Salter's handbag.' Hardcastle glanced at Yardley, who was standing to one side of the cabinet. 'Don't look so surprised, lad. It's called solving a murder.'

'But does it solve it, sir?'

'Not by itself, no,' said Hardcastle, 'but the button, and where it was found, and the Tindall girl's statement describing this room gives us a big stick to beat the reverend with.'

Marriott and Yardley continued to search the room meticulously. It was Yardley who found the piece of evidence that undoubtedly pointed to Creed's guilt.

'I found this in the drawer of that bureau, sir.' Yardley indicated a walnut escritoire, and then held out his hand to display what he had found. 'It's a gold crucifix with the letters INRI on it, sir.'

'That looks very much like the crucifix that Rose Salter said that Daisy always wore,' said Hardcastle slowly. 'First of all, we'll check with the Salters, and then we'll get confirmation from the jeweller in Winchester where they said it was bought.'

'Is that necessary, sir?' asked Yardley. 'If the Salters say it's the one, won't that be enough?'

'Oh, you think so, do you, Yardley? Supposing defence counsel suggests that the Salters' evidence should be discounted because they were so distressed by the murder of their daughter that they would say anything to get the suspect convicted? But if we get corroborative testimony, that'll take care of it.'

'Yes, of course, sir. I understand.'

'Now we'll see what the good reverend has to say for himself. Come, Marriott.'

The scene in the sitting room of the vicarage was like a Victorian tableau. Cyril Creed sat in one chair and his wife Esmé sat in another, facing him. PC Jessop stood by the door. Each of them was quite motionless and none of them was talking.

'I'd like you to come with me, Mr Creed, and you too, Mrs Creed,' announced Hardcastle.

Still in his nightshirt and barefooted, Cyril Creed had taken off his nightcap. For a moment, Esmé Creed appeared to be on the point of refusing the DDI's request, but then she clutched her peignoir more closely around herself and followed.

The little procession entered the study and stopped at the open door of the room beyond.

'How did you get in there?' demanded Creed accusingly.

'With this.' Marriott held up his skeleton key and waggled it in front of Creed's face.

'D'you mean you broke in without my permission? How dare you do such a thing? Policemen are just as much required to comply with the law as everyone else. I shall make a formal complaint.' Even now, Creed was attempting to preserve his reputation in the face of what he must have known was the inevitable outcome.

'My sergeant told you that our warrant empowers us to break down doors, Creed,' snapped Hardcastle, by now tiring of the vicar's posturing. 'So think yourself lucky that Sergeant Marriott was considerate enough to open it with his key. He was quite entitled to kick it down.'

While this short exchange was going on, Esmé Creed had pushed past her husband to enter the room and stood in apparent amazement at the vast array of railway memorabilia.

'What on earth *is* all this stuff, Cyril?' she demanded haughtily as the vicar and the detectives crowded into the room after her. 'I've never seen any of this before. You told me this was a lumber room full of old suitcases and trunks, and boxes of hymn books and hassocks, and all that sort of thing. It looks more like a cross between a museum and a junk shop.'

'It's just my little hobby, my dear,' said Creed lamely. 'I was rather afraid that you would chide me for spending my stipend on my passion.'

'I think you were probably spending my inheritance on it,' retorted Esmé who, ever since their marriage, had been the financial mainstay of the union. 'And what's that?' She pointed at the huge chaise longue. 'Why d'you need that in here, Cyril? Do you sit down on it to admire all this rubbish?'

'I've been looking at your collection of railway uniform buttons, Mr Creed,' said Hardcastle before a full-scale row broke out between the vicar and his wife.

'It is rather comprehensive, isn't it?' said the vicar in his sanctimonious voice, seemingly relieved to be rescued from his vituperative spouse.

'But one is missing.'

'What?' Creed made a passable impression of being shocked.

'The GWR button 1899–1905 isn't there.'

'That wretched girl must have taken it.'

'Which girl would that be?' asked Hardcastle mildly.

'The Salter girl. The one who was murdered. I told you we had to dismiss her for theft.'

'I wonder why she would have stolen that particular button,' said Hardcastle airily, implying that he was not really interested in the answer, but in fact was delighted that, without realizing it, Creed had just made a damaging admission.

'I had them out of the case and was cleaning them all on that table.' Creed waved a hand at a baize-covered table close to the display cabinet. 'I didn't notice that one was missing.'

'Oh, I see.' Hardcastle appeared to accept that explanation, but he was already thinking ahead to the trial. 'However, on another matter, one of my officers found this.' The DDI showed Creed the crucifix. 'Do you have anything to say about that?'

Creed smiled the sort of smile that he reserved for members of the uneducated masses who were struggling to understand the scriptures. 'It's hardly surprising that you should find a crucifix in a house occupied by a clerk in holy orders, is it, Inspector?'

Hardcastle did not for one moment imagine that Creed would make an admission of guilt, but Marriott had noted the question and the reply in his pocket book.

'I have a written statement from a young woman named Marjorie Tindall who will state on oath that you sexually assaulted her in this very room, Mr Creed.'

Creed's face went white with shock and he began to tremble. He attempted to speak, but the words would not come.

Hardcastle paused to give weight to his next statement. 'Cyril Creed, I am arresting you for sexually assaulting Marjorie Tindall on or about Wednesday the eighth of August this year. You will now be taken to Alton police station where you will be charged with that assault contrary to common law and Section Forty-eight of the Offences against the Person Act of 1861. I must warn you that other charges may follow.'

There was a small whimper from behind Hardcastle, and he turned to see Esmé Creed lying on the floor in a dead faint. 'Do something about that woman, Yardley,' he said. 'I presume you have some knowledge of first aid.'

'It might be a good idea if you got dressed, Mr Creed,' said Marriott, and followed the shocked clergyman upstairs to his bedroom.

The station sergeant at Alton had twenty-nine years' service, during which time he had been stationed in most parts of Hampshire over which the county constabulary had jurisdiction. It is fair to say, therefore, that it would take a great deal to surprise Police Sergeant Cornelius Lovibond. However, the arrival in the charge room at Alton police station of a clergyman in frock coat and gaiters whose arms were held firmly by Marriott and Yardley did cause the sergeant to raise his eyebrows, albeit slightly.

'I'm Divisional Detective Inspector Hardcastle of New Scotland

Yard, Sergeant, and this is the Reverend Cyril Creed, Vicar of Thresham Parva.'

'I see, sir,' said Lovibond. 'Am I to understand that you've arrested the reverend gentleman?'

'You understand correctly, Sergeant.'

'Well, I'm blessed,' said Lovibond.

'In the circumstances, I somehow doubt that you will be,' commented Hardcastle drily. 'Mr Creed has been arrested by me for sexually assaulting one Marjorie Tindall on or about Wednesday the eighth of August 1917 at the Vicarage, Thresham Parva, Hampshire. I propose therefore to charge him with that offence, after which I will interview him in connection with another matter.'

'Very good, sir.' Lovibond opened a drawer in the high charge-room desk and took out several official forms before settling down to the business of charging Creed.

Fifteen minutes later, Hardcastle escorted Creed into an interview room. In accordance with the Chief Constable's standing orders, Sergeant Lovibond had deprived Creed of his braces and bootlaces for fear that he may attempt to commit suicide. As a consequence, Creed now presented a rather pathetic, shuffling figure holding up his trousers. In the comparatively short space of time since his arrest, he appeared to have aged by about ten years, and the rather rubicund cherubic face of earlier had given way to a drawn and pallid countenance.

'Sit down, Creed,' said Hardcastle, and without further ado produced the crucifix that Yardley had found in the secretaire in Creed's railway museum. 'Where did you get this?'

'I took it from that Salter girl.'

'D'you mean Daisy Salter who lived with her parents at their coal business in Thresham Parva?'

'I don't know of another Daisy Salter,' said Creed sarcastically.

Hardcastle leaned across the table and grabbed Creed by the lapels of his frock coat. 'Don't try getting clever with me, mister. You're in a lot of trouble and you'd do yourself a great deal of good by telling the truth.' He released his grip and sat back down again. 'When did you take this crucifix?'

It took Creed a few moments to recover from the shock of Hardcastle's physical attack. 'Just before I dismissed her for stealing,' he said eventually. 'She was a common whore who prostituted her body to any man willing to satisfy her. She had no right to wear a crucifix and the implication by so doing that she was entitled to God's love, forgiveness and protection.'

'You told me this morning that you were a man of the cloth, a man of God,' said Hardcastle.

'And so I am.'

'That doesn't sound like a very forgiving Christian attitude to me,' observed Marriott quietly.

Creed glared at Marriott as though becoming aware of his presence for the first time.

'As a Christian and a priest, will you swear by your God that you will answer my next question truthfully?'

'Of course.'

'Did you murder Daisy Salter on or about Monday the sixth of August this year?'

There was a long pause while Creed stared at the scarred top of the interview room table. And then he looked up. 'No,' he said, and crossed himself.

SEVENTEEN

'What about antecedents, sir?' asked Marriott as Creed was put into a cell.

'I was just thinking about that,' said Hardcastle. 'I shan't need you in court tomorrow morning, Marriott, so get back to the Smoke and see what you can find out about the reverend gentleman's background. You never know, we might get some surprises.'

Consequently, early in the day following Creed's arrest, Marriott travelled back to London to begin his enquiries into the vicar's background.

It was fortunate that the Alton magistrates were in session on that Wednesday morning. The court calendar was never sufficiently full to warrant sittings more than once a week, and sometimes not even that often.

Richard Yardley had arranged with the station sergeant at Alton police station to have Creed escorted to the police court next door in time for the commencement of the proceedings.

The usher cried 'All rise' as the three justices of the peace filed into the court and when the usher's one moment of glory was over, the three JPs seated themselves.

The chairman, a man with full grey sideburns and a florid complexion that betrayed a liking for gin, was well into his sixties, and looked as though he would be more at home riding to hounds than sitting on the bench. He was flanked by two other men, one of whom had the appearance of a fishmonger; the second, ashen-faced and painfully thin, blinked through his horn-rimmed spectacles as he peered around the courtroom with a vacant expression as if wondering what he was doing there. Other members of the bench often wondered why he was there too; he rarely made any contribution to the proceedings.

The usual handful of layabouts, having nowhere better to go, occupied the public gallery. Adjacent to the bench a sole reporter sat at a table that was dignified with a cardboard sign, upon which were the handwritten words 'Press Box'. One or two lawyers, in court for later cases, lounged about on counsel's benches.

When Creed was escorted into the dock, attired in his customary clerical collar, frock coat and gaiters, there was a hush followed by a few whisperings from the well of the court and from the gallery. The chairman, although forewarned of the charge that was being brought that morning, was unaware that the accused was a clerk in holy orders, and tried to give the impression that the presence of a clergyman in the dock of his court was commonplace.

'The Reverend Cyril Creed, Your Worships, a charge of rape,' shouted a policeman in a voice that could be heard throughout the court building if not beyond.

The clerk of the court, a local solicitor, glanced briefly at the charge sheet and then looked directly at Creed. 'Are you the Reverend Cyril Creed, and do you reside at the Vicarage, Thresham Parva in the County of Hampshire?'

'Yes, I do, and I must protest that this charge is one that is entirely without foundation, and furthermore I—'

'It is not the intention of the court that a plea will be taken today, Mr Creed,' said the clerk, wearily interrupting the clergyman's outburst. He looked at Hardcastle. 'Are you the officer in the case?' he asked.

'I am, sir.' The DDI walked round to the witness box. 'Ernest Hardcastle, Divisional Detective Inspector attached to New Scotland Yard, Your Worships,' he announced to further whisperings from around the courtroom. 'I respectfully ask for a remand into police custody in order that I might make further enquiries.'

The chairman of the bench was clearly out of his depth. Not only did he have a clergyman before him charged with a despicable crime, but he was also faced with a Scotland Yard detective of some rank who looked as though he knew his business. Already he was beginning to wish that he had ceded the chair to another justice for today's sitting.

'Are you not in a position to proceed this morning, then, Inspector?' The chairman had never before presided over any hearings of this magnitude, the inevitable outcome of which would be a remand to the county assizes, and could not think of anything else to say.

'Certainly not, Your Worship.' Hardcastle allowed the slightest trace of a smile to play around his lips, mocking the chairman's ignorance of legal procedure in major criminal cases. 'There is the possibility that other more serious charges will be brought that would require the fiat of the Director of Public Prosecutions.'

'The Director of Public Prosecutions? Fiat?' Hardcastle's pronouncement clearly disturbed the chairman, and he leaned forward to engage in a whispered and earnest conversation with the clerk of the court. 'God dammit!' he muttered, loudly enough to be heard in court. 'Is there no other way?'

The clerk whispered a reply, and the conversation ended.

'Mr Creed, you will be remanded into police custody for eight days, after which you will appear before this court for the matter to be further considered.' The chairman scribbled a few words in the court ledger, and sighed with relief as Creed was escorted from the dock.

'Frederick Nesbit, Your Worship,' cried a policeman as he ushered a scruffy individual into the dock. 'Charge of drunk and disorderly.'

'Oh, not him again,' muttered the chairman of the bench.

'What happens now, sir?' asked Yardley as the trio left the police court.

'Locking up clergymen always gives me an appetite, Yardley. And what happens now is that we find a decent pub where we can have a pint and, if we're lucky, a fourpenny cannon. D'you know of such an alehouse, Yardley? Come to that, d'you know what a fourpenny cannon is?' It was clear from his jocular comments that Hardcastle was in a very good mood.

'No, sir. What is it?'

'A hot steak-and-kidney pie, my lad.' Hardcastle rubbed his hands together in anticipation.

'In that case I know the very place, sir. The Royal Oak serves very good pies. It's on the corner of High Street and Turk Street.'

'I don't care where it is, Yardley, just take me there.'

'But what I meant earlier, sir, is what happens now that the Reverend Creed is in our custody?'

'Until we've gathered sufficient evidence to charge him with the murder of Daisy Salter, he'll stay there. Every eight days he'll appear before the magistrates for a further lay-down.' Seeing Yardley's bemused expression, he added, 'A lay-down is a remand in custody, Yardley. You really must learn the language if you're going to be a real detective.'

The young Hampshire officer had always been led to believe that London policemen had a different professional vocabulary from the rest of the country's police forces, and here he had proof of it.

'Now comes the hard part, Yardley,' continued Hardcastle as the two of them boarded their taxi. 'Getting it down on paper. We have to gather together all the relevant statements and write a report for the Director of Public Prosecutions. And Sir Willie Mathews always goes through a murder report with a fine-tooth comb. After that, he will brief counsel and the rest is in the lap of the gods or, more particularly, in the hands of the gentlemen of the jury.'

'But can we keep him that long at the police station, sir?' The machinations of investigating murder, and subsequently charging the person responsible, was new territory to Yardley, although he was learning fast.

'Of course we can,' said Hardcastle, 'unless that pompous arse of a magistrate starts getting worried or someone sees fit to apply for a writ of habeas corpus. And the only interested party I can see wanting to do that is Esmé Creed. But after she's found out a bit more about the reverend gentleman she's married to, she'll probably be happy to let him stay where he is.'

At two o'clock that afternoon, Marriott arrived back at Alton police station, where Hardcastle had set up an office. He had surprising news.

'There is no trace of Cyril Creed in any official records, sir.'

Hardcastle put down his pen and for a moment or two stared at his sergeant. 'What exactly d'you mean by official records, Marriott?' he said eventually.

'Precisely that, sir. There is no record at Somerset House of his birth or of his marriage. What's more, I had a look in *Crockford's Clerical Register*, and his name doesn't appear there, which it should as he's a clergyman. Just for good measure, I checked all the records at the Yard, including criminal records, and his name doesn't show up anywhere there either.'

Hardcastle leaned back in his chair, took out his pipe and slowly filled it as he considered the ramifications of Marriott's announcement. Applying a match to the tobacco, he expelled a cloud of smoke into the air and leaned forward again.

'Who's Creed's boss in the church's chain of command, Marriott?'

But it was Yardley who replied. 'It's the Bishop of Winchester, sir.'

'I think it's time we went to Winchester and had a talk with him, then.'

'He's not at Winchester, sir. The bishop's residence is Farnham Castle.' Yardley paused. 'Er, that's Farnham in Surrey, sir.'

'Damned funny set-up,' muttered Hardcastle. 'The Bishop of Winchester, which is in Hampshire, living in Surrey. It sounds to me as though the Church and the Metropolitan Police have a lot in common. But seeing as how you know everything, Yardley, you can tell me how we get there.'

'We'll use our taxi, sir. It's only about ten miles from here.'

'This is an impressive sort of place, Marriott,' said Hardcastle as the three detectives climbed the flight of stone steps that led to the entrance to Farnham Castle.

'Built in the twelfth century, sir,' volunteered Yardley.

'Really? That's useful to know,' said Hardcastle with a hint of sarcasm. Although ready to impart his own smattering of historical knowledge to anyone prepared to listen – or, like Marriott, unable to avoid it – the DDI did not take kindly to being 'lectured' as he called it.

The sight of two men in bowler hats and one wearing a straw boater momentarily disconcerted the young housemaid. Nevertheless, she bobbed a curtsy.

'Good afternoon, sir,' she said, directing her greeting at Hardcastle, clearly the eldest of the trio.

Hardcastle raised his hat. 'We're police officers, lass, and we'd like to speak to the bishop.'

'If you'd care to wait in here, sir, I'll fetch His Lordship's chaplain.'

The maid crossed the hall into which she had shown the detectives, her shoes clack-clacking on the stone-flagged floor. Moments later a youthful clergyman appeared.

'Good afternoon, gentlemen. I'm Luke Gregory, the bishop's chaplain-cum-secretary. Mary tells me that you're police officers.' The chaplain's face took on a grave expression. 'I hope it's not bad news. The bishop's son is a Machine Gun Corps officer serving on the Western Front, you see.'

'What we're about to tell the bishop might be regarded as bad news,' said Hardcastle, 'but I can assure you it has nothing to do with his son.'

'In that case, I'll see if he's free. I won't keep you long.' A couple of minutes later, the chaplain returned. 'If you come this way, gentlemen, I'll take you to the bishop's study.'

The primate was seated behind a desk with his back to a window that afforded a view of an enclosed courtyard. The large windows on the opposite side of the room looked across the sweeping grounds of the castle. As the police officers entered, the bishop rose and walked across the room with his hand outstretched. He was a large man with a jolly, round face, twinkling eyes behind gold-rimmed pince-nez, and a thatch of thick grey hair. Hardcastle estimated him to be about sixty years of age.

'Good afternoon, gentlemen.' The bishop took off his pince-nez and shook hands with each of them in turn.

'I'm Divisional Detective Inspector Hardcastle of New Scotland Yard, sir, and this is my assistant, Detective Sergeant Marriott, and our Hampshire colleague, DC Yardley.'

'Please, sit down.' The bishop waved towards a pair of settees and seated himself in an upright wooden armchair opposite the policemen. 'Luke, I'm sure these gentlemen could do with a cup of tea. See if you can arrange it, there's a good fellow. Now, how can I be of assistance to the police, Inspector,' said the bishop, once Luke Gregory had disappeared to find some tea.'

'It concerns the Reverend Cyril Creed, sir.'

'Has something happened to him?' The bishop sat forward, a concerned look on his face.

'In a manner of speaking, sir,' said Hardcastle. 'I arrested him yesterday on suspicion of having committed rape. He appeared in court this morning and was remanded to police custody while further enquiries are made.'

The bishop sat back in his chair, his mouth slightly open and a stunned expression on his face. 'But what on earth . . .? This can't be right, surely? You are talking about the Creed who has the living of Thresham Parva, aren't you, Inspector?' He began toying with the large crucifix that hung from a gold neckchain, shining brightly against the purple rabat that the bishop wore.

'I am, sir, and there is a very strong possibility that he might also be charged with murder.'

'Murder? Great heavens! I'm finding this very difficult to follow, Inspector. Murder? But who has he murdered? Not his wife, surely?'

'No, sir, but the matter is sub judice, so to speak, so I'd rather not reveal any more than I have to.'

'No, of course not. I quite understand.'

'Was there a particular reason why you asked if he'd murdered his wife, sir?'

'Not really. It was just that I couldn't think of anyone else he might have murdered. But surely there must be some mistake.'

'I don't think so, sir, but there is another aspect to the case that Sergeant Marriott discovered earlier today during a visit to London.'

'Mr Creed's name doesn't appear in *Crockford's*, sir,' said Marriott.

'Does it not?' Once again surprise was evident on the bishop's face. 'Was it an up-to-date edition?' he asked hopefully, as if wishing that Marriott might have examined an outdated copy.

At that moment, Luke Gregory reappeared, accompanied by a young woman bearing a tray of tea.

'Put it down over there, my dear,' the bishop said in a distracted tone of voice and dismissed the young woman with a wave of the hand. 'I think it would be a good idea if you brought in the whisky decanter, Luke. And perhaps you'd bring in a copy of *Crockford's*. I can't seem to find mine.'

When the book was produced and the bishop had satisfied himself that Creed's name did not appear within its pages, he leaned back with a sigh. 'I think I know the reason,' he said eventually. 'Creed came to us from Africa and not all overseas clergy of the Church of England are listed.' The bishop waited until Gregory had served everyone with whisky and took a goodly sip from his own glass before continuing. 'He told me that when the war broke out he was a curate in Tanganyika which was German East Africa at the time, and claimed that he and his wife had to make a hurried departure before they were arrested. He said that his vicar in Dar es Salaam was shot by the Germans for helping British residents in Tanganyika to escape across the border to Northern Rhodesia. Eventually, he told me, he obtained a passage to England. He said something about coming here via South Africa.'

'However, I'm assuming that you didn't see any actual proof that Creed is a clerk in holy orders. No certificates or anything like that? You just took his word for it, did you, sir?' Hardcastle sounded slightly accusing.

'One tends to trust the clergy, Inspector,' responded the bishop, his tone implying that one never did other than trust a clergyman's word, but not immediately appreciating the irony of his comment. 'The living of Thresham Parva had fallen vacant when the incumbent joined the Army Chaplains' Department only a week before Creed's arrival, and so I offered Creed the post. It was as much an act of Christian charity as anything else. Apparently he and his wife fled Africa with just the clothes they stood up in.'

'When did all this occur, sir?' asked Marriott.

'He told me that he and his wife – Esmé, I think her name is – arrived in this country a year ago. If memory serves me correctly, it was last June.' The bishop glanced at his chaplain. 'Is that your recollection, Luke?'

'Yes, I'm pretty sure that was the date, My Lord. If you'll give me a moment, I have a record of comings and goings in my office.' Gregory returned almost immediately. 'It was Monday the fifth of June last year that Creed was appointed, My Lord.'

'Well, there you have it, Inspector,' said the bishop. 'Now you know as much as I do, although you appear to know more of the matter than do I. However, I'd be grateful for a favour, if it's at all possible.'

'Certainly, sir.'

'Would it be permissible for you to keep me informed of the outcome of this shocking affair? A report of the matter will have to be sent to the Archbishop of Canterbury, you see.'

'I'll let you know what happens, sir,' said Hardcastle.

'If it should transpire that Creed is *not* an ordained priest there will be recriminations, and I shall have to explain why he was appointed without the proper checks.' The bishop paused and for a moment or two gazed out of the window. 'Lambeth Palace will be rather cross, I imagine,' he added, looking at Hardcastle once again.

'If that's the case, sir, might I suggest an answer?' Hardcastle had far more experience of talking his way out of difficult situations than any bishop.

'Any help would be gratefully received, Inspector.' The bishop leaned forward, an earnest expression on his face.

'Well, sir, as Creed escaped from German territory and there is a war on, you had no way of checking the man's credentials,' said Hardcastle. 'You could hardly write to the Kaiser and ask him if Creed had been a clergyman in German East Africa, could you? And as you yourself said, sir, it was an act of Christian charity on your part. And as you implied, sir, the clergy always tell the truth.'

'God bless you, Inspector. I would never have thought of that,' said the bishop with a wry smile.

'Thank you for your assistance, sir,' said Hardcastle as he and the other two detectives stood up. 'And thank you for the whisky, Chaplain,' he added, turning to Luke Gregory.

'A pleasure, Inspector.'

'May God go with you in your onerous task, Inspector,' said the bishop by way of a farewell.

The three CID officers stood outside the palace for a few moments admiring the view.

'I feel sorry for the right reverend bishop,' said Hardcastle. 'If Creed turns out to be a charlatan, His Lordship will be writing reports until doomsday, and no doubt finish up getting his knuckles rapped by Lambeth Palace. I'm even more certain now that the Church and the Metropolitan Police have much in common, Marriott.'

'What's next, sir?'

'Next, Marriott, we visit the supercilious Esmé Creed and frighten the life out of her. For all we know the pair of 'em could be German spies.'

'A word with Special Branch, then, sir?' asked Marriott mischievously. He knew how much the DDI hated having anything to do with what he called the 'secret police'.

'Not bloody likely, Marriott,' said Hardcastle adamantly.

EIGHTEEN

The three detectives arrived at the vicarage at Thresham Parva at just after five o'clock, but instead of Violet the maid answering the door it was opened by Esmé Creed herself. It was immediately obvious to Hardcastle that she was not the same woman he had met on their previous encounter. She was pale and drawn, and had obviously been crying.

'I thought you'd be back,' she said listlessly. 'Come in.'

'Where's your maid?' asked Hardcastle.

'Gone,' said Esmé bitterly. 'The minute word got out about why Cyril had been arrested she was out of here as fast as her legs would carry her.'

'We've just been speaking to the Bishop of Winchester, Mrs Creed,' said Hardcastle when all four of them were seated in the front room of the vicarage. There was no doubt in his mind that the change in domestic circumstances and in Esmé's attitude resulted from her husband's arrest and the realization that the Creeds' whole fictional world had suddenly collapsed.

'You know the whole story, then.' Esmé Creed cast a wistful glance into the empty fireplace. 'I knew it was too good to last.' She looked back at Hardcastle, the pompous disdain and pretence of social superiority that had been evident during the detectives' previous encounter with the Creeds now revealed as having been play-acting. 'I didn't mean what I said about you, Inspector, the last time you came; it was all part of trying to maintain the act. I knew you were still in the hall because the front door always creaks when it's opened and I was listening for it.' She half smiled and then shrugged.

'I know,' said Hardcastle and took out his pipe. 'D'you mind, Mrs Creed?' he asked, holding it aloft.

'Not at all. Go ahead.'

'It might help your husband if you told me your side of the story.' Hardcastle filled his pipe and lit it before leaning back to make himself comfortable in the armchair, for all the world like a man about to listen to an interesting story rather than information that might assist in a murder enquiry.

Yardley listened intently, interested to know how this conversation would progress. He knew that Hardcastle did *not* know the whole story, but he had spoken so convincingly that Esmé Creed doubtless believed him. Now, like an expert fisherman playing a reluctant trout, it was obvious that the DDI was about to tease the information out of her.

'Cyril's not a clergyman at all,' Esmé began. 'In fact, his name's not even Cyril, it's Charles. Good old Charlie Creed: everyone's friend and drinking partner, and the life and soul of the party. Until he ran out of money, that is.'

'What were you doing in German East Africa, Mrs Creed?' asked Hardcastle. 'The bishop mentioned it in passing, but I'd like to hear the true story.'

'I met my first husband in England. I was on the London stage then and he was on leave from Tanganyika. It was, I suppose, a whirlwind romance and he took me back to Africa; all very romantic.'

'What happened to your first husband, Mrs Creed?'

'We'd only been married for six months when he was killed on safari by a stampeding elephant. That was in 1912. Not long after that I met Charlie at a dance in Dar es Salaam and we were married there in 1913. Charlie owned a coffee plantation that he'd inherited from his father and we settled there. Unfortunately, Charlie was a gambler, and he gambled the estate away. But my first husband had been extremely well-off and he left everything to me. The future looked bright, and Charlie and I even talked about having children, but we decided to wait awhile because things were starting to get a little unsettled for the British in Tanganyika even before the war started. It was as if everyone, particularly the Germans, knew it was coming. There was increasing hostility towards us from the German settlers, and when war was declared they just walked in and took over our land. We were given twenty-four hours to get out of the country or face internment.'

'The bishop said your husband told him something about the vicar of Dar es Salaam being executed by the Germans for helping people to escape to Northern Rhodesia,' said Marriott.

Esmé Creed glanced at Marriott and laughed, but there was little humour in it. 'I daresay he did,' she said. 'Charlie was a great raconteur, and could always be relied on to tell a good story, but there's not a vestige of truth in that. We didn't even know the Vicar of Dar es Salaam.'

'What I don't understand is why you should have wanted to come back to this country at all, Mrs Creed. Surely you'd have been safer staying in Northern Rhodesia.'

Esmé Creed emitted a tired sigh and for a moment remained silent, as though explaining the downfall of Charlie and herself was even worse than the downfall itself. 'Charlie managed to get a job as an assistant overseer at a maize farm in Luapula Province, down near Kawambwa somewhere,' she said eventually. 'I think that was the name of the place, but we were more or less chased out of Northern Rhodesia within months. As it turned out, Charlie was no better at running a maize farm than he was at running his father's coffee plantation. But to make matters worse, he could never resist a pretty woman, and he had several affairs in Tanganyika after our marriage.' She paused and sighed. 'And probably before we married.'

'Why didn't you leave him, Mrs Creed?' asked Marriott.

'*Leave him!*' Esmé Creed sounded appalled at the suggestion. 'And what would have happened to me? I'd have become a social outcast, Mr Marriott. In the colonies, whenever a couple splits up, it's always the woman who gets the blame. It's a male-dominated society.'

'You said just now that you were chased out of Northern Rhodesia. What exactly did you mean by that?'

'It all came to a head with this young native girl who worked on the farm. She was fifteen and ran home to her father in tears, complaining that Charlie had raped her in one of the storage huts on the farm. He told me later that it was one of the perks of the job on his coffee plantation, and he thought it would be the same in Northern Rhodesia. Whether the girl's claim was true or not, she certainly finished up being pregnant. Well, that caused uproar among the African community, as you can imagine, and all sorts of threats were made against us. And as if that wasn't enough, because we'd come across from German East Africa, the Northern Rhodesians were convinced that we were actually Germans and were probably spies.'

'And that, presumably, is why you left.'

'Not voluntarily. The local police inspector paid us a visit and said that he would have charged Charlie with rape if he thought a court would believe the word of a young black girl against that of a white boss. In any event, he suggested in the strongest possible terms that we leave the country if we wanted to avoid serious injury or even death at the hands of the native population. He went on to say that he couldn't guarantee our safety as it was a very volatile time; no one knew exactly what was going to happen with the war and everything. After a long trek we managed to get down to Durban Harbour in South Africa, obtained a passage in a cargo boat and eventually finished up here.'

'Couldn't you have stayed in South Africa, Mrs Creed?' asked Marriott. 'Safer than here, surely? There aren't any Zeppelins there.'

'We were treated with suspicion there, too. Because we'd originally come from German East Africa, we were thought to be spies. Apart from anything else, we'd no idea how things would work out in Africa. The whole continent was rife with rumour. Would the British win the war or would the Germans win and take over all our colonies in Africa? It was a very worrying time. We knew we had to get to England to be safe.'

'But why did your husband pretend to be a priest? That's the part I don't understand.' Once again Hardcastle asked a question to which he was certain he knew the answer.

'Charlie is not the bravest of men, Inspector.' Esmé Creed laughed scornfully. 'We arrived in England at the beginning of 1916 and found a place to live in London. Charlie had several jobs, none of which paid very much. In fact, there was barely enough to pay the rent for the rooms we were renting in Brixton. But then conscription was introduced and Charlie was terrified that he'd finish up in the trenches. He read somewhere that clergymen were exempt. He's always been a good actor; in fact, he was quite the star attraction in amateur dramatics among the British community in Dar es Salaam. And to my shame I helped him with advice that I'd gained from my acting career. He started going to Westminster Abbey or St Paul's Cathedral in his clerical garb and mixing with clergymen socially. He told them that tale about the vicar of Dar es Salaam, and that he'd been the curate, and one of them mentioned a vacancy that had occurred here. I never thought he'd get away with it, but he managed to pass himself off as a vicar and did so very successfully. Well, he convinced the bishop.'

'Why exactly did you dismiss your maidservants, Mrs Creed? I understand you had several.'

'They weren't dismissed.' Esmé Creed glanced out of the window. A breeze was rustling the trees in the vicarage garden. A stray cat stopped, peered in at the French windows and then went casually on its way. 'It was Charlie. It seemed I wasn't enough to satisfy his appetite,' she admitted frankly, 'so he started on the servants. Some of them were willing, and some just accepted it as part of their job, I suppose. But some objected and left. As for Daisy Salter, she screamed the place down, and when I heard that she'd been murdered, I knew it was only a matter of time before the police turned up here.'

'Did you really not know about your husband's collection of railway stuff, Mrs Creed?'

'Of course I knew. He had a similar collection in Tanganyika, but we had to leave it all behind. He had two obsessions, Mr Hardcastle: railways and young girls. I knew what was in that room and I knew why that great chaise longue was in there. I pleaded with him to stop, but he wouldn't listen. I said it would ruin every-thing we'd been lucky enough to achieve, but I don't think he could help himself. He said no one would believe that a vicar would do such a thing as to take young women against their will.'

'But you stayed with him and said nothing,' said Hardcastle accusingly.

'What else could I do? I had no friends here. If I'd told the police, I'd have been left destitute.' Esmé paused momentarily. 'And that's how I'm going to finish up anyway,' she said.

'Thank you for being so frank, Mrs Creed,' said Hardcastle, and then changed the subject. 'Where was your husband on the night that Daisy Salter was murdered? That was the night of the sixth and seventh of August: Monday and Tuesday.'

'He went out at about nine o'clock, Inspector, and returned at just before midnight. He said he'd had to meet someone on a confidential matter. A sort of confession, he told me. I didn't believe him, of course. I knew what he'd been up to, but I didn't think he'd murdered that poor girl.'

'Where exactly were you married to Charles, Mrs Creed?'

'I told you, in Dar es Salaam.'

'Yes, but where?'

'Oh, I see. In the Anglican church there.'

'And do you have a valid marriage certificate?'

'Of course, although it's all written in German.'

'Yes, I suppose it would be.' Hardcastle nodded. 'Does your husband have any civilian clothes?'

Esmé Creed appeared puzzled by the sudden seemingly irrelevant question. 'Yes, of course, but why d'you ask?'

'If he appears in court dressed as a clergyman, one of the first pieces of evidence I'll be obliged to give is that he is not a clerk in holy orders. And that is likely to prejudice the case against him. However, if he's dressed in ordinary clothes, his deception need only come out after the verdict.' That was only half true. Hardcastle knew that prosecuting counsel would almost certainly use Creed's masquerade as tending to prove his guilt.

'Oh, I see. And do you think he will be convicted, Mr Hardcastle?'

'I think you should reconcile yourself to the prospect of his spending some time in prison, Mrs Creed.' Even Hardcastle, hard-nosed detective that he was, had begun to feel sorry for Esmé Creed, and did not have the heart to say that the most likely outcome was that Charlie Creed would be hanged for the murder of Daisy Salter. But Esmé Creed was an intelligent woman and had probably already guessed as much.

The interview room at Butts Road police station in Alton was a cold and austere chamber, as indeed it was intended to be.

When Creed was escorted into the room he was still possessed of all the pomposity of the indignant clergyman. And he was still wearing his frock coat and clerical collar.

Hardcastle and Marriott were already seated and Yardley was standing near the only wall to have a window, and that was narrow and close to the ceiling.

'I wish to make a complaint in the strongest possible terms, Inspector,' said Creed in his sermonizing, holier-than-thou voice. 'As a man of the Church I seriously expect to be treated rather differently from a common criminal.'

'Sit down and shut up, Charlie Creed,' said Hardcastle. 'You *are* a common criminal.'

'Oh, bugger it to Hell!' said Creed, his voice returning to normal. 'You've found out.' He collapsed into the only vacant chair, a look of despair on his face as he realized that the game was up.

'Of course I have. I'm a detective. Anyway, your wife's told us all about your shenanigans.'

'But how did you guess?' Creed was convinced that his act as the vicar of Thresham Parva had been faultless.

'Vicars don't wear frock coats and gaiters, Charlie. That's a bishop's outfit. As a result, we spent a very interesting hour with the Bishop of Winchester yesterday. We know all about you, Charlie Creed. You're going down for rape, and that's only the start.'

'I hope you don't intend to take the word of that common tart over mine, Inspector. I didn't rape her or anyone else.'

'You'll be kept locked up here until I have enough evidence to hang you, Creed. You might think that it's all a big joke, pretending to be a clergyman and raping and murdering, but it's not. You might've got away with it in Northern Rhodesia, but you won't get away with it at Winchester Assizes.'

'Murder? What are you talking about?'

Hardcastle ignored Creed and stood up. Opening the door of the interview room, he beckoned to the constable waiting outside. 'You can lock this bugger up again, lad.'

'Why did you ask Mrs Creed about her marriage certificate, sir?' asked Yardley as the three of them returned to the room Hardcastle was using as an office.

'If she and Creed are lawfully married, Yardley,' said Hardcastle, 'she can't be compelled to give evidence against her husband about his assaults on these young girls, or his whereabouts on the night of the murder. That's why I asked if she had a marriage certificate. If she produces it to the court, or to prosecuting counsel, that's an end to the matter.'

'But supposing she offers to give evidence, sir?'

'I'm not a lawyer, lad, but I think that would be all right,' said Hardcastle. 'Let's hope we can prove it without having to worry about that.'

* * *

'It's nothing personal, Inspector, but I'm not sure that I can view your arrival with any degree of equanimity,' said the Bishop of Winchester as he welcomed his visitors into his study at Farnham Castle. 'I have this fear that you are not the bringer of good tidings.'

'Much of what you told us the day before yesterday, sir, has been confirmed by Mrs Creed. When I interviewed Creed himself earlier today, he admitted that he was not, nor ever had been, a clergyman. And his name is not Cyril Creed, it's Charles, known to all and sundry apparently as Charlie Creed, a gambler and a womanizer.'

'I suppose he wasn't a lay preacher by any chance, was he?' asked the bishop hopefully.

'I doubt it, sir,' said Hardcastle, 'but his wife said he was very good at amateur dramatics.'

The bishop emitted an audible groan. 'How on earth am I to explain all this to Lambeth Palace?' It was a rhetorical question. 'The Archbishop of Canterbury, Randall Davidson, was my predecessor here, you know, Inspector, but I'm not sure how he'll take this news.'

'Mrs Creed mentioned that they fled German East Africa in a hurry and that most of their belongings were left behind. It seems that they left in what they stood up in, but managed to bring their passports, marriage and birth certificates with them.'

'That may be some justification, I suppose,' said the bishop, 'but it's no great comfort.'

'I understand that Creed conducted a number of weddings, as well as christenings and funerals, sir,' said Marriott. 'It's nothing to do with us, of course, but I was wondering about their validity.'

The bishop remained silent, put his hands together in an attitude of supplication and gazed at the ornate ceiling of the episcopal study.

Over the next week, Richard Yardley learned that the preparation of a report for the Director of Public Prosecutions was, if anything, harder than the detective work that resulted in the identification and arrest of the murderer.

Hardcastle had him running everywhere. The young Hampshire detective found himself taking further statements, making copies of statements, organizing exhibits and acting as a general dogs-body. But all of it was under the strict and demanding supervision of Marriott, who on several occasions, unbeknown to Hardcastle, had been obliged to undertake some of Yardley's tasks in addition to his own. It was obvious to Marriott that the DDI was taking an interest in Yardley's development as a detective. Despite his unforgiving approach, it was something at which Hardcastle excelled, although his detectives at Cannon Row would not have thought that that was what motivated him. They regarded his attitude as one of overbearing and unreasonable demands, but the result was that each and every one of the A Division CID officers was good at his job. Not that Hardcastle would ever have told them, but that was the way of the Metropolitan Police. Marriott, if anything, was the exception rather than the rule when it came to giving the occasional word of praise or encouragement.

After Creed's second remand hearing, Hardcastle decided that Alton police station should no longer bear the burden of accom-modating him, and the DDI asked the magistrate that Creed be remanded in custody to Winchester prison.

Finally, after having been rewritten several times, the report was ready, and was presented to the Chief Constable for onward trans-mission to the Director of Public Prosecutions.

'I have to say, Mr Hardcastle, that I am extremely impressed with the speed and efficiency with which you apprehended Daisy Salter's murderer. What's his name?' The Chief Constable glanced down at the report. 'Ah, yes, Creed, that's his name.'

'He's not the murderer, sir,' said Hardcastle.

'Eh? What d'you mean, he's not the murderer? You've written here that—' The Chief Constable broke off and prodded the report with his forefinger.

'Creed's the suspect, sir,' said Hardcastle, rather smugly. 'He's not the murderer until the jury says so.'

For a moment the Chief Constable stared at Hardcastle, but then he burst out laughing. 'I stand corrected, Inspector,' he said. 'By the way, how was that young detective I assigned to you? Any good, was he?'

'Yardley has the makings of a good detective, sir,' said Hard-castle, which was praise indeed. 'I'd be obliged if you could spare him for the conference with counsel when it takes place. It'll be useful experience for him.'

'By all means. The more my young officers can learn from old hands like you, Mr Hardcastle, the more use they're likely to be to the Hampshire County Constabulary.'

'The conference will probably be in the Temple in London, unless the DPP decides to brief a local man. But I think he's more likely to select a London silk.'

In the event, Hardcastle was proved to be right. At the beginning of October, he received a message that he was to meet a barrister called Sir Harry Cork at his chambers at Paper Buildings in the Temple, for the purpose of reviewing the evidence and assessing the witnesses in terms of their ability to stand up to cross-examination.

'Send a telegraph message to Hampshire County Constabulary's headquarters asking for Yardley to meet me here at eight o'clock next Tuesday morning the ninth of October, Marriott. The appointment with Sir Harry is at a quarter past ten.'

NINETEEN

'Divisional Detective Inspector Hardcastle, sir, and Detective Sergeant Marriott. And this is Detective Constable Yardley of the Hampshire County Constabulary.' 'Find yourselves seats, gentlemen. It's all a bit cramped in here, but I've yet to come across a set of barristers' chambers that ain't packed to the gunnels. As a matter of fact, I'd half a mind to ask you to come to my house in Parsons Green, but it's a bit out of the way.' One's first impression of Sir Harry Cork, baronet and King's Counsel, would be that he was a large, jovial man, but devious witnesses soon found that he could be ruthless when it came to cross-examination.

'I trust the report provides you with all that you need, sir,' said Hardcastle.

'Indeed, a most comprehensive document, Inspector.' Cork tapped the pile of paper with an elegant forefinger. 'I see that this fellow Creed purported to be a clergyman. To coin an apt phrase, God knows how he got away with it.' The lawyer paused and chuckled. 'I prosecuted a vicar about six years ago who had an unhealthy predilection for choirboys.' He thumbed through a few statements. 'This girl, Marjorie Tindall. Will she be all right in the box, or is she likely to change her story?'

'She made a written statement, sir,' explained Hardcastle. 'It'll be difficult for her to go back on that.'

'Ah!' Cork thumbed through a few more statements. 'So she did, and here it is. Made it to a Mrs Annie Jessop.' He looked up. 'Who's Annie Jessop?'

'The local village constable's wife, sir. She's forty-one years old.'

'Oh, she'll be all right in the box. Salt of the earth, copper's wives. But then you'd know that, Inspector.' Cork broke off and chortled. It seemed that he was full of little quips.

'Mrs Jessop said that Marjorie Tindall, although frightened to start with, is now confidently looking forward to pointing out her rapist at the trial, sir.'

'Excellent.' Cork turned a page. 'Why did this Creed person pretend to be a vicar?'

'Apparently to avoid military service, Sir Harry,' said Hardcastle. 'From what I gathered from Esmé Creed, his wife, he's a bit of a white-feather man.'

'Is he, be damned?' Cork had a particular dislike of such people whom he unhesitatingly described as yellow-bellied cowards, particularly as his only son – twenty-year-old Tom – had died in Charing Cross Hospital last year after losing both his legs at the Somme. 'I see you got Spilsbury to do the post-mortem examination. Splendid. That should frighten the defence.'

'I always get Doctor Spilsbury if I can, sir.'

'Very wise, Inspector.'

'What's happening about Esmé Creed, sir? I included the fact that she was aware of Creed's activities with young women.'

'Tricky business, husband and wife,' said Cork. 'There might be evidence of conspiracy there, but one also has to consider the possibility that Esmé Creed was so afraid of her husband that she remained silent under duress. In the circumstances the DPP ruled against prosecuting her. But, my dear Inspector, that ain't necessarily the end of the matter. Now, is there anything you want to ask me before we go to trial?' Cork turned to Marriott and Yardley. 'Or either of you?'

'Only one question, sir,' said Hardcastle. 'Have you any idea who defending counsel is?'

Cork laughed. 'Always a good question for a Crown witness to ask, Inspector, but not as yet. I'll let you know as soon as I know. Shouldn't be too long before we find out.'

On a cold February day in 1918, a German Giant R-plane dropped a one-thousand kilogram bomb on the Royal Hospital, Chelsea, killing five people. That day was also the day upon which the trial of Charles Walford Creed began at Winchester Assizes.

From time to time over a period of two hundred and fifty years, Winchester Assizes had been held in the Great Hall of Winchester Castle. It was an impressive setting, the entire proceedings overshadowed by the huge Arthurian table that hung on the back wall of the stone-flagged chamber. It was, Hardcastle thought, a suitable venue for a murder trial.

The court crier opened the proceedings with the customary proclamation. *'Oyez! Oyez! Oyez! All persons having business before this court of oyer and terminer and general gaol delivery pray draw near.'*

The red-robed judge appeared on the bench and exchanged bows with counsel.

'Harry Cork, My Lord,' said Cork as he struggled to his feet. 'I appear for the Crown with my learned friend, Rupert Strange.'

'Always a pleasure to see you in my court, Sir Harry.' Mr Justice Cawthorne and Cork were old friends and had shared many a bottle of port at Bar mess dinners. 'I trust you found your way from London without too much difficulty.' It was a light-hearted reference to the fact that Sir Harry Cork was rarely seen anywhere else but the Central Criminal Court at Old Bailey.

'It's much easier now that Winchester is connected to the railway, My Lord,' quipped Cork in return.

'Oh, is it really?' queried the judge. 'I didn't realize,' he added, and turned his attention to the defence lawyers.

'Cosmo Lockwood for the defence, My Lord, with my learned friend Dudley Skinner.'

'Ah, you seem to make a habit of appearing before me, Mr Lockwood. Why is that?' The judge beamed at defence counsel.

'I need the money, My Lord,' responded Lockwood with a straight face.

'Is that so? Poverty is an awful state to be in.' The judge raised his eyebrows and laughed. After that short exchange of badinage with the two silks, he began in earnest. 'Put up the prisoner.'

Charles Creed had taken Hardcastle's advice, passed on to him by Esmé, and now wore a dark suit with a white shirt and sober tie. A gold-plated albert was strung between his waistcoat pockets, but there was no watch at the end of it.

'Charles Walford Creed, you are charged in that you did murder Daisy Salter on or about Tuesday the seventh of August in the year of Our Lord one thousand, nine hundred and seventeen at or near South Farm, Thresham Parva in the county of Hampshire. Against the Peace. How say you upon this indictment?'

'Not guilty,' said Creed.

'You are further charged that on a date unknown at the Vicarage,

Thresham Parva in the county of Hampshire you did rape the same Daisy Salter, contrary to Section Forty-eight of the Offences Against the Person Act 1861. How say you upon that indictment?'

'Not guilty.'

'You are further charged that in the afternoon of Wednesday the eighth of August in the aforementioned year at the Vicarage, Thresham Parva in the county of Hampshire, you did rape Marjorie Tindall, contrary to the aforementioned act. How say you upon that indictment?'

'Not guilty.'

The mention of a vicarage in the last two counts of the indictment caused an outbreak of whisperings in the court, not least among the journalists in the press box. It meant that Hardcastle's assurances to Esmé Creed had, after all, been proved worthless, and it was clear that Creed's deception would have to be explained sooner rather than later. In all honesty, the DDI knew that it would have to come out.

'Perhaps you would be so good as to enlighten me, Sir Harry,' said the judge. 'How does a vicarage feature in this case?'

'With Your Lordship's indulgence, I shall explain that in due course.'

'Very well. Bring in the jury.'

The twelve men who were to try Charles Creed now filed into the jury box. Each was a man of property and standing, and each was soberly dressed. Unusually, neither of the leading counsel saw any reason to challenge any one of them.

Once the jury had been sworn in, the judge glanced at Crown counsel. 'Sir Harry.'

'If it please, My Lord.' Cork rose to his feet and turned to the jury box. 'Gentlemen of the jury,' he began, 'it is the Crown's contention that the prisoner, Charles Walford Creed, murdered a young woman by the name of Daisy Salter on Monday the sixth, or Tuesday the seventh of August last year in the village of Thresham Parva in Hampshire. You will hear evidence that the young woman met her death by strangulation and, at the time of her death, was two months' pregnant.'

At that point in Cork's opening address, someone in the public gallery laughed loudly. Whether it was the fact that the victim had been pregnant that caused the unseemly merriment or that the offender had been sharing a private joke with his neighbour did not matter.

Mr Justice Cawthorne glared. 'If there is any repetition of that sort of behaviour, I shall have the public gallery cleared,' he said sternly. 'Please continue, Sir Harry.'

Cork had used the interruption as an excuse to take a pinch of snuff. 'A significant factor in this case,' he continued, 'is that Creed masqueraded as a clerk in holy orders and had, by some devious means, secured a post as Vicar of Thresham Parva. How he managed to do so is of no interest to the court, but, suffice it to say, it was because the deceased believed him to be a clergyman that she trusted him until it was too late. In the confines of a private room at the vicarage, he raped her and she became pregnant. But, gentlemen of the jury, when she threatened to tell the police what he had done to her, he convinced her that no one would believe that a man of the cloth was capable of such a foul act. Nevertheless, her threats of exposure were so vehement that to make absolutely sure that she remain silent, Creed made an assignation with the girl at South Farm in Thresham Parva, and murdered her.'

Cork was so confident of Dr Bernard Spilsbury's expertise that he allowed his junior, Rupert Strange, to lead the pathologist through his evidence about the cause of Daisy Salter's death, and the fact that she was pregnant. Wisely, Cosmo Lockwood declined to cross-examine; he had jousted with Spilsbury on a previous occasion. And lost.

Hardcastle was the next witness to be called for the Crown and Sir Harry Cork explored every twist and turn, every minor detail, of the DDI's investigation.

Hardcastle's testimony lasted three hours but it was still not over. Cosmo Lockwood rose to cross-examine.

'Mr Hardcastle, is it not fair to say that until you questioned . . .' Lockwood paused and glanced down at his brief. 'Until you questioned the young woman, Marjorie Tindall, who is, I believe, only sixteen years of age . . .' He paused again to glance meaningfully at the jury. 'Until then you had absolutely no reason to suspect my client of the murder you were investigating.'

'None at all, sir,' admitted Hardcastle disarmingly.

'So it was merely on the word of a sixteen-year-old child

that you went ahead and arrested my client and charged him with murder.'

Hardcastle looked at defence counsel with a blank stare but remained silent.

'Well?' demanded Lockwood.

'I'm sorry, sir, was that a question? I thought you were making a statement.' It was a comment that produced a wry smile on the judge's face. 'But if it is a question,' Hardcastle continued, 'the reason I arrested your client and charged him with murder is that I found sufficient evidence to warrant such a charge being brought once I had searched the vicarage where he was pretending to be a clergyman. It is, of course, as you know, sir, a charge that cannot be brought without the consent of the Director of Public Prosecutions, who was satisfied that there was a case to answer.'

Lockwood turned to the judge. 'My Lord, I would be grateful if Your Lordship would direct the officer not to introduce prejudicial comments into his evidence. There was no need for him to mention the vicarage or that my client was allegedly masquerading as a clergyman. That, My Lord, is evidence that has yet to be adduced if, indeed, it is forthcoming.'

'I seem to recall that the word vicarage was included in the second and third counts of the indictment, Mr Lockwood, and the masquerade of your client was mentioned in the Crown's opening,' said the judge mildly. 'It's hardly prejudicial to repeat what's already been mentioned in open court. And I think the inspector was merely attempting to answer your questions as fully as he was able.'

'I'm much obliged, My Lord.' Lockwood accepted the rebuke, but inwardly was seething. 'I have no further questions of this witness.'

When Marjorie Tindall was called to give evidence the misgivings shared by Sir Harry Cork and Hardcastle were dashed the moment she stepped into the witness box. Although only sixteen years of age, she was completely unmoved by the panoply of an assize court. The red-robed judge, the bewigged barristers and the policemen had no intimidating effect on her. The frightened child, barely able to describe her ordeal to Annie Jessop, had recovered her confidence and been replaced by an assured young woman. She had become, Hardcastle decided, like a little Cockney sparrow, and he was sure that Annie Jessop was responsible.

Sir Harry Cork started gently to lead her through the ordeal she had suffered at the hands of Charles Creed, but he need not have worried. She replied in a firm voice, detailing exactly what had happened to her. She described the room in which Creed kept his railway memorabilia with great clarity and emphasized that she was only allowed to enter when, as she put it: 'The reverend was there an' all.' Quite unembarrassed, she told how he had pushed her on to the chaise longue – which she described as a sort of bed – and raped her. Her evidence was in such graphic detail that the jury had no alternative but to believe her absolutely.

And when finally asked who had been responsible for raping her, she unhesitatingly pointed to Charles Creed in the dock, and said, loudly, 'It was 'im, sir.'

Cork asked Marjorie Tindall what Daisy Salter had told her about her ordeal at Creed's hands. Lockwood immediately objected because, he said, it was hearsay. But the judge drily observed that the victim was not able to give evidence in person, and he allowed it.

Despite Marjorie Tindall's convincing testimony, Cosmo Lockwood was duty-bound to attempt to discredit her evidence, but he failed.

'I put it to you, Marjorie,' he began, using her first name in an attempt to be friendly, but got no further.

Marjorie Tindall immediately objected to that. 'I'd rather you called me Miss Tindall, like what he done,' she said, pointing at Sir Harry Cork. 'It's only polite.'

'Oh, I do apologise, Miss Tindall,' said Lockwood in a slightly sarcastic voice, but it was apparent from the facial expressions of the jurymen that they were unimpressed by Lockwood's condescension and attitude towards such a young and vulnerable girl. 'I put it to you that your entire testimony is a fairy tale: a hotchpotch of fantasy and make-believe.'

'No, it ain't.'

'You have a dubious reputation in Thresham Parva, do you not, *Miss* Tindall? A reputation for being free with your favours and that you find men—'

'My Lord!' Cork stood up. 'There is no evidence to support my learned friend's preposterous suggestion. Unless he intends to adduce such evidence, he is just attempting to smear the witness.'

Lockwood changed tack, but it was to no avail. However, as much as he tried to undermine Marjorie Tindall's evidence, she would not budge. In fact, the effect of Lockwood's hectoring was to make the jurors more sympathetic towards the young girl than they had been at first. Lockwood's cross-examination of her did nothing to help his client's case.

When Marjorie Tindall finally left the witness box, her head held high, she glanced almost contemptuously around the court. It had been, Harry Cork later confided to Hardcastle, a bravura performance by one so young, the like of which he had never before witnessed in all his years at the Bar.

Over the next weeks, a succession of witnesses made their way to the witness box. Freddie King, the Boy Scout who had found Daisy Salter's handbag under the hedge, had his moment of glory and, to add to his enjoyment, he was congratulated by the judge on the clear and concise way he gave his evidence.

Detective Constable Richard Yardley, oddly much less confident than Marjorie Tindall had been, gave evidence of the information he had received 'from an informant' that led police to interview Marjorie Tindall.

Much of the evidence consisted of the routine requisites of a criminal trial that is necessary to prove the case against the accused 'beyond all reasonable doubt'.

But then came the big surprise.

'I call Esmé Creed,' said Sir Harry Cork.

'My Lord, I must protest.' An outraged Cosmo Lockwood was on his feet in an instant. 'Mrs Creed is not a compellable witness, as my learned friend must know.'

'Send out the jury and hold the witness outside the court.' Mr Justice Cawthorne glanced at Crown counsel once the jury box was empty. He knew that Cork was too experienced a barrister to have made a mistake. 'Sir Harry?'

'My Lord, I am perfectly aware that Mrs Creed is not a compellable witness, but she is a *competent* one, and she has come to court today to give evidence of her own free will. The DPP has wisely decided to afford her immunity from prosecution for involvement in any of her husband's alleged crimes, and, of course, my learned friend was advised, some *weeks* ago, that I would be calling the prisoner's wife.'

'Mr Lockwood?' The judge switched his gaze back to defence counsel. He was beginning to feel like an umpire at a Wimbledon tennis tournament, although those tournaments had been suspended for the duration of the war.

Lockwood waved a hand of defeat. That he had not stood up to withdraw his objection verbally was a discourtesy that further irritated the judge.

'Very well. Bring back the jury,' said Mr Justice Cawthorne, a little wearily. He was rapidly tiring of Cosmo Lockwood's attitude, but recalled, from his own days at the Bar, that attempting to defend an indefensible case was a tiresome task for any barrister, and tended to make him short-tempered. But, as he had pointed out in jest, poverty is a dreadful thing, and a barrister has to earn a living.

TWENTY

Esmé Creed's appearance in the witness box immediately drew admiring glances from the men in the court and one or two sighs of envy from the ladies in the public gallery who leaned forward to get a better view of the prisoner's wife. Her fashionable grey serge costume comprised a jacket with a 'nipped-in' waist and a cream silk jabot, a flared skirt, the hem of which was a good six inches from the ground, and high button boots. A black straw boater and an *en-tout-cas* umbrella completed the picture of an attractive, elegant woman.

She took the New Testament from the usher and spoke the oath in a strong, educated voice.

'Please state your full name,' said Sir Harry Cork as he rose to begin his examination.

'Esmé Florence Creed.'

'Mrs Creed, would you please assure My Lord and the gentlemen of the jury that you are here today to testify of your own free will?'

'Yes, I am.'

'Would you please tell the court how you came to be living in Thresham Parva.'

For the next twenty minutes, Esmé Creed told the jury about the life she and her husband had lived in German East Africa, followed by details of their flight to Northern Rhodesia when the war broke out and finally to South Africa. She went on to reveal how they had finished up, penniless, in rented accommodation in Brixton. Asked to tell the court about her husband's masquerade as a vicar, she was quite open about his desire to avoid military service.

'Were you aware of your husband's sexual appetite for young girls, Mrs Creed?' Cork asked bluntly.

'Yes, sir. It became obvious the moment we were married.' Esmé went on to tell the court the story of how she and her husband were forced to leave Northern Rhodesia and the reason for it.

'Please now tell the court what took place on Wednesday the eighth of August at the vicarage, Mrs Creed.'

Esmé Creed related how she had heard screams coming from the room where her husband kept his railway memorabilia, and how she saw a distressed Marjorie Tindall run from that room straight out of the front door of the vicarage. At this point, Esmé broke down in tears and the judge ordered that a chair be brought into the witness box for her.

'And now I come to an important question, Mrs Creed,' said Cork. 'I want you to consider your reply carefully before you make it, and remember that you are on oath. Where was your husband on the evening of the sixth of August last year?'

'He went out at about nine o'clock, sir.'

'And when did he return?'

'Just before midnight.'

'Did he say where he had been?'

'Only that he'd had to meet someone on a confidential matter. He said he was taking a confession.'

'And did you believe him, Mrs Creed?'

'No, sir.'

By the time that Sir Harry Cork had elicited all the evidence he required, Esmé Creed had been in the witness box for an hour. But her ordeal was not yet over.

Cosmo Lockwood rose ponderously from his seat on the front bench and adjusted his gown. 'I put it to you, Mrs Creed, that you only agreed to give evidence for the Crown because you have been given immunity from prosecution,' he said, and pushed his spectacles a little further up his nose.

'Mr Lockwood.' The judge intervened before Esmé Creed had the opportunity to reply. 'I would suggest that it is most unwise of you to criticize a decision made by the Director of Public Prosecutions, and I will not allow Mrs Creed to answer.'

'As Your Lordship pleases,' said a disgruntled Lockwood. Changing tactics, he asked, 'Do you love your husband, Mrs Creed?'

'Yes.'

'Why then have you come to court today apparently intent on denigrating his character and attempting to have him convicted of murder?'

'Quite simply because I want him to stop before he harms any more young women, sir.'

Lockwood spent a further twenty-five minutes attempting to discredit Esmé Creed's testimony, but she would not be moved. Defeated, he sat down.

'Mr Lockwood, do you have witnesses for the defence?'

'No, My Lord.' Lockwood half rose from his seat.

Mr Justice Cawthorne now addressed Creed directly. 'Prisoner at the bar, you may give evidence on your own behalf under oath. If you do so, counsel for the Crown is entitled to cross-examine you. Alternatively, you may address the court from the dock without taking the oath, in which case you cannot be questioned. I must warn you that to take the latter course means that less credence will be put upon what you say.'

'I have no desire to say anything, My Lord, other than to say I am entirely innocent of these crimes,' said Creed, whose sanctimonious voice had returned for the occasion.

Cosmo Lockwood stood up to embark on the nigh-impossible task of convincing the jury that there was insufficient evidence upon which to convict his client. He particularly invited the jurors to disregard Esmé Creed's evidence as unreliable and merely the testimony of a spiteful woman, although he did not enlighten them as to why he thought her to be spiteful. He spoke eloquently and convincingly for thirty minutes, wisely deciding that to go on for longer would antagonize the jury.

Mr Justice Cawthorne adjourned the court for the day and announced that he would sum-up the case tomorrow.

The following morning, a bright and sunny day, marred only by a cold wind, Mr Justice Cawthorne began his summing-up.

It was a scrupulously fair assessment of the evidence that had been placed before the jury, and carefully drew attention to the points that were favourable to the accused as well as those that supported the Crown's case.

The jury took a total of seven hours and forty-two minutes to arrive at their verdict. It was eleven o'clock the following morning when they filed into the jury box.

'Gentlemen of the jury, are you agreed upon your verdict?' asked the clerk of the court.

'We are, sir,' said the foreman.

'On the count of murdering Daisy Salter. How say you?'

'We find the prisoner guilty, sir.'

'And is that the verdict of you all?'

'It is, sir.'

And so the ritual continued until it was clear that the jury had found Creed guilty on all three counts of the indictment.

Throughout the unfolding drama of the jury's verdict, Charles Creed had gripped the dock rail, his fingers becoming whiter by the second as his grip tightened.

'Prisoner at the bar. Have you anything to say before sentence of death is passed upon you?' asked Mr Justice Cawthorne.

'It's wrong. I didn't do any of those things.'

Seated in the well of the court, Hardcastle turned to look at Creed. Gone was the supercilious play-acting clergyman he had first encountered to be replaced by a broken man whose sins had finally caught up with him. Esmé Creed was not in court to hear the verdict and sentence. Hardcastle later heard that she had changed her name and gone to live in Cornwall.

The judge did not waste his time by reciting a judicial homily on Creed's wrongdoings, a custom so beloved of Cawthorne's brothers on the bench. He simply donned the black cap and, favouring the slightly older form of the death sentence, began.

'Charles Walford Creed, you have been rightly convicted of the foul crime of murder. The court doth order you to be taken from hence to the place from whence you came, and thence to the place of execution, and that you be hanged by the neck until you are dead, and that your body be afterward buried within the precincts of the prison in which you shall be confined after your conviction. And may the Lord have mercy upon your soul.'

Beside the judge, his chaplain intoned the single word, 'Amen.'

In the dock, Creed cried out the one word: 'No!' before being dragged, whimpering, down to the cells by the prison warders who had been beside him throughout the trial.

One week after the Court of Criminal Appeal had confirmed the verdict, the Home Secretary, Sir George Cave, read the docket containing details of Creed's conviction, sat in silent contemplation for an hour, read the docket once more and then wrote 'Let the law take its course' on the cover of the docket.

The usual crowd of ghouls gathered outside Winchester Prison on the morning of Creed's execution. At two minutes past eight o'clock, a warder appeared and placed a black-framed notice on the prison gates. It stated that the execution of Charles Walford Creed had been carried out according to the law. At the same time, a black flag was raised over the prison.

It rained all day that day.

One day in July, Hardcastle was sent for by Detective Chief Inspector Frederick Wensley.

'Ernie, the Commissioner's received an application, through the Chief Constable of Hampshire County Constabulary, from a young copper called Richard Yardley who wants to transfer to the Metropolitan Police.'

'What's that got to do with me, sir?'

'I thought I'd ask your opinion of the lad because he worked with you on the Creed murder job?'

'Yes, he did, sir.'

'Well, what d'you think, Ernie? Should we accept him?'

'He's all right,' said Hardcastle grudgingly.

Wensley laughed, and after Hardcastle had left his office, he wrote on the docket: 'This application is strongly supported by DDI Hardcastle of A Division.'